A
COAT
DYED
BLACK

A COAT DYED BLACK

A NOVEL OF THE NORWEGIAN RESISTANCE

—

Don Pugnetti Jr.

LEGACY HOUSE
PRESS

Published by Legacy House Press, Gig Harbor, Washington
www.donpugnettijr.com

Edited and designed by Girl Friday Productions
www.girlfridayproductions.com

Cover design: Emily Weigel
Project management: Sara Spees Addicott
Editorial production: Jaye Whitney Debber
Image credits: cover © Shutterstock/Iakov Kalinin, Shutterstock/ Melissa Madia, Shutterstock/Benoit Daoust

ISBN (hardcover): 978-1-7375953-0-4
ISBN (paperback): 978-1-7375953-1-1
ISBN (ebook): 978-1-7375953-2-8

Library of Congress Control Number: 2021920749

To all the courageous Norwegian resistance fighters—men and women—who risked and gave their lives for the cause of freedom from Nazi tyranny

CHAPTER 1

April 8, 1940

From five miles off the Norwegian coast, Anders Kongsgaard cast a wary glance from his wheelhouse window. Odd shapes bobbed on the sea ahead. He stroked the stubble on his unshaven face. His trawler was too far away for him to identify what was out there. What he could pick out were objects scattered in jagged heaps across the rolling waves of the North Sea.

The captain of the *Hildur VI* had seen debris of all sorts on these waters since he was a small boy fishing with his father and grandfather. But this morning was a first. Never had he come across what appeared to be a large floating junkyard at sea.

Rotten for fishing, he thought, but the peculiar sighting had to be checked out. The skipper adjusted the wheel and pushed the boat's course a touch more on a north-northwest heading.

Behind him, thick fog enshrouded Norway's south coast and his home port of Lillesand, a fishing town of about 750 people. The dense white air hung wet and heavy when he set out before daybreak. The conditions kept most of the fleet in port. Now, the fog was dissipating, the sun was rising, and seas were calm. If only, Kongsgaard thought, he could combine such a glorious day with a good catch.

As the trawler chugged closer toward the mess, Hans Martensen, the lone crew member, stood at the bow and spotted the debris, too. He pointed forward, turned back toward the wheelhouse, and shrugged his shoulders. The captain grabbed binoculars and shouted back, "Take the wheel, would you?"

They traded places. From the foredeck, the captain aimed the glasses dead ahead where sea swells jostled the unfamiliar objects.

The *Hildur VI* closed in, handing Kongsgaard a better view. His eyelids flickered, clearing his vision. There were bodies riding the waves. Not human bodies. Larger than human. The four-legged kind. Horses.

Bloated horse carcasses were entangled in a wide swath of floating wood debris. He counted ten horses. Then a dozen. He stopped counting at twenty-one. A long piece of a ship's rail drifted among the rubble.

He motioned for Martensen to throttle down. Dead horses thudded against the hull as the boat chugged forward.

As the trawler broke clear of the gruesome carnage, muffled shouts reached Kongsgaard over the drone of the engine. He raised the binoculars and scanned across the boat's path. After a couple of swipes, he spotted men in a listing lifeboat waving their arms and yelling. He stuck one arm high to acknowledge them.

When *Hildur VI* pulled alongside, the lifeboat rode low in the water with waves splashing over the rail. The skipper wondered what kept it afloat. Inside, five men sat waist deep in sloshing seawater, three moving and two still.

One by one, the captain and his mate pulled three men up onto the trawler. The men's long military coats shed steady streams of water onto their boots. They collapsed to their knees on the deck, folding their arms across their shivering bodies.

Kongsgaard pointed at the two still in the raft. "Are they alive?"

One of the rescued men shook his head. *"Nein."*

The captain nodded. The bodies would be left behind.

The survivors were taken belowdecks. The skipper looked them over. Swastikas on uniforms beneath their coats identified them. German soldiers. These were not the grizzled battlefield faces of Third Reich warriors he had seen in newsreels. These were the youthful faces of boys who looked like they belonged in a classroom.

The soldiers received heavy blankets. Kongsgaard pulled a pack of smokes from his pocket, gave each man a cigarette, and struck a light. The soldiers nodded their thanks but said nothing.

Curiosity about the accident filled the captain's head. Why was the wreckage of a ship carrying German soldiers so close to Norway's coast? War in Europe created military skirmishes on the North Sea, though usually much farther out. He also wondered about the horses. The captain wanted to ask, but language was a barrier. So, he refrained from questioning the soldiers. One of the men, however, did volunteer a word the two Norwegians understood: "Torpedo." As the man in a soggy uniform said it, he lifted his arms up and out.

"Makes sense," Kongsgaard muttered. He surmised that an Allied submarine must have chased a troopship into Norwegian territorial waters and launched a torpedo that blew it apart.

The *Hildur VI* turned back to port, and the captain radioed on his ship-to-shore to alert the harbormaster's office that he was returning with shipwrecked German soldiers. The fishing was over before it had begun.

—

Bjørn Erliksen built a fire in the brick living room fireplace. He then brought a bottle of Hansa beer from the kitchen, poured a glass half full, and put them both on a small square table next to his favorite chair. He had become a creature of habit. Each evening imitated the one before. He turned on his Huldra radio and set the lighted semicircular dial to NRK, Norway's national network, to catch up on the day's news. Finally, he nestled into an upholstered wingback chair.

Bjørn leaned toward the fire and stretched out his arms with open hands, savoring the warmth and listening to the crackle and snap of birch and fir. He knew how to build a fire. Growing up, he had risen early for an assigned chore to heat the house with a well-fed blaze. The responsibility was critical during those cold Norwegian winters. Electricity had come to his small farming village of Erlikvåg on Norway's west coast in the early 1920s, and, with it, increased use of electric heaters. But in his household, the central fireplace remained a primary heat source.

Bjørn glanced up at a framed photograph gracing the white wood mantel. The photo was a portrait of his parents. He thought of his mother, Kerste. As he had done so many times, he wondered what she was like. His eyelids softened. He had been told about her, but he never knew her. She had died in 1920 from complications giving birth to him.

Then six months ago, he had lost his father, Sigfried, whose heart gave out. His father's deteriorating health had forced him to retire at age sixty-four as the longtime district sheriff, and his death followed just months after. Bjørn dropped his head and stared at the leaping flames. He was glad the demands of farmwork helped him deal with the sadness.

Bjørn, at twenty, now owned the five-acre family homestead perched atop a hill overlooking Erlikvåg. Sigfried's will had deeded the farm to him, the youngest of three. Neither of his two siblings wanted to farm, and they had moved on. So he lived and worked there by himself, the latest of multiple generations to stake a livelihood from animals, crops, and hay.

Workdays were long, and Bjørn relished the evenings to sit back. The radio was his companion. That stylish square box of polished birchwood was his window to the outside world.

This night's NRK broadcast started just after he put his legs up on a cowhide-covered footstool and took a gulp of beer. The news led off with a British announcement that its Royal Navy had laid mines in the outer fjords leading to Norway's northern town of Narvik. Nazi Germany was mining iron ore across the border in Sweden and transporting it by train to Narvik's port, where it was loaded on German cargo ships.

"The British stated they took this action in concert with France to prevent Nazi Germany from using Norway's ports to obtain war resources," the broadcaster said. "The Norwegian government, along with Germany, protested the British mining of Norwegian territorial waters and demanded the mines' removal."

Bjørn scowled. He didn't like hearing that the war waged across the southern sea in Europe was reaching Norwegian shores. He wished Great Britain, France, and Germany would fight it out in their own backyards and leave his homeland alone.

He was confident Norway could stay out of the fight. The Norwegian government of Prime Minister Johan Nygaardsvold had formally declared the country's neutrality just like it had during the Great War. After two decades of peace, the new conflict had broken out seven months ago when England and France declared war on Nazi Germany after Hitler's blitzkrieg invasion of Poland.

Public sentiment in Norway after the Great War had called for peace at all costs, and the government acted accordingly. Its budgets consistently focused on providing for the nation's social well-being over defense. Norway's military armament and troop strength had fallen to bare bones.

Bjørn's opinion that war wouldn't come to Norway was no different than what he heard from his fellow villagers. To them,

Hitler was simply a cartoon character appearing on the newspaper editorial pages of Oslo's *Aftenposten* and the *Bergens Tidende*. They didn't see him as their menace.

Yet disturbing reports invaded Bjørn's living room with increased frequency. Weeks earlier, there had been news about warship movements on the North Sea, ship sinkings by submarines, and the British navy chasing a German tanker into Norwegian waters to rescue three hundred English prisoners and seamen on board.

When the radio announcer moved to the final item of the news broadcast, Bjørn looked at his watch. *Right on time,* he thought. He intended to stay tuned after the news for one of his favorite serials, *En Feil Sving* (*A Wrong Turn*).

"This morning, a fishing trawler rescued three men floating in a life raft on the North Sea off the southern coast," the newscaster said. "They all were taken to Lillesand, where the local sheriff interviewed them with the assistance of an interpreter.

"The men were German soldiers who said their transport ship, the *Rio de Janeiro*, was sunk by a torpedo presumably fired by an Allied submarine. The ship reportedly carried hundreds of German troops, military equipment, munitions, and horses.

"The soldiers told the sheriff they were on their way to Bergen to save Norway from a British and French invasion."

Bjørn lurched to the edge of his chair and leaned in closer.

"The trawler captain reported seeing many horse carcasses among the wreckage," the broadcast continued. "According to the soldiers, the horses were kept in an enclosure on the ship's deck. Most of the troops were belowdecks, and there were few survivors.

"In Oslo, government cabinet members, the Storting, and military officials met behind closed doors to discuss the report. But the government made no further comment."

He put his hands to his chin. Why would a German military ship be sailing to Bergen, Norway's largest urban center on the west coast, only thirty-five miles south of Erlikvåg? And for such a far-fetched reason? Perhaps the German soldiers were mistaken, or their explanation had been misinterpreted in translation. He dismissed the news item as another unsubstantiated rumor. He poured the rest of his beer into his glass and listened to the radio serial before turning in for the night.

Bjørn went to bed a little unsettled by news of British mines and rescued German soldiers. He couldn't worry about it. He needed sleep. Tomorrow, farmwork had to begin early.

CHAPTER 2

April 9, 1940

Bjørn sprang out of bed at four thirty the next morning. By five, he had washed, dressed, gulped down coffee, and headed out the door.

Heavy fog drifting up from the fjord further blinded the still-dark morning. Bjørn expected the thick, cold air that whited out Erlikvåg to hide the sun all morning. But he knew every square inch of the farm, and he was able to keep his bearings with the help of a flashlight. After pulling down hay from the loft for the cows, he set out slop for the pigs, collected eggs from the chicken coop, and let the sheep out of their pen to feed off the pasture grass.

Then he toured the outer reaches of the farm, checking for any overnight damage caused by predators. Bjørn corralled a piglet that must have squirmed under the fence overnight. He recognized it as the runt of the newest litter. He knew better than to get attached to the farm animals, but he couldn't help but pat the scrappy escape artist on the snout as he returned it to the pen.

Coming back to the house, he shed his damp blue pullover cap and heavy coat and hung them in the back mudroom to dry. He sat at the kitchen table for a breakfast of two soft-boiled eggs opened on top of toasted bread accompanied by another coveted cup of coffee.

The Huldra in the adjacent living room delivered the morning news over Bergen radio. The broadcast brought him to his feet. His leap skidded the chair backward and crashed it to the floor. He rushed into the living room and hovered by the radio.

The broadcaster, in a tense voice, reported that explosions and firing from large guns had erupted early in the morning in Byfjord, the main shipping lane linking Bergen and the North Sea. Warships of unknown origin had entered the fjord and were steaming toward the city. Bjørn's deep-brown eyes widened. He stood riveted to the words emanating from the Huldra.

"Norwegian military authorities ordered coastal beacons and navigational lights turned off," the broadcast went on, "and the navy laid mines on the fjord's approaches to Bergen."

The announcer signed off, pledging to return as more details became known. The radio fell silent.

The news left Bjørn motionless. He stared at the receiver as if he were expecting someone to step out from behind the radio speaker's mesh fabric covering. His mind raced with questions. What in the holy hell was happening?

He turned the dial to NRK's frequency. The Oslo-based network reported an armada of German warships was closing in on the capital city. Air-raid sirens blared and streetlights darkened. The government advised Oslo citizens to stay off the streets and move to their basements if possible.

Like Bergen radio, NRK announced the suspension of its regular programming and promised to return as further details arrived. The radio went silent again. Bjørn flicked the dial back and forth between Bergen's radio station and NRK for several minutes. The room hummed with radio static.

He held a sliver of hope that the next report would say everything was a terrible mistake, even a hoax, like Orson Welles's 1938

"War of the Worlds" broadcast in America. But separate news-casts from two cities had given similar accounts that Norway was under siege. How could it not be true? Then he remembered last evening's news about the rescued German soldiers. Things began to add up.

Confirmation came within the hour. NRK returned, and the newscaster read a statement issued by Norwegian Foreign Minister Halvdan Koht on behalf of King Haakon VII and the government.

"It is with great regret that I announce our nation is at war with Nazi Germany." A shiver rushed through Bjørn. Koht's radio message reported a convoy of warships in Oslofjord had engaged defending Norwegian naval forces in the early-morning hours, with losses on both sides. The foreign minister said that the Norwegian military was battling invasion fleets at other port cities on the coast, including Bergen.

His report went on to say that Germany claimed it was Norway's protector against Great Britain and France. The Nazis accused those two enemy nations of planning bases of operation in Norway to attack Germany and of plotting to take over the Port of Narvik to prevent ore shipments.

"German propaganda," Bjørn uttered aloud.

The foreign minister added that Nazi Germany had demanded that Norway surrender its troops, military equipment, and sup-plies. Norway also had to provide information on the location of any mines laid, black out all its territory to help with aerial defense, and put Germany in control of media, mail, and other communications services. The Norwegian government had rejected the demands.

Bjørn continued to listen, numbed to the words. Other reports came across the airwaves. The government announced a general mobilization of all military troops and reserves.

By midmorning, reality had set in for Bjørn. Norway was swept up in war.

———

A telephone ring jarred Bjørn's already frayed nerves. Upon hearing his sister on the other end, he released a deep sigh.

"I've been trying to get through, but lines are jammed," Åsta's hurried voice bolted from the receiver.

His questions came rapid fire. "Are you safe? What's going on? Is there fighting in the city?"

"I'm fine. Need to be quick. Don't know how long I can talk before I'm disconnected. At my apartment now, but I'm leaving Bergen. Coming to stay with you, at least until things settle down. That OK?"

"*Ja, absolutt.* Don't delay. Get here as soon as you can."

Åsta's voice held its urgency. "Leaving in a few minutes with a friend who has a car. She'll drop me off at Salhus. I'll catch the ferry, then make my way to the farm."

Bjørn's thoughts turned to his brother and his family. "What about Arne?"

"They're fine. Spoke to them a short while ago. They should be far enough out of the city center to avoid problems."

Bjørn pressed again. "What's happening in the city now?"

"No fighting, yet. German ships are in the harbor. They're beginning to unload. I heard guns going off early. Farther out in the fjord. Loud enough to wake me up. Then planes came over. Couldn't see them in the clouds. But I heard them. They dropped leaflets. Millions of 'em came down all over the city. Signed by a German general. They said they're coming as friends to defend us from the British and French."

Åsta's voice slowed from its machine-gun pace. "This is horrible. Don't know what will happen when they come into the city.

How can they be friends when they bring warships and soldiers? They want to take us over."

Bjørn frowned. "Looks that way. Leave as fast as you can. Don't delay. Don't do anything to put yourself in danger."

The distance from Bergen to the small settlement of Salhus was only about twelve miles north by car. A ferry from Salhus crossed Osterfjord to the village of Frekhaug. From there, a road followed the fjord about twenty miles to Erlikvåg. Normally, the trip took little more than an hour. But this day was anything but usual, and Bjørn couldn't help but worry.

"Traffic's very heavy, I'm told," Åsta said. "May be several hours before I get there. *Farvel.*"

Bjørn released a long, slow breath. For the first time since the streams of disturbing news had started, he showed a smile. *Whatever happens in Bergen,* he thought, *Åsta will be safe here.* And he relished the idea she would stay with him.

She was nearly ten years older and was more than a sister. She was like a mother. After Kerste died, Åsta had helped raise him. Sigfried hired a nanny to care for Bjørn as a baby while he tended to his sheriff duties and Åsta was at school. She liked to remind him how she held him in his infancy and rocked his cradle in the evenings.

The demands of being sheriff took Sigfried away from the farm frequently, and it fell on his children to do the work. There were eggs to collect, a chicken coop and barn to clean, cows to milk, sheep to shear, pigs to feed, hay to cut, fencing to repair, and a large garden to tend.

Beyond Åsta's household chores, she knew her way around the farm and became Bjørn's tutor as he grew. Chores and responsibilities increased with age. To her and their father's delight, Bjørn took to farming. He soaked up Åsta's instruction like fertile earth after a good rain.

He and his sister had been inseparable. Bjørn remembered how crushed he was when she announced she was leaving for Bergen to attend business school and pursue a bookkeeping career.

His thoughts shifted to his brother, Arne, a Bergen police officer who had a home in the city with his wife and young daughter. Arne's passion was in police work like his father. Growing up, Bjørn wasn't as close to Arne, who had seven years on him. He had grieved their mother's death by taking it out on Bjørn. Arne blamed him for the loss. As they got older, Arne admitted misplacing the blame and their relationship mended.

Arne could take care of himself. Bjørn's primary concern was Åsta's safety. But Bjørn still felt anxious about his brother. Arne's police beat placed him in the heart of Bergen and in the eye of a potential Nazi onslaught.

Bjørn brought his untouched breakfast from the kitchen table into the living room and picked at the cold toast and dried eggs. As morning light filled the room, he sat enveloped by the radio airwaves that brought gloom.

Reports from Bergen confirmed Åsta's description. No bombing or battle had ensued. After the Germans landed, the Norwegian Army had decided against defending the city to spare its destruction. But panic and uncertainty had prompted many citizens to leave as Åsta had.

Bjørn pulled in a deep breath and huffed it out. German troops were in the city by now, he assumed. Just marching right in and taking over. What had Norway done to them? What would they want with a small, peaceful nation?

NRK issued new reports. German planes had dropped a bomb on Oslo's public square at Akershus Castle. They had flown just above buildings and fired machine guns across the roofs and along streets. Pedestrians had scrambled to recessed doorways to avoid getting hit.

Farther down Oslofjord, never-used cannons installed at Oscarsborg Fortress just after the Crimean War had fired on the advancing German fleet and sunk the lead battleship. That had forced a waterborne German force to retreat, delaying its arrival at the capital city.

Bjørn's head dipped, but he kept his gaze pointed at the radio. More details arrived. South of Bergen, Nazi paratroopers captured Sola Air Station near Stavanger. The Germans were everywhere, taking over Trondheim, Kristiansand, and Narvik to the north. It was as though they had cast a large fishing net over Norway's strategic cities.

As the grim reports piled up, Bjørn's emotions moved well past disbelief and the shock of it all. They forked into resignation. He slumped forward. His hands felt weightless folded in his lap. His mind wrestled with questions of why it had happened and how it could be allowed to happen.

As his emotions flowed, Bjørn's anxiety grew into frustration, then advanced to a feeling of anger. How dare the Nazis invade Norway. Nazi Germany was a menace to the world and had to be stopped. The Reich should not be allowed to take over the country without a fight. Norway must fight back!

Bjørn rose from his chair, strode to the front window, and peered out. Much of Erlikvåg below the farm remained enveloped in damp fog. The gray screened out the waters of Osterfjord just beyond the village. A few houses and outbuildings near his farm were becoming visible. It was peaceful. No war. Just quiet. In his imagination, he visualized German soldiers and tanks bursting through the fog toward the house.

In that instant, helplessness washed over him. All he kept was a rifle that he had used for shooting competitions in school. It was a far cry from a military weapon. Useless against an army with many soldiers, tanks, and big artillery. He also had no training. Military service was mandatory for young men in Norway,

but he held a temporary deferment because of family responsibilities on the farm.

Bjørn pushed his frustrations away by pacing in circles around
the living room. Then came pounding on the front door.

CHAPTER 3

The banging on the front door commanded attention. It wasn't a polite rap that a neighbor made to borrow milk or to visit. This knock echoed down the hallway.

A voice behind the door shouted, "Bjørn! Bjørn! It's Jon. Need help."

Bjørn hustled to the door and swung it open. The chilly, moist outside air rushed in, sending a quiver through him.

Jon Møland, Bjørn's best friend, was hunched over on the small landing at the top of the steps, struggling to catch his breath. It appeared he had run most of the three miles from his farm at another end of Erlikvåg.

Jon burst out words between breaths. "It's the Germans . . . They're trying to take us over . . . I need help . . . Gotta get to Voss . . . Units are . . . mobilizing near there . . . Can you help me? . . . Your boat?"

Bjørn stepped back and took in Jon's full battle dress. His field-green Norwegian Army uniform was slightly visible beneath a heavy double-breasted military coat. The coat was cinched tight by a leather belt that held an ammunition pouch and first-aid kit. A soft wool field cap covered his head with flaps pulled down over his ears. He held a Norwegian-made, standard-issue Krag-Jørgensen rifle. A bulging knapsack was slung on his back.

Standing in the doorway, Bjørn looked skyward as he pondered a response. Given their tight bond, Bjørn didn't want to let Jon down. Still sucking in air, Jon looked at his friend and waited.

Bjørn lowered his gaze toward Jon. "You're right. The boat's the best way to get there. Can't think of any other good options."

Bjørn shared a boat that his father passed down to him and his siblings. Since it wasn't solely his, he felt reluctant to lend it, even to Jon. It was a speedy, eighteen-foot runabout with a varnished mahogany deck. The British-made Marston Seagull outboard motor pushed it between twelve and fourteen knots an hour, sixteen knots in calm seas.

Primarily used for sheriff duties, the boat had given Sigfried an efficient way to reach coastal communities with limited road access. He had emblazoned his job title *"Lensmann"* on the transom.

A brief time elapsed before Bjørn turned his head sideways away from Jon again, staring into the distance. He pulled out of his brief trance and found Jon waiting with wide eyes.

"I'm taking you myself and going with you to fight. Maybe I'm crazy. Soldiers fight wars, not farmers. I'm only a farmer. You're a farmer, too, but also a soldier. You're trained to fight, I'm not. But I can't sit on my hands at home. We must protect our farms and families. And our country."

Jon's face brightened. His heavy breathing had by now eased. "I wasn't asking you to go with me. But I was nervous about going alone."

"If we leave now, we can reach Bolstad before nightfall," Bjørn said. "Then we'd be only twenty miles from Voss."

Bjørn left Jon at the doorway and rushed down the hall. Moments later, he returned with a heavy coat, gloves, knit pullover cap, and a knapsack stuffed with cured meat and cheese along with a few extra items of clothing.

He also had stopped at the hallway closet to retrieve his own Krag-Jørgensen and a box of ammunition. His was not the same model as Jon's army-issued weapon. It was a guttekarabin that Bjørn used for target shooting in school physical-education class. The rifle featured a shorter barrel and accepted only a few cartridges at a time. It was not designed to kill. But if aimed with intent, it could be lethal.

Bjørn and Jon bolted from the house and made their way down the road. When they reached a neighboring farm, Bjørn halted in midstride. "Wait for me here. I need to tell Nils Tellevik to keep an eye out for Åsta. She's getting out of the city and will stay at the farm."

After that was accomplished, they raced through Erlikvåg to the waterfront. A boathouse along the fjord a half mile north of the village housed *Lensmann*.

They found the sleek boat snuggled in its slip. Bjørn retrieved a black slicker from a hook inside the door and wrestled into it. He then pulled down four ten-gallon petrol cans, enough fuel to cover the fifty-mile trip, he estimated.

He unlatched and slid open the large barn-type doors facing the water. With Jon and their gear on board, Bjørn pushed the boat out of the slip into the foggy abyss and jumped in. He yanked hard on the motor cord and fired up the outboard, which sputtered to life with its trademark whiny hum.

———

Bjørn and Jon arrived at their destination well before dark. Their journey by boat had been steady and uneventful in the calm waters of Osterfjord. They had seen little sign of war on the way. Only a Norwegian patrol boat crowded with soldiers had sped by headed north. The friends had motored the northern length of Osterfjord, turned southeasterly into an intersecting fjord, and maneuvered an intricate network of waterways to the settlement of Bolstad.

The village sat in rugged beauty. A lush forest of fir rose steeply from the fjord banks. In some places, massive granite faces jutted straight up from the sea. Situated on a flat spot at the end of Bolstadfjord, the village itself was nothing more than a few businesses, a centrally located church, and a handful of scattered farms.

After obtaining permission from the harbormaster, Bjørn tied the boat at the community dock. When he told the harbormaster why they'd come, the man agreed to store *Lensmann* in an unused boathouse and directed them to an army unit camped on a farm at the end of a dirt road uphill from the village.

The farm resembled Bjørn's place except for a much larger, green-painted barn. Beyond a tight cluster of farm outbuildings sprouted an army encampment. Bjørn sighted a dozen or so soldiers scrambling to put up large camouflage-covered tents just inside the tree line of a gently rising forest. Tall firs created a canopy to hide the tents from German warplanes that might loom overhead.

Bjørn and Jon were pointed to the barn that now found use as unit headquarters and were told to see a Lieutenant Brittvik. The friends were less than fifty paces away from reporting for duty.

———

Lieutenant Konrad Brittvik let them know he was in charge. He was as stiff and stern as he was emphatic.

The officer fixed his gaze on Jon, whose posture was at full attention. "I'm assigning you to my unit. I'll clear it with command. Your unit commander will understand. I need men, and you have military training."

Bjørn tried to emulate his friend, standing with his chest out and eyes pointed straight ahead. But without military experience, he doubted his stance met army regimen.

The barn turned unit command center was roomy and sparse. A desk and chair held down the far corner on the dirt floor. A couple of radios and a shortwave transmitter were on the desk. A large table was positioned in the center with a map spread out across the top. The lieutenant was on one side of the table, and Bjørn and Jon stood on the other.

Brittvik posed ramrod straight. His six-foot-two frame fit perfectly in his uniform. He looked a military man through and through. His gaze alternated between the new arrivals. With both hands, he gestured toward them.

"Look, Corporal Møland," he said, "new recruits are showing up here from all over. They're willing to fight, and thank goodness for that, but they have no military knowledge or skill. We must train them and do it quickly. I need people like you with experience. The enemy is already trampling our land. The Germans are potent fighters. They have a superior army, and our challenge is to prevent them from overtaking us."

The commanding officer leaned forward and relaxed his hands on the table, then shifted his eyes toward Bjørn. "And you. Can you shoot?"

Bjørn's stiff face converted into a half-grin. Brittvik's stare intimidated him, but he tried his best not to show it. "I earned a marksman medal in school competitions. And I hunt."

Brittvik put his hand on his chin. "Let's see about that."

The lieutenant turned to another soldier, who had been introduced as Brittvik's aide-de-camp. "Draw a target and pin it to a tree outside. Make sure there's space for at least fifty paces. And check that no one is behind the tree. I don't want any casualties before we fight."

The aide took a large piece of notepaper from the desk, drew a circle the diameter of a dinner plate, and sketched smaller circles and a bull's-eye. They followed Brittvik out, and the aide nailed the paper to a thick fir along the tree line.

Nightfall neared but there was enough light to see. It had been a long day for Bjørn and less than ten hours since German warships had landed in Bergen. He felt weary, but he had to show proficiency.

Brittvik directed him to back up fifty paces and shoot at the target with his school carbine. Bjørn pumped five rounds at the target. One went through the small bull's-eye, three hit inside the next circle, and another shot hit just inside the larger perimeter circle.

"That will do," Brittvik said. "All right, report to the tent next to the barn and we'll get a uniform together for you." He turned to his aide. "Get him a good rifle."

Brittvik's focus returned to Bjørn. "The sergeant here will take you to your quarters for the night.

"You're now members of . . ." Brittvik glanced down at a chart on the table. "I'm putting you in Second Platoon, G of the Tenth."

Jon interpreted for Bjørn. They now officially belonged to Second Platoon, Company G, Tenth Infantry Regiment of the Norwegian Army's Fourth Division.

———

Bjørn got his uniform and shed his civilian clothes. His military greens fell short of a perfect fit. The pants were a little big and the shirtsleeves slightly short for his five-foot-ten, two-hundred-pound frame.

He exchanged his rifle for the same model Krag-Jørgensen weapon that Jon shouldered. The supply clerk also issued ammo, a sleeping bag, rations, a first-aid kit, and other supplies, as well as a large pack to hold them.

In their assigned sleeping tent, they joined fifteen soldiers. During introductions and handshakes, Bjørn learned that most of his tentmates hailed from the mountain and fjord-side towns and villages near Voss. The others were from the west coast in places north of Erlikvåg. Jon and the platoon leader were the only regular or reserve army troops. The rest were green volunteers like Bjørn.

The army's Fourth Division was commanded by Major General William Steffens, the officer who had decided to mobilize in the mountains at Voss to spare Bergen from bloodshed and destruction.

—

Bjørn huddled around a portable kerosene stove with Jon and their tentmates near the end of a traumatic, eventful day. He struggled to keep his eyes focused and was ready to roll out his sleeping bag. But a soldier stopped by their tent and poked his head through the front flap.

"Report to the farmhouse," he commanded. "Vidkun Quisling is about to speak over the radio."

Jon looked at Bjørn. "Quisling? The fascist?"

"He must be in bed with the Germans," Bjørn said.

Another soldier in the tent spoke up. "That Quisling guy heads the Nasjonal Samling political party. It's like the Nazis. Never gained much traction in Norway. Don't know how they've hung around this long. But the Germans come, and Quisling must be the center of attention now."

When Bjørn and his comrades entered the house, Brittvik and other soldiers were jammed in the front room. They had been invited by the home's owners, a family of five who were hosting the encampment on their property. The receiver was tuned to NRK. The men's chatter died away to a presenter's crackling words: "Here is Vidkun Quisling, the new head of the Norwegian government, to issue a proclamation to the people of Norway."

The Norwegian Nazi's voice then filled the air. "Men and women of Norway. After England violated Norwegian neutrality by laying mines in Norwegian territorial waters without meeting any opposition other than the usual half-hearted protests from the Nygaardsvold government, the German government offered the Norwegian government their peaceful help accompanied by a sincere reassurance that they would respect national independence and Norwegian life and property."

Bjørn shook his head and mumbled, "A mouthful of crap."

Quisling's voice droned on. "As an answer to this offer to help solve our country's totally unbearable situation, the Nygaardsvold government called for regular mobilization and gave the Norwegian military the unreasonable order to oppose the German help by means of armed force."

He went on to accuse the national government of putting the country's independence at risk by resisting. He then declared himself the "new chief of government" and called on all Norwegians to remain calm, for all national and local government officials to submit to the new order, and for the country's military to put down their arms. Quisling then abruptly stopped.

Looking around the room, Bjørn felt his anger grow and sensed it building in others. What began as a murmur of resentment rose to borderline rowdiness.

"Bastard traitor," someone shouted.

"I'll never submit to his puppet government, never," Bjørn overheard someone else say.

Brittvik's voice lifted above the clatter. "Let's keep it down. Let me have your attention." The room quieted, and he continued. "We all know there's an enemy in our country. We have a duty to fight on behalf of our king and remove this evil. Let us recommit ourselves to what we are ordered to do. There are many countrymen and women counting on us. We must focus all our attention and energy on the German enemy and traitors in our country who brought them here. So, return to your quarters and get rest. I've been informed that we move out in the morning."

Angry words filled the night air as the soldiers returned to their tents. In Bjørn's tent, fuel was added to the stove and everyone crawled into their sleeping bags. Even then, discussions were hot.

Bjørn zipped up his bag and glanced over at Jon, who was wrapped up in his sleeping bag to one side of him. The two had been friends since they were six, meeting at school. They had grown up as best buddies and stayed that way.

Jon liked to remind Bjørn about what had happened when they were teenagers and a school tough had challenged Jon to a fight. He didn't want to involve Bjørn and had showed up alone in the woods near the school playground prepared to defend his boyhood. He didn't know that Bjørn had sensed trouble and trailed him. Bjørn broke in between the two before the fight began. "When you take on my friend, you must take me on, too," he had told the bully, who backed away.

Like Bjørn, Jon had been running his family's farm since his father retired early and handed it over to his only son. Two years ago, at eighteen, Jon married Liv, a school classmate, and Bjørn was the best man. The couple became parents to a son, Mikal.

The friends had always shared their thoughts openly. Now Bjørn needed to level with Jon, who he noticed was still awake.

"Just before Quisling spoke, I began to question why I came with you," Bjørn said in a near whisper. "I thought maybe I'd reacted too quickly. I know nothing about the military. I just left the farm and put everything in Åsta's lap. Then I heard the fascist. I've got to go on and fight. Everyone is depending on us."

Jon answered in a soft voice. "We're putting our lives at risk, isn't it true, and I've got Liv and Mikal to think about. But I agree with you, we must defend our country."

After a brief silence, Bjørn spoke again. "We've always looked out for each other. We must do that now more than ever before. Help me be a good soldier."

"*Ja.* I will be watching your back, and I know you'll do the same."

Bjørn's eyelids were heavy. But he couldn't stop Quisling's voice from replaying in his head. Bjørn remembered a cartoon in the *Bergens Tidende* newspaper portraying the fascist leader as a pouting child with a swollen, baby-faced head stomping his feet and stammering in front of a government building, demanding attention to be heard on his views. But passersby paid no heed.

Now that cartoon figure was trying to take over the government with the support of Nazi invaders. In one day, Norway had been turned on its head. The Germans invaded and now held Norway's two most major cities, Bergen and Oslo. If radio reports were accurate, several more important coastal port cities had fallen, and the king and government had fled the capital. It had all happened so suddenly.

Risks and farm responsibilities aside, Bjørn vowed to do what he could to defend his homeland.

CHAPTER 4

April 18, 1940

A fresh recruit with little more than a week's worth of military training, Bjørn moved out with his platoon headed for battle. His shoulders felt all sixty pounds of his full pack. He gripped his rifle. An accompanying bayonet inside a slender holster was strapped to his leg, and an ammunition belt banded around his waist.

In the ten days since he had joined the army, this was the second time he was on the move. The first had been an uncomfortable 150-mile journey from Bolstad, where he'd enlisted, to Hagafoss, a small village nestled at the upper end of a valley named Hallingdal in the central mountainous part of southern Norway. He and twenty-four other troops had been packed tightly in the bed of a transport truck over rough roads that were narrow, curvy, and rutted. Bjørn had felt every bump and turn as the truck slogged through mud and skidded on snow.

His unit had been joined by another company of mostly untrained volunteers at Hagafoss, where they had set up a temporary base. There, Bjørn and other new recruits learned the fundamentals of soldiering. They were drilled on firing their weapons and marching and were put through an abundance of physical training.

Then orders had come to go by foot southeast to the valley of Ørhandal. They were to trek the length of the valley to its southern end, set up defensive positions, and prepare to take on a large German fighting force. Their mission was to repel the enemy. En route, they would link up with another Fourth Division unit, but they still expected to be outnumbered.

Lieutenant Konrad Brittvik had told them that fierce fighting was already being waged in Gudbrandsdal, just one mountain range to the east of them. The king and government had fled through that valley only days earlier with the Germans in hot pursuit. Norwegian forces were playing defense, attempting to hold back the Nazi onslaught advancing north from Oslo.

Bjørn broke camp in Hagafoss with 118 other soldiers. Crisp, early-morning mountain air whipped around his face as he marched near the end in one of two columns following a steep, windy road to Ørhandal. Jon was at his heels.

As Hagafoss disappeared behind him, Bjørn's stomach churned. Despite a little military training and a growing number of comrades, his confidence wavered. In the days ahead, he anticipated a major battle, facing tanks, artillery, and even the Luftwaffe in addition to seasoned Wehrmacht ground troops. He clenched his rifle tight to keep his hand from shaking.

A steep mountain pass stood between them and Ørhandal. They made their way through a long climb of switchbacks. The road was paved, but cracks and potholes from a long, hard winter made the ascent arduous. At the summit, Bjørn rubbed his overworked thigh muscles and drew in deep breaths.

The soldiers descended the mountain and reached the northern edge of the valley, and Brittvik and the other company's lieutenant called a halt. Bjørn and the others dropped their packs. He gulped water from his canteen and dipped into rations. Jon perched on his pack beside him.

Bjørn had a clear view of the valley. Ørhandal appeared to be a long, thin slice of flat land cut through high mountains. A small river flowed through the valley floor, which was barely wider than two *fotball* fields. Mountains on both sides of the valley rose to majestic heights.

The march resumed, and after about five miles, the military contingent arrived at Gjelldal, a spot in the road that was nothing more than two farms. Here, the other Fourth Division element of company size appeared and joined the units. A heartened smile filled Bjørn's face. By his count, the addition tripled the contingent's size.

"Now we have more to fight with, true?" he said to Jon.

"The more, the better."

The newly arrived unit took the lead, and the soldiers again formed lines on both sides of the road, each troop five to six paces apart. Bjørn marched near the back of the formation. He guessed the procession now was strung out about a half mile.

As they passed a few more remote farms, families emerged from their houses to view the troops, watching the procession as if it were a parade. A grandmotherly woman waved a Norwegian flag. Bjørn pushed his chest out and looked straight ahead with gritted teeth. He saw himself in them—patriotic Norwegians living a simple life in an isolated place far from the world outside and untouched by war. Except he had a rifle in his hand and was equipped to keep it that way.

CHAPTER 5

April 19, 1940

After a night on hard ground in sleeping bags, Bjørn and the other troops were on the march again. His back ached and his legs were sore. But he had no complaints about the overnight accommodations. Roughing it in the mountains during hunting, hiking, and ski trips was the way of life in Norway.

Back in double-file formation, the men were well on their way to reaching the southern end of Ørhandal, where they would establish strategic positions against the Germans.

Before long, they reached a point where the valley narrowed to about one hundred yards with steep, tree-filled terrain on both sides leading up to high mountain ridges. Brittvik was about a hundred yards farther up the line, and Bjørn and Jon maintained their positions near the rear. The shuffle of boots echoed across the valley.

Suddenly the air around them exploded. From the left, a volley of rifle shots rang out and continued in rapid fire. Bjørn saw soldiers not far ahead of him crumple to the ground. Instinctively, he hit the earth. He saw Jon and others around them do the same. As he hugged the ground, Bjørn fidgeted with his rifle's bolt action lever, preparing to shoot back. The rattle of other weapons being prepared surrounded him, but it was muffled by the sound of rifle fire coming at them. They lay flat on open ground like ducks on a pond. Bullets whizzed above Bjørn's head.

He felt a tug on his coat sleeve, looked up, and saw Jon hunched over him, pulling on his arm with a firm grip.

"Follow me. Do as I do," Jon hollered.

They sprinted for the trees roughly thirty feet away. Bjørn duplicated Jon's lead, crouching low in a zigzag pattern. Bjørn crashed through the trees with a headlong dive between two tall firs and crawled tightly behind one. A bullet shaved off splinters of bark above him. He maneuvered to get a good shot at the enemy. Bjørn pushed his legs under him and shimmied up with his back firmly against the trunk of the tree. Jagged bark scraped his back. He spun around into a kneeling position and quickly leveled his rifle around the tree to return fire. He squeezed the trigger and emptied the five-round magazine into the tree line across the valley.

German soldiers weren't visible on the other side. Like him, they were hidden in the dense thicket. But he aimed and shot at the gun smoke curling up from their rifles. Bjørn reeled himself back behind the trunk to load again. He could see Jon huddled behind a nearby tree, firing his weapon from a kneeling position. Machine-gun fire thundered their way, sending volleys that tore into the trees, spraying splinters all around them. The barrage forced Bjørn to stay tucked behind the tree.

It was an ambush, plain and simple. His Norwegian force had planned the same thing. But the Germans must have advanced faster than expected and beat the Norwegians to the punch.

The intense exchange of gunfire continued minutes more, a span that seemed like an eternity to Bjørn. Then it gradually tapered off, with sporadic shooting. Both sides still took cover in their respective tree lines. After a short lull came heavy pounding more violent than before.

A dreaded whistling, then deafening explosions stung Bjørn's eardrums, forcing him to drop his rifle and cover his ears. He realized what it was. Artillery. Big German guns took over the ambush. As shells collided with treetops, explosions set off flashes of brightness that matched fireworks at a Constitution Day celebration. Bright colors painted the sky.

Limbs and blown-apart chunks of tree trunks rained down. Bjørn pressed his head firmly against the tree. His senses dulled and motion slowed to a crawl. He slumped to the ground beside the tree and curled his body into a tight ball. Bjørn was gripped by pure terror that froze him in place. But it became clear that he had to move or be crushed.

Bjørn looked across at Jon, who stared back from his adjacent, still-standing tree. With a nod of his head, Bjørn sent a signal. He grabbed his rifle and raced uphill. A thick falling branch struck him on the shoulder, and he dropped to one knee, wincing in pain. Again, he felt the clutch of Jon's hand hoisting him up. They were in full retreat.

The two moved beyond the heart of the shelling. Explosions landed behind them with thunderous booms. The hillside grew steeper and Bjørn's legs churned harder. His shoulder throbbed.

They scrambled and clawed their way up as the terrain steepened. They were deep in trees on a mountainside well away from the valley floor. As they continued to climb, the forest gave way to more open rocky terrain where tree cover was spotty. They found a trunk of a decayed, fallen tree and crawled under it into a pit. The divot was smaller than a shell crater, but deep enough to put them below ground level. They curled up there until the shelling ceased.

Jon looked at Bjørn with still-fearful eyes. "How did we make it through that?" Bjørn was silent. He could only close his eyes and suck in all the air his lungs could handle.

———

Bjørn was now on top of a solid rock ridge high above the field of bombardment, Jon next to him. There were others. Bjørn counted twenty-nine, including himself. He recognized the same exhausted, anguished looks on the faces of Jon and other soldiers spread out along the ridge. He felt equally spent of energy.

He lay down, resting his head on his pack that somehow had stayed strapped on while he'd dodged sizzling bullets and artillery shells. He ran his hand across a rip in the corner of it about the size of a bullet. Had a bullet torn through it while he hugged the ground in the valley meadow? That might have put him inches from death. His shoulder continued to throb, but it didn't feel to him like anything was broken or displaced.

He didn't move a muscle. But as his initial trauma began to fade, he was gripped by a fear that he and his fellow soldiers might be hunted. Bjørn bolted upright, jammed fresh bullets into his rifle, and scanned the ridge.

The ridge looked like a long, solid formation of Ice Age granite with a cliff-like face. It appeared to stretch for miles, overlooking an open meadow of grass and brush at the base of the cliff about two hundred feet below the top. The forest of thick fir was just beyond the meadow, extending down the steep mountainside where they had climbed.

If German forces emerged from the trees onto the meadow, they would be exposed to the Norwegians' strategic advantage on the ridgetop. The only way up that Bjørn could see was a tundra-filled gully that he and other surviving Norwegians soldiers had found to make their way to the ridgetop. Now they had that access covered.

"We have to be ready," he told Jon, who nodded and then sent signals down the line to the others. Like Bjørn, the survivors fought through fatigue and prepared their weapons. They stretched out along the solid ridgeline, forming a line of defense. Bjørn also kept his eyes peeled for more Norwegian stragglers. But neither friend nor foe appeared. Quiet returned to the steep-sloped mountain.

Bjørn's vantage point gave him a sweeping view of the treed hillside below. Farther down, it looked like a tornado had swept through. Gaps were blown through lush green treetops. Tree trunks stood topped and delimbed, and debris lay scattered and piled. He couldn't see enough of the valley floor to spot any activity.

He sat absorbed in his thoughts. Then he turned to Jon. "I wonder if anyone is alive down there. I saw so many lying on the ground."

Jon nodded with a frown. "Can't go down and get them."

"You're right. But I hate thinking that some might still be alive. So many were with us, and"—Bjørn snapped his fingers—"in an instant, they weren't."

He looked away from Jon off into space. "Don't know how we survived it. God must be looking out for us. Why do we deserve to live?"

Jon shrugged and his chest collapsed in an exhale. "We need to find out if anyone else made it up the mountain farther down the ridge."

He left Bjørn's side and moved down the line of resting soldiers along the ridgetop. He returned a half hour later.

"Found a regular army sergeant," Jon said. "Best I can tell, he's the highest ranking of all of us. I'm second because I'm a corporal, even if I'm in the reserves. Like you, the rest seem to be volunteers."

Bjørn managed a slight smile. "*Ja*, I'm green. I don't want to get tested like that again."

He lifted his arm to check his shoulder and grimaced. "What happens now?"

Jon was quick to reply. "We decided to send four out in pairs in both directions to see if anyone else made it up the ridgeline farther down and to keep an eye out for Germans. I didn't volunteer you. You've got to rest that shoulder.

"We'll stay put for the night," he continued. "The sergeant and I agreed we can't stay here. Nazis probably'll sweep the area before long. At first light in the morning, we're leaving. Heading north over the mountains toward Sognefjord. Hoping we can meet up with some other units at Lærdal.

"For now, we'll all spread out and take turns on watch. You and I, we'll move down to the end and watch our right flank."

Bjørn nodded.

About two hours later, one pair of scouts returned with four other Norwegian troops. The soldiers reported they had scrambled up the ridge about two miles south. By Bjørn's count, the new arrivals grew the survivors' ranks to thirty-three.

At night, he took his turn on watch. He lay prone but with his head raised and eyes vigilant for anything stirring below or approaching along the ridgeline. All he could see was darkness. If there was moonlight, cloudy night skies shielded it. But the night was quiet.

Bjørn's mind wandered. He replayed the day. He couldn't remember a more traumatic period in his life. He was spared. So many of his comrades weren't. He wondered whether Lieutenant Brittvik survived.

He looked at Jon, who was asleep. It was silent all around him. At that moment, Bjørn was alone. He had this part of the night to himself. Tears began to roll down both cheeks. He couldn't stop them.

CHAPTER 6

June 1940

For Bjørn, the fighting had ended before it had begun. It had been eight weeks now since the German ambush in Ørhandal that had decimated the 350-member Norwegian force he'd marched with. He had survived enemy fire and shelling with thirty-two others. He didn't know how many additional soldiers might have escaped it. He wondered if he'd ever know. Bjørn had spent the weeks since the massacre in retreat.

The surviving group he and Jon were with had fled the mountain ridgetop the morning after the German attack and had headed northward over barren, snow-covered, mountainous terrain. They had sought to put distance between them and any pursuing German troops and eventually reach the picturesque town of Lærdal on the banks of Sognefjord's upper reaches. There, they hoped to find vestiges of Norwegian Army forces and regroup to fight another day.

The trek had proved sluggish and strenuous as they traversed a formidable plateau at an elevation of more than five thousand feet. In places, Bjørn and his fellow soldiers had left knee-deep imprints in the frozen white. Relying on compasses, they had climbed and descended a rugged contour, crossing still-frozen lakes, circumventing massive rock outcroppings, and facing subfreezing temperatures while camping under open skies. If there was any comfort, it was in not encountering the enemy along the way.

After crossing the mountain plateau, Bjørn and the contingent eventually had dropped into a slender valley with a river running through it. When the valley floor widened, they approached two farms standing side by side. Both were set back from the river, which meandered through fields of meadow grass. There were large patches of snow, and the homesteads didn't seem quite awake from their winter slumber.

When the farm families identified Norwegian flag patches on the soldiers' uniforms, they had greeted them as heroes. The farmers provided them with food and shelter in their barns for the night.

The farmers also had delivered news that changed the course of Bjørn's retreat. The soldiers learned that the Norwegian military had abandoned the southern part of the country and moved to northern Norway, where the king and the government would carry on the fight. It had left a large section of the country with most of the populace, including the capital city of Oslo and the second-largest metropolis of Bergen, firmly under Nazi control. One farmer said Norwegian units in the south were ordered disbanded and soldiers dismissed. He also advised them not to proceed to Lærdal. German ships had landed troops and taken over the town.

With that disappointing news, the ranking sergeant decided the contingent would split up and the soldiers would go their separate ways home. He had reasoned that continued travel as a group invited conflict if they encountered Germans.

Facing a long journey home, Bjørn had wondered how he and Jon would get there. His feet were wet and cold, his legs and back were sore, and he was physically exhausted. But the friends had left the next morning, traveling in now-enemy territory in their own homeland. Bjørn and Jon kept their rifles and all their gear. They had to stay in uniform. It was the only clothing they had. Their route westward had followed Sognefjord, often along high mountain ridges overlooking the fjord and in tree lines well back from the main road winding along the water. Sightings of German transports shuttling troops and equipment were frequent, and they also had to stay hidden from enemy planes buzzing overhead.

On the way home, Bjørn had shivered beneath his heavy coat in frigid temperatures and soaking rain. Their rations didn't last long, and they went days without food. Stomach growls had been constant. To refresh their aching feet, they soaked them in streams of glacial runoff. On occasion, they basked in sunshine and approached an occasional homestead that flew a Norwegian flag. The loyal Norwegians shared food and on one stop allowed them to bathe.

They had covered most of the 127-mile length of Sognefjord when they reached Ytre Oppedal, a town near the fjord's entrance. The men stopped at a friendly house and faced crushing news. A retired ferryboat captain who lived there told them that Norway had surrendered completely to Germany on June 10, and the king and government officials had fled to England. Norwegian soldiers, he said, were guaranteed safe passage home if they surrendered their weapons. But Bjørn and his friend were not about to relinquish their rifles. They buried them in hay on a farmer's truck that took them the rest of the way home.

———

Bjørn now found himself standing in the rutted dirt road looking at a two-story farmhouse of worn white paint and a gray slate roof. Sheep and cows grazed in a fenced pasture that sloped gently down the left side of the house toward a half-moon-shaped lake. He was home.

When he and Jon had reached Erlikvåg, they had separated. Jon proceeded to his farm, and Bjørn trudged through the main part of the village and up the winding road to his homestead.

When Bjørn was about fifty steps from his house, he stopped to take in the welcome sight. His bulging backpack had been strapped to his back for so long, it seemed permanently affixed. He couldn't wait to discard it. Sweat caused by the warm, sunny day dampened his uniform. A once-shiny new rifle, now scratched and used, hung on his shoulder. That, too, he was ready to retire. After cheating death and spending months surviving on little food and many anxious moments avoiding enemy troops, the sight of his farm enveloped him like a warm blanket.

He saw the front door fly open. His sister appeared in the doorway.

There hadn't been much for him to smile about on his trip home. But seeing Åsta bounding down the front steps produced a broad one.

He bolted toward her, forgetting about his fatigued, aching legs. Her cheeks glowed as she flung herself toward him. Bjørn slid the straps of his rifle and pack off his weary shoulders and dropped them to the ground, all as he approached her.

They met in a warm embrace, gripping each other tight. When he softened his hold on her, Åsta put her hands on his whiskered cheeks and, on tiptoes, kissed his forehead. She hugged him a second time.

"This is all I wanted," she said. "To see you again."

His words came out in a whisper. "Me, too."

He felt her tears on his face.

"We've been so worried," Åsta said. "We heard the fighting was horrible. It drove me mad. I assumed you were in the middle of it."

Bjørn's eyes drifted away from his sister. "We had some difficult moments, it is true. But that's in the past. I'm here now."

He looked back at Åsta and turned the subject. "How have you been getting on here?"

She responded with a soft smile. "It's been quiet. We have been removed from any war. I feel relaxed being away from the city. Except for the circumstances that brought me here, I'm glad I came."

"I owe you. I made a sudden decision when Jon showed up needing help. I believed I had a duty to go. And I left the place all in your lap."

Åsta shook her head. "You did what you had to do. All I wanted was for you to come back alive."

She turned toward the house. "I bet you're hungry. I'll fix you something."

———

After a refreshing bath and putting on a clean change of clothes, Bjørn puttered around the farm. Åsta insisted on making him a special homecoming dinner—*fårikål*, a savory stew of lamb and cabbage served with boiled potatoes. His favorite dish. He inspected the farm while she cooked.

First stop was the barn just behind the house. Bjørn rubbed the large, heavy ring handle of the barn door, closing his eyes as he felt the cold, smooth iron. He found it tidy inside. The dirt floor was raked smooth, the separate enclosure for the cows cleaned, and hay piled in the loft. He smiled, thinking how well Åsta maintained it.

He strolled back outdoors and peered in the chicken coop, a separate low-rise building next to the barn. He wandered past the pigsty and covered pens for the sheep and goats. Bjørn then opened the gate to the pasture and stepped through, brushing the grass with his boot. The animals busily picked apart the pasture grass. They ignored him until he got close. Then they merely raised their heads, eyed him, and resumed feeding.

Bjørn spotted a loose board on the fence with a nail popped out. He picked up a stone and pounded it back into place. Today, there would be no heavy lifting. Farm chores could wait. He just wanted to savor the moment. The fighting was over. He was back. He was alive.

Norway's defense against the invaders had crumbled in only two months. King Haakon VII and the government had fled the country aboard a British destroyer to live in exile in London. The Nazis now ruled Norway. While Erlikvåg outwardly seemed untouched by war, Bjørn anticipated uncertain days ahead.

CHAPTER 7

The summer of 1940 brought glorious blue skies and warmth as Bjørn settled back into the routine of farming. Life pushed on as usual. He saw no physical evidence of Nazi Germany's rule in Erlikvåg aside from an occasional military truck rumbling by the village on the main road along the fjord or a gray German patrol ship on the water.

But mentally he didn't feel right. Memories of his short-lived war experience plagued him. Soldiers falling dead around him in Ørhandal and jarring artillery explosions played out in his head at night.

He shared his troubled thoughts with Jon, who visited him one hot day in early July.

"Don't know if you're feeling the same thing, but I'm having nightmares about Ørhandal," Bjørn said as they shared a beer. "Some mornings, all I want to do is stay curled up in bed. Åsta has to get me up to do chores.

"I get angry, too. The other day, I replaced a fence post and my shovel hit a rock. Hurt my wrist. Should have been no big deal. You know, happens all the time. But I got so mad, I banged the shovel on the ground so hard I broke the handle. Made me so unhappy, I broke down."

Jon cast a side glance at his friend. "My dreams aren't good, either. Same thing's happening to me. I dream about it and wake up sweating."

Bjørn dropped his head. "I keep asking myself why we survived when others didn't."

Jon reached out and touched his friend's shoulder. "You can't answer that. So you need to try to forget it. You'll drive yourself crazy otherwise. Give yourself time. I'm hoping it'll pass."

———

In the ensuing weeks, Bjørn erased noticeable evidence of his military service. He folded his field fatigue uniform, stashed it in the rucksack, and tucked it away in the recesses of the attic. His army-issued Krag-Jørgensen rifle went up there as well.

Since he had traded his winter jacket along with other civilian clothes for military gray-greens when he'd enlisted, he needed a winter coat. His army coat had kept him comfortable in the mountains when he was away at war. Its multiple pockets made it useful on the farm.

But Bjørn didn't want to stand out in military apparel. So, he soaked the coat in a lye solution to wash out the army green and colored it with black dye. The coat retained its military styling but now had a functional civilian look.

While he made easy stow of his military remnants, his emotions were more difficult to bury. Over the summer, Bjørn's disappointment and even guilt that he'd failed to save his country advanced in another direction. His anger reawakened. It was fueled when he and Åsta listened to the evening news from NRK and the BBC and learned about Nazi oppression beyond the borders of Erlikvåg.

Josef Terboven, a German hard-liner close to Hitler, had been appointed to oversee all nonmilitary functions in Norway as

Reichskommissar. Norwegian Nazi Vidkun Quisling hadn't lasted long as the self-declared ruler of the national government. He was demoted to a position with little authority when the Germans quickly recognized he didn't have the support of the people as he'd claimed.

All summer, Terboven's venom against the exiled king and government spewed into the Erliksen living room over the propagandized, Nazi-controlled radio waves of NRK. Bjørn caught himself balling his hands into fists as he listened. He sometimes rose out of his chair and huffed around the living room.

One evening brought them news of a Terboven-issued decree ordering Norwegians to surrender their firearms and establishing severe penalties for violators. Despite that, Bjørn refused to part with his army-issued rifle. He pulled it down from the attic, wrapped it tightly in a bedsheet, and hid it in the root cellar under the house.

To get censorship-free news, they, like many Norwegians, tuned in to the BBC to keep current about the war in Europe and hear snippets of trustworthy news about Norway. From the BBC, Bjørn and Åsta heard that the occupying Germans were significantly drawing down Norway's reserves of coal, grain, food supplies, and commodities, sending them to Germany. With no merchant ships arriving with needed supplies for import-dependent Norway, food shortages surfaced in large and small cities alike. Rationing was imposed.

As the summer neared an end, they were unable to buy what they needed from the depleted shelves in the village's general store.

———

Bjørn took good care of his chickens, and they rewarded him with eggs by the dozens. His father and Åsta taught him early to keep the coop clean, the chickens well fed, and the roosts sufficiently bedded with straw.

He was pleased with the production of the hens. He relied on his birds as a food source and as an important part of his regular income. Since his return to the farm, he discovered his fifty-one hens and five roosters were as productive as ever. One day, Bjørn retrieved forty-nine eggs. He sold two dozen at the general store and another dozen directly to neighbors who didn't raise poultry. He kept the rest for himself.

On a September day when heavy rain pounded the metal roof of the long, narrow chicken coop, Bjørn was bent over, shoveling waste and sediment from the sturdy wood-planked floor.

The hinges of the coop entry door let out a loud squeak. Bjørn's head popped up, and he saw a stranger stepping into the coop. He thought the visitor's tight-lipped smile was a little smug for an uninvited guest, especially one whose closed umbrella was dripping water onto the newly scraped floor.

"Jens Grutermann," the visitor announced in a stiff tone.

Bjørn managed to extend his arm for a quick handshake along with a nod of his head. He had never met Grutermann, but his name was familiar as a farmer from the neighboring community of Nestad. In Norway's sparsely populated regions, everyone knew everyone else for miles around.

Lone wolf was the description that flashed into Bjørn's mind as he waited for Grutermann to break the silence and explain what brought him there. Bjørn recalled talk about this man's extreme views supporting fascism. He was a Vidkun Quisling loyalist, a Nazi. Most people in Erlikvåg and surrounding communities didn't agree with Grutermann, but they seemed to tolerate him. Bjørn's fellow farmers had enjoyed poking fun at the fascist when his name was raised in conversation around the stove in Jonas Seversen's general store.

Now, with the Nazis in control, he appeared before Bjørn as if he carried newfound power.

"Your wife directed me here to find you," he said.

"My sister, not my wife." Bjørn's tone was curt. "What do you want?"

Grutermann didn't mince words. "The new sheriff . . . who took the place of the one who replaced your father . . . commissioned me to take inventory of your animals and produce."

Bjørn shrugged his shoulders. "This new sheriff, he's a Nazi, isn't he?"

Grutermann raised his chin and, with it, his nose. "He's a party member."

At five-foot-four, Grutermann had to look up to meet Bjørn's eyes. His pudgy fifty-ish frame wasn't the build ordinarily formed by the rigors of farming. He had a puffy face, small hands, and skinny wrists.

Bjørn sensed his visitor was a little intimidated. He had half a foot of height on Grutermann. But the way the Nazi carried himself, with an erect posture and his head raised, he transmitted a sense of superiority.

Bjørn's emotional burner was heating up. Taking inventory could only mean one thing: loss of animals and produce. But he resolved to keep his anger in check.

Grutermann turned away and began counting the chickens, pointing a finger at each one as he inventoried.

"Fifty-six," Bjørn interrupted. "There are fifty-six. No need to count."

Grutermann nodded. "I'll accept that." Then his tone grew pointed. "I need to see the other animals. Show them to me. I want to see the garden, too . . . and the hayfield."

Bjørn put his hands on his hips. "I suppose you're taking some from me. Who are you giving it to, Herre Grutermann? The Germans?"

Grutermann's voice turned even more firm and huffy. "Yes, our German guests. They are here to help our country, and we must treat them with respect and do what we can to help them."

Bjørn dropped his arms down to his sides and curled his hands tight.

"Guests!" His voice carried beyond the coop. "They invade our country, kill our people, steal our freedom, and now they intend to steal from us. And you think we should treat them as guests."

He looked into the Nazi's eyes. The stare prompted Grutermann to look away, and he said nothing.

Bjørn tightened his fists. He was tempted. Jens Grutermann had a punchable face. But the chicken coop wasn't a schoolyard.

Picking up a shovel, Bjørn scooped a small amount of chicken manure. Grutermann backed away three paces and stood there alert and silent, positioned to defend himself.

Bjørn knew Grutermann held all the cards. He deposited the shovelful in a pail.

His words remained laced with steam. "How many animals are you giving up yourself, Herre Grutermann?"

"I'm prepared to give what I'm asked to give," the adversary responded. "You must do the same. You must be careful, Erliksen. Do not insult me or our guests. They are here to make our country strong. The old government made us weak."

Bjørn tilted his head and angled his eyes on the Nazi. For several seconds, the two men squared off. No movement. No speech. Just eyes on eyes. Then Bjørn's words filled the vacant air. "You and your Nazi trash are trait—" He stopped himself.

He put down the shovel. "Get on with it, then. Do what you must do, and after that, get the hell off my farm."

Together they toured the farm in the pouring rain. Grutermann noted numbers on a clipboard: two milk cows, three head of cattle, five pigs, thirteen sheep, and four goats, along with the fifty-six chickens. He sized up the garden. Then he left without further exchange of words.

———

Bjørn recognized the belching black smoke from a convoy of military trucks rumbling up the road toward his farm. It was the same dark exhaust that spewed from Nazi convoys he'd evaded while returning home from battle. He peered out the front window as they snaked their way closer. This sighting of military presence in the village came eight days after Jens Grutermann took inventory. Bjørn had a good idea what they wanted.

As they headed up the road, several vehicles peeled off and turned onto roadways leading to other farms farther down the hill. The lead truck continued, coming to a jerking stop in front of Bjørn's house.

The rumble of a truck drew Åsta into the living room. "What is it?"

"Germans. Wait here."

Gripped with dread, Bjørn went out the front door to intercept the Germans soldiers who were exiting the vehicle.

Five soldiers stood by the truck as Bjørn stepped toward them, hands in his pockets. The foul exhaust smell of burning oil reached him. He sized up the troops. Four appeared to be foot soldiers in fatigues, guys used to receiving orders, not giving them. One had what looked like a submachine gun slung over his shoulder.

The fifth German was fitted in a tailored officer's uniform with striped slacks and a coat. He wore a holstered sidearm and carried a pocket-size notebook.

"We have come to collect animals," he said, speaking Norwegian in a matter-of-fact tone. "Where are they?"

Bjørn's head filled with words he wanted to say, all with a
message to get off his property and go back to where they came
from. To say what he was thinking would only lead to trouble. He
felt helpless.

He pointed toward the pasture. The officer motioned his men
to follow and looked back at Bjørn. "Come."

Bjørn took a deep breath and swallowed hard before heading
out to where his animals grazed.

Once they reached the pasture, the officer looked over the
stock and pointed at what he wanted. He directed Bjørn to help
the men round them up. Bjørn and the others tied ropes around
the necks of four sheep, a goat, a beef cow, and a pig and led the
animals to the truck, which had a long bed with high sides of
wood boards. The soldiers lowered thick planks to create a sturdy
walkway for the livestock to get in the truck bed.

They weren't finished. Bjørn was directed to escort them
to the coop, where he had to watch as the soldiers stuffed ten
squawking chickens into burlap sacks.

But he did what he was told without resistance or complaint.
Bile surfaced in his throat. Since his days growing up, he had
cared about the animals he raised. Slaughtering cows and sheep
for meat had always been painful, and many times, it brought
tears to his eyes.

If the German troops noticed his enraged, reddened forehead, they didn't seem to care. Now he could only watch some
of his animals being hauled away, probably to feed the Nazi war
machine. Resentment of the Nazis mounted and melded with
thoughts of the ambush. The invaders had given him another
reason to hate them.

Bjørn's anguish deepened when German soldiers made two
more visits to Erlikvåg in October, hauling away more livestock
from him and other farmers. His stable was reduced to thirty-
two chickens, six sheep, two pigs, three goats, one milk cow, and

a lone beef cow. The personal and financial loss left Bjørn livid. He knew life under Nazi tyranny would become a struggle to survive.

CHAPTER 8

A cold winter arrived in the closing months of 1940 with the Nazis ratcheting up their demands on Bjørn. Besides confiscating almost half of his farm animals, German authorities demanded he convert his garden to potatoes and rutabagas and hand over 70 percent of the produce as well as an equal share of his hay. Other farms were squeezed as well. The new blows to Bjørn's livelihood intensified his anger and resentment.

At the same time, Germans and their Norwegian Nazi collaborators were deepening their attempt to convert the masses to fascist principles. They banned all political parties except the Nasjonal Samling. With that decree, membership mushroomed from a dismal few thousand to more than thirty thousand. Even though that number still represented a tiny slice of Norway's population of three million, it was enough to boost German authorities' confidence that the fascist party could help it rule.

The regime moved against the Norwegian Lutheran Church, seeking to censor sermons and to replace a common prayer for the king with praise for the Nazis. It also imposed Nazism in school curriculum and placed lackeys in state and local government positions. These moves led to resignations, strikes, and protests. Compromises had to be reached.

Nazi censorship of the press gave rise to underground newspapers. These crude, one-page mimeographed papers circulated to receptive audiences unfiltered news of Nazi actions. They found their way to Jonas Seversen's store, and he distributed them to community members whom he could trust not to reveal their source. He gave Bjørn one entitled *Trofast Mot Kongen (Faithful to the King)*. Bjørn shared it with Åsta, and they read about exoduses of military-age Norwegian men for England. These young men left on fishing boats and other vessels across the North Sea, intending to sign up as soldiers and fight.

That got Bjørn thinking.

———

On a cold, dark day in late February 1941, Arne came to the farm with his wife, Inga, and their five-year-old daughter, Kristi, for a Sunday visit. They lived in a comfortable hillside home on the northeast edge of Bergen, overlooking the city and fjord. For them, the serenity of Erlikvåg's rural environment provided welcome relief from the city where life was tense and food rationing put meager portions on the table. The supper Åsta prepared for them fell short of a feast, but she was able to serve tiny portions of cured meat that the visitors savored with every bite. Meat was no longer available in cities.

After dinner, Bjørn and Arne bundled up in winter coats and strolled to the barn with a half-full bottle of Borger aquavit. It allowed the two of them to talk removed from earshot of others. Bjørn sat on a storage box, and Arne grabbed an old wooden chair.

The conversation quickly turned to Arne's increasing challenges in a police department under Nazi leadership. He stared at the barn's raised beams and smiled as a swallow of the distilled potato-and-dill liquor hit his throat.

"I'm allowed to do my usual police work and haven't had to collaborate with the Gestapo," he said. "Glad for that. You can't imagine how malicious they are. I know about their arrest tactics and interrogation methods."

Bjørn grimaced as Arne said he got a circular from the Nazi-appointed police minister of the puppet national government, advising him to join the Nasjonal Samling.

Arne raised his hands and briefly covered his face. "I did not respond, and neither did many of my fellow officers. We're not going to join the Nazis. But some officers did, and now I don't know who to trust."

Bjørn studied his brother. He had rarely seen anguish in him before.

Arne let out a long sigh and resumed. He told Bjørn about an officer named Amund Hoggemann, a known fascist even before the German invasion. Hoggemann had attended an Oslo police school two years before Arne and upon graduation joined the Bergen Police Department.

"When I got my job with the police department, Hoggemann was there and already had a loud mouth when it came to fascist views. We put up with it. Now he's hard to be around. A lot of us steer clear of him."

It was Bjørn's turn. He told his brother about his short-lived army experience. "When I came back to the farm, all I wanted to do was hide from the world and from the war. Now, after all the Nazis have done, I want to do something to fight back."

Arne responded with a nod. "Organizations keep forming in Bergen to resist. The Gestapo is hunting them down. They've arrested people. Executed some. But groups still spring up."

Bjørn was quick to respond. "Thought about doing that but decided against it."

He told Arne about a meeting that he and Jon had attended two months earlier in the community of Resvik south of Erlikvåg.

"A neighbor boy invited Jon to the meeting, and I went along." Bjørn shook his head. "This boy was only sixteen. Sixteen. Yet he was being recruited by the group that put on the meeting. Once we were there, we found out it was the Communists. The man running the meeting said he was associated with Peder Furubotn. You've heard of him?"

Arne nodded. "*Ja*, Furubotn's high up in the Kommunistiske Parti."

"*Ja*, he's the one. So, this man representing Furubotn pleaded with us to put aside politics and unite against a single enemy. I had to agree with that. But I didn't want to be a part of the Communists. Jon felt that way, too."

Bjørn swallowed a shot of aquavit and steadied his eyes on his brother. "I have other hopes. People are leaving for England and joining the Norwegian Army there. I want to do that. I want to learn to fight . . . Be a good soldier so I can come back here and do what needs to be done. I risked my life once and it didn't help. I want to try again. How can I get to England?"

Arne leaned back in his chair and smiled. "Would you pour me a little bit more?" He held out his glass. Bjørn half filled it and waited for his brother's reaction.

"Have you told Åsta?" Arne said after a sip.

"Not yet."

"Talk to her before you decide. She's always had good advice."

Bjørn stared at Arne. "I need to talk to her, *ja*. But my decision's made. I want to leave. Just need to find out how I can do it."

Arne leaned forward, resting his elbows on his thighs. His eyes studied the barn's dirt floor. Then he returned upright in the chair.

"I respect you for what you want to do. Wish I could do it." Arne started to speak again but pulled back. After more hesitation, he said, "What I'm about to tell you must not be shared with anyone. Anyone! I know a man who can help you. He can arrange travel to England."

Arne's eyes narrowed and his look turned stern. "I'm going to give you an address in Bergen. Don't write it down. If it fell into the wrong hands . . . well, you realize how dangerous that would be."

Bjørn nodded.

"When you get to this address, you'll see a bakery," Arne continued. "Next to the bakery, on the right side, is a door. It's set back from the sidewalk and hard to find. Inside is a stairway to the second floor. Take it. Apartment four is down the hallway. Remember number four. Knock four times, no more, no less. Bring a small bag of potatoes and hand them over when someone answers. Say exactly these words: 'I brought these for you from the garden.' That will tell them that you're a good Norwegian. They should be able to instruct you from there."

Arne's eyes remained narrow and focused on Bjørn. "You must be cautious. Do everything exactly as I've told you. This is risky. If you believe you are being followed, do not go there."

Bjørn reached out and clasped his brother's hand. This was the connection he needed to get back in the fight.

CHAPTER 9

March 1941

Bjørn inched down the gangway and scanned the ferry terminal dock in Bergen harbor. The fingers of his left hand gripped the required folded document with "Border Zone Certificate" printed on the front in both German and Norwegian. He lined up with his fellow passengers from the early-morning fjord steamer, the *rutebåt*, and waited to present the identification paper at the dock's Nazi checkpoint.

Bjørn's brown slacks flapped against his legs in the gusty breeze. The cold, moist air penetrated his coat and blue button-down shirt. He shifted from one foot to the other in a swaying motion. He was experiencing the same feelings he had in his early years when his father took him to the big city. Bjørn remembered being intimidated by the hordes of people going here and there, vastly different from the mere handfuls he mingled with in his community.

On this morning, Norway's west coast urban center was still congested. But the hustle-bustle was different. Uniformed, rifle-toting German troops did much of the scurrying. They seemed everywhere. Anti-aircraft guns covered by camouflage netting pointed skyward near the terminal next to a sandbag-encased machine-gun nest.

Assuming he would be allowed to pass through the check-point, Bjørn was on his way to secure passage to London. For that, he needed another piece of identification—the small sack of potatoes he clutched. When he reached the apartment that his brother, Arne, specified, the garden-grown spuds hopefully would get him in the door.

When it became his turn to present his papers, Bjørn's stomach muscles tightened and his hands trembled. He fought to will away the jitters, concerned a visible showing of nervousness might raise suspicions with the German soldier reviewing documents. Standing nearby assessing passengers was another Nazi in the black uniform of the Schutzstaffel, German SS. A submachine gun dangled from his shoulder strap.

Bjørn opened the eight-by-six-inch paper with his name and photo. The guard seized the paper with indifference and studied it. He looked back up and his eyes met Bjørn's. *"Dein Name?"*

Bjørn stated his name in a formal, elevated tone.

The soldier then clawed at the potato bag, tearing a corner as he tugged to peer inside. He pulled back his fingers, handed over the passport, and waved Bjørn through. Two steps beyond the control point, Bjørn drew in a deep breath and felt the knots in his stomach ease.

As he left the ferry terminal, he spotted the distinctive row of historic buildings of the old Hanseatic waterfront section across the harbor. The structures dated back to Bergen's domination by Dutch merchants and traders in the 1600s. The structures were intact, just as they always appeared to him. Perhaps, he thought, it was a good thing the Norwegian military ceded the city to the invaders instead of defending it. Leaving Bergen unguarded and mobilizing elsewhere probably saved the city from destruction and preserved those buildings.

He had put off telling Åsta of his plans to leave until the night before coming to Bergen. Bjørn didn't know how she would react.

But it couldn't have gone better. She didn't want him to leave and put himself in more danger. But she understood.

And he remembered her last words: "Come back safe."

———

Bjørn's stomach churned with tense excitement as he walked briskly through the city on his way to his contact. The destination was Strømsett Gate 47. It was a twenty- to thirty-minute walk through the heart of downtown and into a quaint business district in the southeast section of the city.

His step was lively, and he frequently turned to check behind him. Bjørn felt conspicuous carrying the sack of potatoes and hoped the Gestapo wasn't watching him, especially if they knew what the bag meant. He listened for every sound and footstep behind him. So far, no sign surfaced of anyone following him.

Passing pedestrians, he breezed by without a nod or glance. Many wore long faces. They looked downward as if they wished to keep to themselves and go their way unnoticed. He sensed a city on edge. A city struggling. Its people hoping only to survive.

Bjørn passed by the stately Hotel Norge, vintage 1885. The white four-story building, built in a classic style of elegance, had long been a magnet for the well-to-do traveler.

He recalled what Arne told him during the visit to the farm. Vidkun Quisling stayed at the hotel in October 1940. Thousands of people had gathered in front and began shouting, "We want to see the führer, we want to see the führer." When Quisling answered their cries and appeared on a front balcony, the crowd changed the chant to "traitor, traitor, traitor." They booed him, bombarded the hotel with eggs and stones, and broke front windows. He retreated inside.

Quisling had been scheduled to speak at a large hall near the hotel. Instead, he sequestered himself in his room. The crowds grew. Nazi-party goons rushed to his aid carrying blackjacks. Rioting ensued, prompting German soldiers to form a wedge between the Nazis and protesters.

Arne had been called to the scene to help control the crowd. When he arrived, much of it had dispersed. But in the melee, two people were killed and fourteen hospitalized.

There was no crowd when Bjørn passed by. The hotel stood there as a stately beacon of yesteryear, when no Germans occupied Bergen and the city thrived commercially with factories and an active seaport.

Bjørn reached the large, beautiful Byparken, the city park. It was a central fixture of Bergen. Now, plots of potatoes replaced some of the grass, flowers, and shrubs.

He turned up Strømsett Gate to make the last multi-block journey. Bjørn deliberately walked on the opposite side of the street from number forty-seven. He wanted to get a good look at the bakery and the doorway next to the address to see if any potential threat lurked there. He saw nothing that alarmed him.

The building at Strømsett Gate 47 was more like an over-size house than a commercial building. It had a wide front and appeared to run long to the back. Large windows spread across the front of the bakery. A "Closed" sign hung on the front door. To the side, he saw the entryway to the second floor. It was a small brown door with a compact window in an upper frame.

Bjørn crossed the street and approached the door. There was no lock. He entered, climbed the narrow stairs, and walked softly down the long hallway. It was as quiet as a church. No one seemed to be around. He felt conspicuous again, hearing his rapid breathing and his shoes tapping the wooden floor. When he stood in front of apartment four, he took a deep breath and knocked four times.

He expected the door to open. It didn't. Instead, a timid voice called out, "Who's there?"

Bjørn certainly could not give the sack to an unopened door. He had to go off script.

His voice crackled. "My name is Bjørn. I have brought you these potatoes from the garden."

The door opened only enough for an elderly woman with tied-back white hair to poke her head from behind it. Eyeing the sack in Bjørn's hands, she widened the door and grabbed it.

"You must leave now," she said. "The Gestapo came early this morning looking for your contact. They may be watching. A stairway in the back goes to the alley. Get out of here."

With that, she shut the door.

Bjørn did as told and headed toward the back. As he approached a rear stairway, he questioned whether going out that way was wise. Gestapo agents could well be surveilling the alley. He halted, turned around, and went the other way. Exiting the front door, he reasoned, seemed more normal.

Bjørn walked out the front door to the street, trying to act nonchalant as if he were a resident. After a block, his pace picked up. He kept his head locked straight ahead, but he was on the lookout for anything suspicious.

His mind raced. He had no idea who his contact was, but the Gestapo seemed to be on that person's trail. It appeared he was able to flee. The woman must have been the contact's wife.

Only after Bjørn boarded the *rutebåt* and it motored away from the Bergen dock did his heart rate begin to slow down.

CHAPTER 10

Like the prior year, 1941 delivered a wet spring and magnificent summer. Wildflowers bloomed in brilliant colors, and the sun was out most days. A wet, mild spring had turned Bjørn's pasture and hayfields a lush green. The few animals still on the farm basked in comfortable heat and had plenty of grazing food. But in the sun's orange glow, Bjørn burned with anger when he kept hearing about more oppressive conditions imposed by the Nazis.

On May 17, the Germans had made good on a threatened prohibition of celebrating Norwegian Constitution Day. No parades. No customary dress with regional flair and national colors. No patriotic songs. And no flying of Norwegian flags. Some caught defying the order were arrested and sent to concentration camps. It was typical Nazi justice in which the penalty didn't fit the infraction. Norwegians had to honor the day on their own behind closed doors. Bjørn and Åsta hung their country's flag from the fireplace mantel.

Shortages of food, products, and raw materials worsened. The list of scarce foods grew. Even fish was rationed. By the summer, milk all but disappeared in major cities. If it could be found, it was rationed at one-quarter of a liter per person a day. Fortunately, Bjørn still had a milk cow that hadn't been taken by the Nazis.

Despite giving up a major share of their garden produce to the Nazis, Bjørn and Åsta managed to harvest an adequate supply of vegetables to get them through the winter. From fishing in the fjord, Bjørn stashed two barrels of cured herring and pollock.

The BBC reported that the German occupiers continued to pilfer Norway's stockpiles of commodities and raw materials and send them to the motherland. Factories had to scale back production or close altogether. Many more things, even clothes, were rationed. The quality of clothes and other items suffered as businesses found different ways of making them with what materials they had. Factories made shoes with wooden soles and layered paper tops. Even those were rationed and could only be bought by filing a special application with German authorities.

One BBC broadcast cited a report that it now took fifteen months for a Norwegian man to get enough ration documents to buy an ordinary suit. Even at that, suits were hard to find.

Bjørn turned to Åsta. *"Så du det,"* he said in a matter-of-fact tone.

News of the German Reich's invasion of Russia that June caught them both by surprise.

"At least it's another enemy for the Nazis," Bjørn told his sister. "I keep waiting for the Americans to join the war and become a German enemy. Then the Nazis are in for a fight."

The newly established Russian front raised more pressure on Norwegians to contribute to the Nazi war effort. Jens Grutermann made the rounds again in Erlikvåg, knocking on doors to collect boots, blankets, and warm clothing for the Russian front. Bjørn handed over one blanket and not-so-politely sent Grutermann on his way.

Nazi authorities began to realize that fewer Norwegians regularly tuned into the NRK network and other sources of their propaganda and dictates. Incensed by increased listenership of BBC programming, authorities acted to cut off news and information from the exiled Royal Norwegian government. On August 2, 1941, an order was issued requiring all Norwegians to surrender their radios and receiving sets to Nazi authorities within five days. Anyone caught with a radio after that date was threatened with execution.

Securing and keeping inventory of all radios was easy for the Nazis. Before the German occupation, Norwegians were required to register radios they owned with the government. Those sets were taxed at five kroner a year. So, the Nazis had lists of all radios in the country.

Bjørn wore a twisted scowl as he handed in his prized Huldra unit to the quisling district sheriff. The sheriff had set up a table in the community hall behind the Erlikvåg general store to collect them. The radios then were locked up in a storage room in the attic of the hall.

But later in August, the district's deputy sheriff, a friend who remained loyal to the king, slipped Bjørn a key to the community-center storage room. The deputy had replaced Sigfried Erliksen as sheriff, but was moved aside when the Nazis took over. Bjørn and Jon snuck into the community center one night not long after the seizure and retrieved several radios, including the Huldra.

As Nazi repression grew worse, Norwegian unity and the will to resist intensified. Some showed their disdain in passive ways. Norwegians greeted each other with a split-fingered *V*, to signal *"vi vil vinne"* (we will win). Paper clips appeared on lapels, a simple symbol of loyalty to the king.

Bjørn's commitment to finding a way to join the fight for his country had only strengthened.

———

For Jonas Seversen to visit a villager's farm was uncharacteristic of the storekeeper. When he did, there was a good reason. On a warm overcast day in late August of 1941, he called on the Erliksen farm, catching both Åsta and Bjørn by surprise.

There was no need for him to drop by any farm to socialize. Residents of Erlikvåg flocked to him and his store. The village had a community hall for large meetings. But Jonas's store was the community's social gathering place. His pleasant greeting and warm stove were magnets to young and old, men and women alike. He was the storekeeper, postmaster, *rutebåt* ticket seller, and village crier of news and gossip. He even maintained a community telephone for those who didn't have one.

Officially, the village wasn't a town. It had no government. It was only a place on a map, a rural community. But in every resident's eyes, Jonas was the unofficial mayor.

His family had lived there for generations, and Jonas was clearly homespun. He loved where he lived and loved those he lived with. Jonas had grown up on a small farm in the heart of the community, the middle child among three brothers and two sisters. Besides farming, his father had run the store since the early 1900s.

When the elder Seversen died, Jonas had taken over the store. He was thirty-five at the time. For the past fifteen years, Jonas had operated the store as the community centerpiece.

From his boxy little office in the back of the building, he managed Bjørn's and the other farmers' accounts, forging relationships with all the country's commodity cooperatives to ensure the farmers got their produce to market for a fair price. For a small cut only enough to cover what he needed, Jonas received and paid out the earnings and kept meticulous records of every krone and øre. He had earned a high level of trust, respect, and fondness from the people of Erlikvåg.

When Jonas appeared at the Erliksen farm asking for Bjørn, Åsta wrapped him in a big hug and directed him to the barn where her brother was pitchforking hay down from the loft. Jonas entered the barn and quickly put aside small talk and got to his point.

He handed Bjørn a small piece of folded white paper. Saying nothing, Bjørn looked back and forth between Jonas and the paper before unfolding it and reading handwritten scribbles.

"*Torsdag* 6 September. 2130. *Hildur VI*. Hernar."

Bjørn focused on the paper. He understood Thursday, September 6, nine thirty at night. He didn't recognize the name "*Hildur VI*" but knew of Hernar as an island west of Bergen on the edge of the North Sea.

He took a moment to absorb it and looked up at Jonas with wide eyes. "Is it arranged? Am I going to England?"

Jonas smiled. "It's what you wanted, isn't it? By boat to Shetland. From there, you can make your way to London."

The pace of Bjørn's words quickened. "My God, yes. How did this happen? How did you know I wanted to go?"

"It's better for you not to know how this was arranged," Jonas said as his grin vanished. "Limit whom you tell. The Gestapo is watchful of those leaving for England."

"*Ja*, I understand. The Gestapo stopped one chance of mine already. I'll be careful and only tell Åsta of this. I'd like to tell Jon, also. You know he is trustworthy. Now, what do I have to do?"

Jonas gave instructions, then carefully pulled an envelope from his pocket. "One more thing," he said, handing it to Bjørn.

"What's this?"

"Take a peek."

Bjørn peeled open the envelope's flap and pulled out a square four-by-four-inch photo. He squinted. The photo was taken from a distance and the image was small. It looked to him like the stern of a sunken ship protruding from the water.

"Photo of the German warship, *Königsberg*, in Bergen harbor," Jonas said. "Our shore batteries hit it and damaged it the day of the invasion. British bombers later sunk it. But I was told the Brits were unable to confirm that it sunk and believe it still might be operating. This photo confirms the sinking and will be useful to them. They'll know they have one less warship to worry about. Deliver it to our government when you reach London, and let the Norwegian military turn it over to the British. That would be the appropriate thing to do."

He added, "Hide it well as you begin your journey. If the Germans stop you and find it, you'll be arrested for sure."

Bjørn nodded. "You can count on me."

He then clasped Jonas's hand with both of his. "Will you look after Åsta for me?"

"Åsta is very resourceful, as you know," the storekeeper said. "She can handle things. I'm here to help if she needs anything."

He turned toward the barn door. As he left, he called back to Bjørn. "I wish you good luck. Your country needs you for what you're about to do."

CHAPTER 11

September 1941

As Bjørn stepped off the local ferry on Hernar Island, the night blacked out his view of the local fishing village. It had been a half-hour hop from Seløyna, one of the larger and more populated of the string of islands west of Bergen forming a barrier between the sea and the coastal fjords. A brisk wind blew chillier and more aromatic sea air into his face than when he'd left the city. Seas were choppier out here. He was at the outer edge of Norway's west coast civilization. Beyond was two hundred miles of nothing but sea.

He inhaled a deep whiff and let the moist salt air fill his lungs. It seemed to refresh his soul. The remoteness of the place gave him a sensation of seclusion and freedom away from German dictates and repression.

Bjørn had followed Jonas's instructions. His trip by *rutebåt* and the local ferry to get to Hernar Island had been uneventful. But the start of the journey at the Bergen boat terminal had been unnerving. His rucksack was stuffed with personal belongings packed for a trip and the sunken *Königsberg* photograph was taped to his back under his shirt. He felt noticeable.

Presenting his Nazi-issued credentials, Bjørn had drawn a prolonged stare from the Nazi soldier who shouldered a submachine gun. Bjørn had answered with a stare of his own and fisted one of his hands tight. The guard had looked down at the document and returned it without checking his pack.

With the boat travel between Bergen and Hernar Island now behind him, a much greater leg of the journey across the North Sea awaited him. Bjørn shuffled down the narrow finger of dock to step onshore. Fifteen others disembarked with him. All carried rucksacks and wore warm clothing to combat the cold. Bjørn wondered how many of them were going with him. His question was soon answered.

A figure stood near the end of the dock, unrecognizable in dark clothing and a face recessed in a hooded jacket. It made him almost invisible in the night.

As the passengers approached, he said, "Anyone taking a trip? *Hildur VI*? Stop here."

Almost everyone stayed by him, except for two men who peeled off and went away from the dock into the night.

The greeter extended his right arm, pointing the way. "Follow me, please." Bjørn and the thirteen who would be his fellow passengers trailed the man in a single-file procession.

Bjørn focused on his footsteps to find stable ground. Occasionally he looked ahead and could make out shadows of buildings in the darkness. He assumed they were homes. Razor-thin strips of light squeezed through windows likely covered by so-called blackout blinds. The Nazis required the coverings. They wanted no light that could serve as night beacons for Allied aircraft or ships on the coast. It was like that throughout Norway.

Butterflies fluttered in Bjørn's gut. It struck him that this could be a Gestapo trap. For all he knew, there could be SS soldiers waiting ahead to arrest them.

They were ushered directly to a fishing boat secured to a wooden bulkhead. Traces of light shone from the cabin. A man on the boat in a slicker and a wool cap tight over his ears called out in a husky voice, "Welcome, come on board . . . *Hildur VI.*"

The group's original hooded guide disappeared, and the man on the boat took over, directing Bjørn and the others up a sturdy gangway. Then, in single file, they all descended steep, ladderlike steps to below deck. There, the exposed wide, wooden planks of the hull held by thick wood ribs put the vessel's seagoing hardiness on display.

Bjørn exhaled long and deep, loosening his tense upper back and neck muscles. No SS waited. This looked right.

He took in his surroundings. Accommodations below were not built for comfort. Long benches were bolted to the inside ribs for seating. Blue cushions, worn and faded, provided padding, and short stacks of life jackets poked out beneath the benches. The fishing trawler seemed to take on the function of a makeshift ferry. Below deck, the bow was enclosed and accessed through a small door. Sleeping quarters for the captain and crew, Bjørn guessed. Aft was an enclosed compartment, likely the head.

Everyone took a seat on the benches and spread out. Seating was more than ample for the fourteen of them. Bjørn sat at the end of the portside bench at the foot of the stairway. No one spoke. There were nods of recognition and a few polite greetings, but none of the passengers seemed in a talkative mood. He attributed the silence to anxiety anticipating the long trip across the sea. He felt it.

The man in the slicker with the booming voice came down the polished wood steps. "My name is Anders Kongsgaard. I'm your captain, and this is my boat, the *Hildur VI.* I can assure you she's seaworthy. She's seen many storms and rough waters. But we're hopeful that the North Sea will treat us well. Seas are moderate, and there's nothing we know of to make this trip difficult."

Kongsgaard introduced the man with him as Hans Martensen, whom he described as the boat's chief mate and machinist.

"Hans is good at keeping the engine running, and we have plenty of fuel," Kongsgaard continued. "We'll be underway in just a little bit. Sorry the accommodations might not be ideal. This is not like the liner SS *Bergensfjord*. But it'll get you to where you need to go.

"Our destination is the town of Lerwick on the Shetland Islands. It'll take us about twenty-four to twenty-six hours to get there, depending on weather and seas. I wish each one of you a good trip."

Kongsgaard and his mate returned to the wheelhouse. Bjørn adjusted his rear end on the bench to get comfortable. His watch read 9:17 in the evening as he felt the *Hildur VI* pull away from its moorage.

He tried to picture in his mind what the Shetland Islands looked like. He seemed to remember hearing his father talk about a way-back ancestor who had come from the islands, and that the family's name was somehow rooted there. He didn't care knowing the family history at the time. But now his dad's words registered with him.

Shetland, a thinly populated archipelago of two hundred islands—most of them uninhabited—strung out sixty miles north to south. The northern tip of Scotland lay a hundred miles from the chain's southern point. The islands had been first colonized by the Vikings in the tenth century. In the late 1400s, the Shetland Islands were ceded to Scotland as a dowry for the marriage of Danish princess Margaret to Scottish king James III.

To see the islands, he had to get there first. The thought of the trip caused the butterflies in his stomach to spread their wings again. Two hundred miles of unpredictable, untamed water lay ahead.

CHAPTER 12

After just three hours at sea, a gale blew in from the northwest, turning the sea violent. The storm attacked *Hildur VI* with a vengeance. Winds whistled like a hot teakettle, rattling the wheelhouse door and demanding to be let in. Driving rain battered the windows of the wheelhouse above them. Bright lightning flashes shimmered down the stairway opening. In the subdued light below deck shining down from the wheelhouse, Bjørn swore he could see the whites of his fellow travelers' wide eyes. He grabbed the stair railing next to his seat with his left hand and gripped it tight.

The vessel rocked viciously, crashing through rapidly building seas. Torrents of water pushed the bow toward the sky and sent it smashing down in deep ocean gullies. Seawater cascaded over the deck, and Bjørn heard it crash against the wheelhouse. The boat shook from the blow. He leaned over from his bench and pressed his upper body closer against the railing, wrapping his arms around it and clutching it with both hands.

The engine's steady chug changed to a high whine as the propeller came out of the water. Crewmate Martensen scrambled below to check on the engine, hanging on to anything he could to keep his footing on the stairs. Bjørn caught a glimpse above of Kongsgaard shaking his head as he fought to guide his boat and keep it afloat.

The passengers, who moments earlier passed the time with idle conversation, grew silent as they were thrust into the eye of the storm. They held on to anything affixed to the boat. Any bags and belongings not lashed down slid across the planked floor.

Martensen emerged from the engine room and staggered back up to the wheelhouse. Bjørn heard the crewman tell the captain the engine was fine. He sighed, but he could feel his heartbeat pound against the wall of his chest. His inner thoughts still debated the peril, seesawing between survival and death. The engine worked for now. But what if it died? Surely the boat couldn't stay afloat. They'd all go down. The boat looked plenty stout. But could a storm this strong break it into mere splinters?

Bjørn heard Kongsgaard and Martensen shouting above the ruckus. They discussed turning back if conditions worsened. Bjørn silently prayed they would complete the journey.

Keeping out the driving rain and seawater crashing over the deck was impossible. Water seeped into the enclosed wheelhouse and streamed below through the stairway opening. With each rise and fall of the boat, the smelly seawater sloshed across the floor below deck before finding its way between planks into the bilge to be pumped out.

The *Hildur VI*'s furious rocking turned Bjørn's stomach sour, and he didn't look forward to what was likely to come next. Before long, the storm inflicted a physical toll on everyone. Retching was in full swing. The reserved Norwegians were forced to share buckets. Some were unable to grab a bucket in time and lost their insides on the floor. Vomit mixed in with the seawater steadily dripping from the wheelhouse floor. The mixture's stench seemed to set off a new round of vomiting.

No one complained. They all faced the same condition. Like Bjørn, they appeared too miserable to focus on their terror. Sickness had become an antidote to fear.

The boat's rock and roll prevented any of them from lying on the benches. Some were doubled over, faces buried in their laps while tightly gripping their bench seats. One was prone on the floor with his head on a suitcase, water ebbing and flowing around him. Bjørn sat upright, his forearms tiring from the tight hold on the rail as the boat tossed about.

Kongsgaard and Martensen didn't appear to be seasick. Bjørn was glad for that. The last thing anyone on board needed was an ill captain unable to give his full attention to controlling the boat through the storm.

———

At last, the storm relented. The wind's howl lessened. Although Bjørn thought he could hear rain pelting the wheelhouse windows, the once-thunderous crash of water no longer reached his ears. *Hildur VI* continued pitching in high seas, but he felt an easing of the violent rise and fall. He hoped the worst of the storm was behind them.

He hadn't checked his watch, so it was hard for him to know how long the seas had been tossing them around. He thought maybe two or three hours had passed. But it had seemed never ending.

Seasickness still had a firm hold on him, but the heaving had stopped. Perhaps he had no more to give up. His stomach was raw and his body ached. He relaxed his left-hand grip on the railing and removed his right hand altogether.

Bjørn no longer heard the sounds of heaving from the other passengers. He looked around the space below. The only light filtered through the open stairs from the wheelhouse. His fellow passengers were still, almost lifeless.

———

Bjørn saw the first glimmer of morning light filling the wheelhouse and managed a slight grin. He realized he had dozed off but didn't know how long he'd been asleep. He looked at his watch: 4:29. Sunrise seemed punctual. At this time of year, daylight lasted for more than eighteen hours. The sleep had refreshed him a bit, though his stomach remained sour. *Hildur VI*'s rocking was ever-present but less so.

There was no movement yet among Bjørn's fellow travelers. The only two female passengers, who had introduced themselves as sisters, lay side by side on a bench, sandwiched by two young men. Each man hung on to his respective side of the bench, sitting but slumped forward. Most of the others were either in the same position or were leaned back with their heads resting against the boat's side ribs and planking.

Bjørn looked up the stairway opening to where the captain sat at the wheel, installed in a swivel chair bolted to the floor. Martensen was in a secured chair next to him. Minutes later, he took over the wheel and Kongsgaard came down the stairs, timing each step with the pitch of the boat. There was a slight stirring among the passengers.

"*Morn, morn*, I know it was a miserable night," he said. "Can't control the weather and didn't expect the squall. Worst is past us. Seas still will be a little rough. But we'll be all right."

A few heads looked the skipper's way as he spoke. But no one said a word.

Once Kongsgaard returned to the wheelhouse, he directed Martensen to check on any damage outside. The crewman pulled on his foul-weather jacket and ventured out. He reentered the cabin and gave the skipper a thumbs-up. Kongsgaard directed him to retire in the forward cabin belowdecks to get some shut-eye. Both had been operating on no rest.

Bjørn decided fresh air would give him relief from the stale stench of the boat's lower dregs. He pushed himself up from the bench and ambled up the laddered stairs to the wheelhouse.

Kongsgaard glanced his way. "How's everyone? I didn't see much movement."

Bjørn forced a smile. "Not well . . . but alive."

"We're not able to clean things up down there for you all. Sorry about that. But when Hans gets back up, I'll have him make hot tea for us. It'll help settle your stomachs."

Hildur VI hit a wave, and Bjørn braced himself against a wall and gripped the edges of a side counter. "How much farther do we have to go?"

"A long way still," Kongsgaard responded, glancing at his watch. "Almost five fifteen now. I figure we're about seventeen, eighteen, hours out. We'll probably get there late tonight if the waters back off a little. Could take us another twenty if the seas keep kicking up. Don't anticipate any more storms, though. But in the North Sea, you never know."

Kongsgaard turned toward him with a quizzical glance. "Why are you making this crossing?"

"Going to join up in the military so I can come back and fight the Germans."

Kongsgaard gave Bjørn a single nod of his head and returned his gaze to the sea. "Good. Norway needs fighting men to stop the Nazis. I've taken others to Shetland for the same reason."

"How many crossings have you made?"

"This is my third."

"You live on Hernar Island?"

"Now, yes, when I'm home. I'm from Lillesand. Maybe you've heard of it. Near Stavanger."

Bjørn's head bobbed. "*Ja,* I remember hearing a story just before the invasion. German soldiers from a sunken ship picked up by a fishing boat near there."

Kongsgaard cracked a wide smile but kept his eyes peeled ahead and steadied the wheel as *Hildur VI* crashed through a high wave. "That was me. I'm the one who found them. We picked them up and brought them in."

"Did the soldiers really say they were on their way to Bergen to save Norway? That's what I heard on the radio."

"The sheriff let me sit in when he interviewed them," the skipper said. "I heard them say it. They were speaking German. So I got the translation."

Bjørn shook his head. "I just thought it was another rumor."

Kongsgaard turned his head and gave the passenger a swift glance. "I didn't believe it, either. We both were proven wrong."

"How did you end up on Hernar?"

Kongsgaard frowned. "The Germans moved into Lillesand and set up a boat station. They took four fishing boats from friends to use for patrolling the coast. I was allowed to keep my boat, this one, but they required me to fish only for cod and herring and to deliver all my catch to a fish oil factory in Stavanger. That was all right, except I was paid only twenty-five percent of what I usually got. Then I heard they were sending the oil to Germany as a lubricant for tanks. I'd have none of that.

"My wife has a cousin living on Hernar. He invited me to join him. There were no Germans around. So I shuttered my home in Lillesand and moved my wife and daughter there. I figured it would be safer for them and me.

"A few months later, I was recruited by an organization in Bergen to take people who needed to leave," Kongsgaard said. "I was told they all faced arrest and maybe death by the Gestapo. I decided it was something I could do for my country. I knew the sheriff, and he gave me additional rations of petrol so I could cross."

Kongsgaard turned again and looked at Bjørn. "I respect you for wanting to fight."

———

After nightfall, Kongsgaard called Bjørn back up to the wheel-house and pointed ahead. "Land." He handed Bjørn a pair of bin-oculars. "There's a light out there."

When *Hildur VI* leveled off during her rise and fall riding the waves, Bjørn peered through the glasses and sighted a slight flicker of light showing itself at intervals.

"Is it a lighthouse?"

Kongsgaard squinted. "Should be."

A map was spread out on a shelf ahead of the wheel. "If that's the correct beacon, we're exactly where we need to be. My instruments are reliable, and we've been able to maintain our heading despite the conditions. The lighthouse we're looking for is on an island just in front of the town of Lerwick. That's our destination."

Martensen, seated in the wheelhouse, nodded his agreement.

Bjørn went below and announced the sighting to the others. Lingering symptoms of seasickness tamped down enthusiasm, but he noticed relieved smiles.

Kongsgaard steered *Hildur VI* toward the light, which flashed larger and brighter the closer they got. The seas still rocked and swayed the boat.

It was pushing midnight when the trawler rounded a point and entered a wide channel between the island with the beacon and another island. The skipper hugged the shore near the light-house. In the channel, the turbulent waters eased a bit. Despite the darkness, Kongsgaard was able to pick out a small dock and pulled the boat up to it.

Bjørn volunteered to go ashore and find the lighthouse keeper. Kongsgaard told him to identify the boat and say it had arrived from Norway carrying refugees. Bjørn then was to ask the keeper to alert the British navy and request an escort through military-patrolled waters to Lerwick.

He jumped over the rail and down three feet to the dock. Despite a hard landing, the dock built over stable pilings provided immediate relief from his seasickness. His legs felt stiff, but it was good to move. The sea air slapped his face with a crisp but refreshing bite.

He moved up a sloping knoll toward the lighthouse on what appeared to be a large swath of pasture. The top half of the structure with the light rotating around a turret came into view.

When he neared it, a man came out and greeted him. Bjørn knew a little English, even though he struggled with the language in school. It was enough to generally make out what the man told him. The keeper said he saw the running lights of *Hildur VI* as it approached the shore and had already called for a military boat to meet them.

"Norwegian?" came his query. Bjørn nodded.

"Have you crossed the sea today?" The ruddy-faced old man kept a hand on his head to keep his short-billed hat from flying off in the wind.

The question induced another nod.

"You're a brave man. It took courage to come across in those conditions."

When Bjørn returned to the *Hildur VI*, the military boat with two uniformed British sailors had pulled alongside and boarded. After inspecting the *Hildur VI*, the trawler left the dock with the escort leading her down the channel. Both vessels turned south into another passage to the small harbor at Lerwick.

After the *Hildur VI* tied up, passengers bade Kongsgaard goodbye and were transported to a barracks-like building adjacent to a stone Anglican church. By then, it was in the wee hours of the morning. They all were wet and sapped of energy, but the seasickness rapidly evaporated. Only two turned down a bowl of stew. It held chunks of lamb, potatoes, carrots, and celery swimming in a rich, creamy broth. Bjørn wasn't one of those who turned it down. He relished every bite.

The female passengers were led to a separate room, and Bjørn and the other men were accompanied to another dormitory-style room and assigned bunks. Dark shades were pulled over the windows, and a single light bulb at the end of the room cast just enough light to allow them to find their beds. Other men were already there sleeping, earlier arrivals from other boats, Bjørn assumed.

The single-story barracks appeared to have been hastily built on church grounds. The bunks had metal springs with thin mattresses, but they were neatly made with clean sheets and blankets. Bjørn stripped off his wet clothing and crawled beneath the bedcoverings. His stomach was satisfied and the bed was warm. No sooner did he close his eyes than he fell fast asleep.

CHAPTER 13

September 13, 1941

This was not the London Bjørn dreamed of visiting. Growing up, he had seen photographs in magazines and studied the city in school. A city with London Bridge, Buckingham Palace, the Tower of London, Big Ben. Now, in time of war, much of the city resembled Roman ruins.

He had been almost giddy with excitement when his train from Liverpool arrived at London's Euston station that morning. Bjørn anticipated what the moment would feel like. Now he was experiencing London but not at all in the way he had imagined it.

He gawked at the devastation from a window seat of a bus taking him and other refugees from the train station to a place known as the London Reception Centre. As the vehicle wound in and around the heart of the city, he felt sickened by the effects of the German Luftwaffe's night bombing raids.

The once-grand city was now filled with rows of buildings and entire blocks and neighborhoods reduced to rubble. Piles upon piles of bricks blasted apart. Splinters of furniture and pieces of other materials scattered about. Sides of buildings collapsed, exposing rooms with tables, chairs, and wall hangings still in place. He wondered how anyone survived but knew the answer. Tens of thousands of lives must have been lost.

Dark clouds and a steady drizzle added to the gloom he witnessed. The subdued daylight cast a cold dreariness on the debris. The bus passed by workers digging through piles. He assumed they were either looking for bodies or retrieving anything worth repurposing. Not everything was piled high. There were deep bomb craters. He also saw greenscapes of fallen trees with some torn out of the ground by their roots. Pedestrians walking along the streets appeared oblivious—perhaps numbed—to city blocks laid to waste.

Some structures appeared untouched by enemy planes. They often stood alone amid the ruin. When the bus crossed a still-standing bridge over the River Thames, Bjørn saw the pointed sandstone-colored north tower of the Palace of Westminster. Part of the structure looked damaged, but the iconic face of Big Ben appeared unblemished in the near distance. His head slowly pivoted to keep the view of the clock as long as he could. Amid all the unimaginable destruction, Bjørn felt relief that such a historic remnant still stood. He realized that could change with the next bombing raid. Nothing was certain in war.

He passed other buildings saved from destruction. Stacks of sandbags up to six feet high surrounded them. Antiaircraft batteries were positioned nearby under camouflage netting in colors that resembled the cityscape.

To him, there was neither rhyme nor reason to German bombing targets. It looked so indiscriminate. The German war machine seemed not to care as long as it harmed and destroyed anyone and anything British.

After crossing the Thames, the bus entered a section of London with a sign labeled: "Metropolitan Borough of Wandsworth." This part of the city showed fewer vestiges of bombing. There seemed to be more green than in other sections of the city he passed through.

Bjørn's fellow passengers on the North Sea crossing had boarded the bus with him in the morning, just less than a week since landing on the Shetland Islands. They all had taken a passenger ship, *Ben-my-Chree*, from there overnight to Liverpool. Now on the bus, he heard other nationalities. He thought he recognized German, Russian, Eastern European, and assumed some were Jewish people escaping persecution and death from Nazi tyranny. England was among the few remaining places of freedom in Europe, despite the ravages of the Blitz.

When Bjørn stepped down from the bus, before him stood a majestic Gothic-style building unscathed by war. "Royal Victoria Patriotic Asylum" was etched in the stone facing over the front entrance. The three-story structure was of light-yellow brick and quarry-carved granite. A slate roof cascaded down, much like the steep pitch of a French chateau. Leaded glass windows in metal frames lined the facade of the building. There were three towers on the front, one on each end, and the other in the middle over the entrance.

A makeshift sign attached to the side of the entrance read "London Reception Centre," the place where British authorities, he assumed, would find out more about him, determine why he'd come, and decide how he could help the Allied or Norwegian war effort. He hoped the stay would be short. While the building kept its stately exterior, Bjørn found the inside showing age, neglect, and the telltale signs of being converted to a cultural catch basin. Only a few steps in the door, he inhaled a pungent, blended odor of must, perspiration, plumbing, and disinfectant. Paint peeled off the walls, and a layer of dust left streaks across the worn varnish on stair railings.

After a check-in process that took two and a half bureaucratic hours, Bjørn entered the assigned second-floor room he would share with two Polish refugees and a Czech. He and the Norwegians he traveled with had been assigned separate rooms.

He wondered whether that was deliberate for some reason or simply a matter of where beds were available.

His quarters were cramped and meager. Wire-meshed cots with thin mattresses were arranged in bunk-bed formation, anchored to the walls by bolts. Clean sheets were neatly tucked into the bunk, and a flat pillow sat on top. A wooden ladder attached to the wall on each side provided access to the upper bunks.

Bjørn used his limited English to talk with his roommates, who also spoke some English. Otherwise, he understood nothing of their conversations and used hand gestures when necessary.

During the first night, Bjørn and his roommates were awakened by the distant boom of antiaircraft guns followed by bombs falling somewhere in London. The attacks weren't close enough to trigger a siren calling everyone to safe shelter in the basement. He wondered what kind of buildings were now crumbling and what the death count was.

For seven days, he waited, uncertain about when he would be delivered to Norwegian custody. He passed the time by pacing the halls of the reception center and the inner courtyard outdoors.

In a conversation with a reception-center worker, Bjørn learned the building originally was built as an institution for orphaned girls of soldiers killed in the Crimean War. Queen Victoria herself ceremonially helped lay the foundation stone in 1857. It then became a girls' school until 1939, when children were shipped to the countryside by train to protect them from an anticipated German attack on London.

On the eighth day, a message delivered to Bjørn's room summoned him to a threadbare first-floor office with only a table and three chairs. There, a British Army lieutenant named Stephen Donovan and a Norwegian translator took him through questioning that lasted two hours.

The interview sought details of Bjørn's background. Who was he? Where was he from? What was his occupation? How did he arrive at Shetland? Why did he come? Questions delved into his family and friends and everything that happened to him during and after the German invasion. Donovan asked about German fortifications and activities in his area and the effects of the occupation on him. Bjørn believed he had relived every waking hour of his life since the Nazis came.

He didn't bring the photo of the sunken German cruiser *Königsberg*. Instead, he adhered to Jonas Seversen's instructions and held it for the Norwegian government.

The questioning left him exhausted and a little worried. Later, replaying the answers in his head, he hoped his responses were acceptable. They were honest. But he couldn't help second-guessing himself. Was there an answer Lieutenant Donovan didn't like? Did he come all this way only to be rejected and sent home? How would he get there? While he wrestled with his nerves, he also reminded himself that he was of military age and physically fit. How could they afford to expel him?

Bjørn was called the next day to another office for a second interview, adding to his anxiety. Arriving for the appointment, a receptionist escorted him into a larger and better-appointed office and invited him to sit in a tartan-upholstered chair in front of a broad desk buried under stacks of paper and files. A nameplate on the desk faced him. It said "Colonel Oreste Pinto."

When Pinto entered the room, he was cordial but business-like. There was no translator. When he spoke, he used perfect Norwegian.

Bjørn didn't expect it. Pinto didn't look Norwegian, let alone Scandinavian. "How do you know the Norwegian language?"

"I studied a great many languages," the British colonel said, flashing a broad, confident smile. "Language is an interest of mine. Your language is one I came to know."

His questions focused on individuals that Bjørn knew in Erlikvåg and its surroundings. Who was loyal to the king and who was a traitor? Bjørn raised Jens Grutermann's name and told of his effect on his farm and the other villagers. These questions were closer to what he expected, and they put him more at ease.

Pinto asked about the passengers who'd traveled across the North Sea with him. "Was there anything they said or any behaviors that were peculiar to you?"

Bjørn shook his head. "I knew none of them, and we made no effort to get to know each other. Sorry I can't be more helpful."

Pinto pursed his lips slightly as he scribbled on a notepad. Then with wide, probing eyes, Pinto delved into the Bjørn's own sympathies.

"Are there any circumstances that would cause you to support what German authorities are doing in your country?"

Bjørn was direct. "They brought war to my peaceful land, stole my animals, and took away my freedom. They made me carry documents to get around. I hate them. I came here to fight them."

When the interrogation ended, Bjørn felt uncertain about what would occur next. He asked, "When will I see someone from my government?"

Pinto looked away briefly and returned his eyes to Bjørn. "For now, we shall have to wait and see."

Three days later, another message arrived for Bjørn at his reception-center room. He was summoned to "Kingston House North, 30 Prince's Gate, Knightsbridge, London, at 11 a.m., 2 October 1941." The address was the residences and offices of the exiled Norwegian government. A car would fetch him at ten o'clock sharp, and he was to bring all his belongings.

Bjørn gave the paper containing the message a soft pat and carefully secured it inside his jacket.

———

Bjørn had hurriedly signed documents to check out of the reception center and was out in front twenty minutes early. He wore the same clothes as when he'd crossed the ocean, and the same rucksack was slung over his back. The photo of the sunken German warship was inside. The car meeting him was punctual. As the clock tower above the reception center's front entrance struck ten o'clock, a dark-blue sedan pulled up in front.

When the vehicle reached Kingston House North, the building caught Bjørn by surprise. It was modern with a plain, clean redbrick face. There was nothing historical Merry Ol' England about it. Nothing ornately Victorian or royal to command attention. Just a nice, large, multistory apartment building. Next to it was an identical building, Kingston House South.

Both buildings had survived bombings. They were surrounded by stacks of sandbags and barriers. Armed security seemed everywhere. Soldiers in Norwegian Army uniforms were armed with rifles and pistols. Camouflage netting hung over the roof to make it invisible from the air.

Bjørn was escorted through a checkpoint to a reception area on the second floor. A slim young woman, her hair rolled into a stylish bun, greeted him with a smile and asked his name in Norwegian. Checking a list and finding him, she nodded and politely directed him to sit and wait. He was fifteen minutes ahead of schedule.

He waited about a half hour before a telephone rang at the reception desk, breaking the dull quiet. Bjørn jumped slightly in his chair.

"Mr. Erliksen," the receptionist said, "please come with me."

She led him down a long hall with a string of closed numbered doors lining each side. About two-thirds of the way down the hall, she stopped and lightly rapped on a door. Hearing a voice inside call out, she opened the door and ushered Bjørn in. At the sight of the man behind the voice, Bjørn's jaw dropped and he reached forward with one hand to steady himself against a chair.

Sitting behind a desk was his old army unit commander, Lieutenant Brittvik.

CHAPTER 14

There was no mistaking Konrad Brittvik as anything other than a soldier. Tall and ramrod straight with chest puffed up and out. He was formal and focused, and he was twice as tough as he looked. Bjørn believed that if all Norwegian Army officers and soldiers were like his former commander, Norway might well have succeeded in turning back the invading Germans. He also knew that Brittvik was fiercely loyal and supportive to the troops that served under him.

On this morning, the two men, who had been left to guess about each other's fate in the Ørhandal ambush, met face to face.

It was Captain Brittvik now. He sported three black stars sewn onto the shoulders of his uniform. At seeing Bjørn, Brittvik abruptly rolled back his wheeled desk chair, rose, and moved around his desk. He was in full uniform, several medals and a few rows of ribbons pinned on the right side of his chest. His smile and handshake were warm.

"Bjørn Erliksen, a pleasure to see you again."

The former soldier of Brittvik's unit was unable to disguise his surprise. His eyes popped like a frog on a toadstool. His mouth wasn't working. "I . . . I, um, I'm happy to see you, too." Bjørn quickly remembered military formality and, though delayed, blurted out a high-pitched, "Sir."

Brittvik seemed to forget the formalities he usually carried with him and flashed a wide smile that filled out his cheeks.

Bjørn collected himself. "Sir, we didn't know what happened to you . . . Feared you were lost." He dipped his head. "So many died that day."

Brittvik buried his commanding smile and turned solemn. "I can't forget it. It's one of those scenes that keeps me motivated."

He extended his arm. "Well now, we have much to discuss. I fear we'll run out of time. Please sit down."

He motioned Bjørn to a small folding chair with a seat of thin polished wood. Bjørn sank into it but sat erect and perched forward with his eyes fixed on his former commander.

Brittvik studied his trooper. "The British notify us of every Norwegian who reaches their shores. When I saw your name on the list, I asked to see you."

"How would you even know who I was?"

Brittvik grinned. "I always remember my men. We were not together long, and like the others, you were green. But you trained well. And, as I remember, you could shoot."

Bjørn kept his reserve, but he was touched. He wished Jon were there with him to see the captain alive and still in command.

The captain swung side to side in his swivel chair while keeping his focus on Bjørn. He checked his watch and seemed to reconsider the direction of the conversation. "We must catch up . . . I haven't talked to anyone else in the unit except those who escaped with me. So tell me, what happened to you and those who, I assume, were with you?"

Bjørn turned his eyes away from Brittvik, tilting his head toward the ceiling. His recollection of the events beginning with Ørhandal valley were fresh from the interviews with the British officers. Now he recounted them for his unit commander. All of them. His attempt to fight back after reaching the tree line. His escape up the steep mountainside to the rock ridgetop. The subsequent retreat over the mountains to Sognefjord, and ulti-mately the long journey home.

Brittvik listened intently with a grim face. He said nothing, except once he interjected, "You were among the lucky ones. We lost more than one hundred men. Those of us who survived were scattered all over that mountain."

Bjørn's weak smile reflected the gloom of the story. He was glad he'd found an empathetic ear. Someone who was there. Someone who fully understood. He knew it was as painful for Brittvik to hear as it was for him to relive it.

When Bjørn finished, he turned the questioning to Brittvik. "Sir, what happened to you? How did you survive?"

The captain leaned back in his chair, moving the wheelbase a half a foot. The springs squeaked. "*Ja*, I owe you that."

He then perched forward, sliding the chair up with him and resting his elbows on the desk. His intense gaze drew Bjørn in. His former charge inched forward in his seat. They were kindred spirits of a shared experience.

"I wish I'd been more leery of enemy troop movements," Brittvik said. "I think of that every day. We should have been bet-ter prepared and more observant."

He shook his head. "So many lives lost . . . so many. But I was under orders to move hurriedly to the south. The Germans simply advanced faster than we expected. They just lay in wait for us."

Brittvik pulled his sleeve back, exposing what looked to Bjørn like a superficial divot in his left forearm. It had healed over.

"As I ran for the trees, a bullet grazed me here," he said, lightly tapping his wound with his right fingers. "It tore my coat and clothing and took off some skin, and it bled a lot. But it only bruised my bone. Like you, I was fortunate.

"I was with about sixty soldiers who made it to the trees. We found a gap in the mountainside just to the south with a small stream flowing through it. We went along the ridge overlooking the creek and took up positions there, preparing to fight the Germans if they came through the gap.

"I sent two men back to see what the enemy was doing. They reported that German forces had moved into the valley to assess the damage. The Germans seemed to stop there. Our men heard a few rifle shots."

Brittvik bowed his head. "They were probably killing our wounded."

Bjørn gasped.

Brittvik lifted his head and directed his eyes at Bjørn. "To this day, it makes my blood boil."

The captain said he and the surviving soldiers with him subsequently joined what remained of General Steffens's forces, who had been forced to evacuate Voss. The Germans obliterated it with bombs and artillery fire, and ultimately took over the town.

After southern Norway fell to the Germans, Brittvik said he dismissed most of his men and, with a handful of soldiers, accompanied the general to northern Norway.

"When the war ended, I was on the British destroyer that took the king and government to England. Now, I'm supervising a section that interviews Norwegian men and women who—like you—come here."

Brittvik looked down at an open file and flipped through pages. "I see you've been questioned by Colonel Pinto."

"He seemed interested in my loyalties," Bjørn answered.

"Colonel Pinto is an interesting fellow," the captain said. "He works for the British Security Service, and he's earning quite a reputation. His main purpose is to identify and intercept German spies. He's caught a few, from what I hear."

Bjørn squared his jaw. "Sir, I came to England for another chance to fight . . . To rid our country of Germans."

He scraped his chair across the tiled floor toward Brittvik's desk. "Can you help me?"

Brittvik stared at him. "I appreciate your eagerness and respect your desire to become a soldier again. I have some ideas on that, but no commitments. Allow me some time. I'll work on it for you."

The captain then told Bjørn he had arranged for him to stay at a nearby hotel. Brittvik reached in his pocket and pulled out a British ten-pound note. "Here, this will get you by," he said. "Use it sparingly so it lasts."

Bjørn then remembered the photo in his rucksack. He sprang from his chair and interrupted. "Sir, I'm sorry, I almost forgot to give you this."

He fumbled through his bag and pulled out the envelope, handing it to Brittvik. The captain opened it and studied the contents.

"What's this?"

"*Königsberg*. The German warship. It was sunk in Bergen harbor."

"Where did you get the photo?"

"The person who arranged for my passage to Shetland."

Brittvik nodded. "This may be of some use to us. I know of this ship. If I understand correctly, its fate was uncertain. Good to see it underwater."

Bjørn had a final request. "Is there a way to get word to my sister, Åsta, in Erlikvåg that I am safe here?"

"Let me work on that, too." Brittvik picked up a pen and scribbled a note.

With that, the captain rose and dismissed Bjørn, who now knew he was in good hands.

CHAPTER 15

October 1941

For more than a week, Bjørn had bided his time waiting to hear from Brittvik about his future. His frequent pacing across the floor of his cramped hotel room began to wear scrape marks on the linoleum.

Then came a handwritten message delivered to Bjørn's box at the County Hotel.

"Bjørn Erliksen: May have something for you. Be at my office 8 in the morning 11 October. I will fill you in." Brittvik's signature was scribbled at the bottom.

On the appointed day and time, Bjørn showed up promptly at the captain's office. Brittvik was his assertive self. Bjørn didn't mind the formality. He had been used to seeing it. He was eager to hear from his former commander.

Bjørn sat alert with his back straight in the same folding chair as before. Brittvik got right to the point. "I've recommended you for a Norwegian special forces company. The unit is an operation of the British Special Services, but they are working with us. You'd be trained as a commando and returned to Norway where you would conduct operations as instructed against the Germans. Is that acceptable?"

The words hung in the air. Words Bjørn wanted to hear. He had made a harrowing trip across the North Sea to hear them. Bjørn's grin was wide. He leaned back before returning to a straight posture. "*Ja*, I won't let you down, sir."

"I'm confident you won't." Brittvik wasn't finished. "I'm told there'll be a bit of a delay before you'd start training. Could be several months. I've arranged work for you while you wait. We maintain gardens near here to help feed the king and all of us in exile. You'll manage some of those gardens. The pay is fifteen pounds a month. It should be enough. We'll extend your stay at the hotel while you're here."

Brittvik slid his swivel desk chair back and stood. "Well, then, let's get you on your way. I've arranged for you to meet with the unit commander, Captain Martin Linge. His office is in the basement. He's expecting you. Good luck to you, Erliksen."

Bjørn left the office and hustled to his next appointment.

———

Down a walled-in basement corridor and past a furnace room, Bjørn stood in front of the narrow office door with "NOR.I.K.1" stenciled on the glass panel in the upper half of the door. He had no idea what the initials meant. He took a deep breath, turned the doorknob, and entered.

Two men in civilian clothes leaned over their small metal desks in a tight front room. They looked up and in unison pointed to a back office where Bjørn was greeted by Captain Linge. The officer stood at six foot three and sleekly filled his Norwegian military uniform. He stepped forward with a slight limp and sized up Bjørn head to toe.

Linge motioned for Bjørn to sit in a stiff wooden chair and returned to his chair behind a desk. He made it clear to Bjørn that Brittvik's recommendation had gotten him through the

door. "Captain Brittvik spoke well of you. We need men like you
to fight the Germans inside Norway."

Linge went on to explain that his unit was formed earlier
that year to recruit, train, and dispatch Norwegians back to
their homeland as special forces for covert operations. It was the
brainchild of a secret British organization, Special Operations
Executive. SOE, as it was called, was created to carry out espio-
nage, sabotage, and reconnaissance in the growing list of Nazi-
occupied countries throughout Europe. So, the Norwegian
Independent Kompani No. 1 was hatched.

"When our agents go back, they report on German military
movements and fortifications and commit acts of sabotage to disrupt Nazi activities," the captain said. "We've stationed some of
our men here, and they've partnered with the British forces for
special operations."

He told Bjørn about a raid in March in the northern Lofoten
Islands. "It was successful for us," Linge said. "We blew up several fish oil factories that the enemy used to ship oil to Germany.
They're using glycerin from fish oil to make explosives and as
tank lubricant. That had to be stopped."

Linge took in a long breath and released it. "But the king was
not happy because the raid caused Nazi reprisals. Arrests, executions. So, the British now are cooperating with our government
on our unit's activities. That's why we're located here at Kingston
House, to improve our coordination."

The captain winced as he pulled his legs, extended under the
desk, back to his chair.

Bjørn noticed it. "Are you hurt?"

"Yeah, I'd been an actor for the national theater before the
war, and I also was a lieutenant for an army reserve unit," Linge
said. "My unit mobilized when the Germans came. When we
were fighting in Romsdal, I took shrapnel from a German stick

grenade in my foot. It was pretty banged up. It still gives me problems."

Bjørn shook his head. "How'd you end up here?"

"After I was wounded, I was evacuated to a British hospital ship and then to England. A Norwegian doctor treated me and thought of me when a British officer he knew mentioned the formation of this unit. They needed someone to run it, and things fell into place."

The captain held his gaze on Bjørn. "I've heard about your war experience. Tell me what happened to you after that and what brought you to England." Bjørn delivered the full story of the farm, Nazi confiscation of his animals and crops, and his desire to fight back.

Linge listened, his chin resting in his hand. At the end, he said, "Well, I think this unit will fit your needs as well as ours. Interested in joining?"

Bjørn's head lifted. "Very much."

Linge slid documents across his desk. His new recruit gave them a quick look and didn't hesitate to put his signature on the final page.

———

Bjørn waited several months before beginning his training in Norwegian Independent Kompani No. 1. The delay left him impatient. He found a distraction, and with it some income, by spending long hours tending to several so-called victory gardens that grew produce to help feed exiled Norwegians in England. It felt good to get his hands in dirt again, albeit English soil. Between his employment and the housing covered by the Norwegian government, Bjørn was able to get by as well as anyone could in wartime London.

As he waited for a call to duty, significant events unfolded, changing the course of the war. On December 7, 1941, Bjørn listened to a news broadcast that the Japanese attacked the United States at a place called Pearl Harbor in the Hawaiian Islands. Despite a significant loss of ships and lives, he hoped the attack would lure Americans into the fight against the Germans and reverse the Nazi's tide.

The next day at one of Bjørn's gardens, he heard joyous shouting and laughter from the street. He asked two men who had been arguing what the commotion was about. They told him that the American Congress had declared war on Nazi Germany as well as Japan.

"Germany is destined for defeat," said one man, who was up in years. "I remember when American troops entered the Great War. It was the beginning of the end for the Germans. It will be the same this time around, too."

"Don't be so confident," the other replied. "Remember that the Japanese just destroyed America's navy. Who can fight without a navy?"

"America has many military-aged men and material to build tanks, planes, guns, and ships," the old man said. "You'll see."

Bjørn stood back, hoping the eldest man was right.

Just after Christmas 1941, Bjørn's mood was lifted upon hearing another BBC broadcast report of a second raid involving the Kompani's commandos in the Lofoten Islands. Soldiers of the Norwegian unit joined British special forces on four destroyers and the cruiser *Kenya*. They knocked out three German coastal defenses and destroyed several more fish oil factories. More than one hundred German soldiers and Norwegian Nazis were captured and brought back to England.

The next day, Bjørn received a handwritten note from Brittvik. In a shoot-out with German forces during the raid, Captain Linge had taken two bullets to the chest and was killed. In delivering the news to Bjørn as a courtesy, Brittvik wrote: "This has no effect on your status. But you have lost a good leader." Bjørn's throat tightened. The news strengthened his resolve to fight.

Weeks later, another BBC report brought news from Norway that on February 1, 1942, Reichskommissar Josef Terboven resurrected Vidkun Quisling's importance, making him minister-president of the country and tasking him with forming a new government.

Reports of Quisling's oppression reached Bjørn in the following days. In the first meeting of his government on February 5, he issued a new law requiring all youth between ten and eighteen to join a Norwegian Nazi organization akin to Germany's Hitler Youth. Parents were protesting the Nazification of their kids, flooding the Quisling government with thousands of letters.

While Bjørn waited for military training, news of the oppressive acts at home piled up. He made a daily ritual of checking his hotel mailbox for his orders. Every time, he returned to his room empty-handed and disappointed.

It was early March before he returned to his room clutching an envelope, this one already torn open in the hotel lobby. He was directed to report for training the following month.

CHAPTER 16

Spring 1942

Bjørn reported for the first phase of his training at the British Royal Air Force Parachute Training School. It was at Ringway Field, Cheshire, England, outside of Manchester. Originally designed exclusively for British troops, the parachute school later opened to all Allied forces. For those first five weeks, Bjørn held the bottom-rung military rank of *menig*, the equivalent of what the United States Army would call a buck private.

At the school, he learned the techniques of folding and strapping on a parachute, jumping, and landing. His first jump of any height was out of a five-story tower. Then he parachuted through a hole in the carriage of a hot-air balloon at one thousand feet. He took a deep breath, crossed his fingers, and plunged to earth.

Anticipating the leap from more than four thousand feet up out of a converted Handley Page Harrow bomber was what really knotted his stomach. Not only was it his first airplane jump, it marked his first time on a plane. He was unable to stop quivering. His legs felt wobbly. It wasn't from the weight of the forty-pound pack on his back and the chute strapped to his front. A piece of him wanted to tell his commanding authorities he wanted out. Pride wouldn't let him do it.

So, in late April 1942, Bjørn lined up with the other trainees and made his way toward the plane's exit door to bail into a white sky on a cool, cloudy, misty day. When his turn came, he froze. It took a firm nudge from his primary trainer, British Sergeant O'Shea McLaughlin, to send him airborne. In the end, he landed with the precision his training had taught him. After his feet touched ground, he tucked and rolled and hauled in his chute. Bjørn stretched on the ground staring at the puffy white sky with an ear-to-ear smile. He wanted to do it again.

Bjørn had graded high on that and subsequent jumps and finished parachute training among the top graduates of his class. Superiors handed him a certificate and a promotion to corporal. Now he had two stripes on his uniform sleeves.

With parachute school done, he and twenty-four other trainees boarded a train in mid-May for Aberdeen, Scotland. The next day, they left Aberdeen in a truck for the unit's training camp at Glenmore Lodge, an old estate in the northern Scottish Highlands near the town of Aviemore. By then, Norwegian Independent Kompani No. 1 had a new name. The unit was referred to as Kompani Linge, in honor of its slain former commander.

Bjørn jumped down from the back of a canopied truck when they arrived in front of the lodge on a rainy afternoon. He was in Norwegian Army combat fatigues, with a beret secured on his head and his kit bag strapped over his shoulder. The newly minted parachute school certificate was tucked inside the bag.

Even though he wore a uniform of his homeland, officially he served at the pleasure of the British SOE. He viewed the reporting structure as merely technical. In his heart, Bjørn considered himself a special forces commando in the service of Norway.

The main manor of the estate was a dignified two-story structure built of graying white concrete. He heard it had served once as a hunting lodge for a Scottish lord. The large estate covering hundreds of acres was nestled in a valley with huge, rugged mountains as a backdrop. When Bjørn saw them, he gasped at the beauty. It was as if he were in Norway again.

The main house was off-limits to trainees. Officers, trainers, and training administrators had commandeered it for their use. Instead, Bjørn and the others were assigned to a simple wood building a short way down the hill. The rectangular single-story building was constructed of repurposed, faded-red boards and looked every bit like a barracks. Adjacent outbuildings held the kitchen and mess hall.

Inside, dormitory-style, two-person bunk beds with individual footlockers filled the place. Many of the bunks were in use by others already training—about twice as many as Bjørn and the other new arrivals. Light bulbs connected by heavy wire were strung along the ceiling. A large room with flush toilets and washbasins was at one end of the barracks. Electricity and indoor plumbing gave the makeshift structure unexpected creature comforts.

The first evening, Bjørn joined the others for a meal in the adjoining mess hall. They crammed together at two tables.

They were joined by First Lieutenant Ian Robertson, who introduced himself as their main training officer. This guy was hard to miss in a crowd. Robertson had entered the mess hall with a stately, put-together stride. He was about six feet tall, with ginger-colored hair and a rugged face that said he had seen war. Their lieutenant was on the young side but had a good five or six years on Bjørn, who had turned twenty-two a month earlier. The officer wore British Army–issued fatigues but had a different beret than those so prevalent among English troops in London. It was black with a red Scottish unit patch sewn on the front.

Around the dinner table, there was lots of curiosity about his background. Robertson told Bjørn and the others he grew up in Glasgow. His parents owned a small bookshop, and he spent hours working there. It fueled his interest in reading. He subsequently studied literature and business at the University of Strathclyde. The swirl of troubling events in Europe that included the rise of Nazism in Germany and the Spanish Civil War called to him to protect his country. In 1937, at twenty-three, he'd enlisted in the Glasgow Highlanders, part of the Highland Light Infantry's 157th Brigade. In 1940, he fought with the British Expeditionary Force in France and was evacuated from the beaches of Dunkirk. When the SOE set up Norwegian training centers in Scotland, Robertson jumped at the chance to return to his country and serve in another capacity.

The lieutenant's expression switched from jovial to stern. "You all are in for a long stretch of six months," he said. "This training will not be easy. You will be pushed further and harder than you've ever experienced. You already know why it's important and what's at stake. I don't need to give you a motivational speech or yell at you like new conscripts. You're all motivated enough in light of what's happened in your country. If I must raise my voice, it will be for a good reason."

He told them that Czechs, Poles, Greeks, and other exiles from Nazi-controlled countries were training at other sites in the vicinity for the same purpose—return to their homelands and clandestinely fight the Germans.

"The few people in England who know about this training say we're Churchill's Secret Army. Some Germans have figured out what we're doing and have adopted another name for us. They call us the International Gangster School."

Robertson added, "Don't get too excited about the beauty of the Cairngorms outside. You'll likely grow to hate those mountains before you're finished."

His demeanor seemed to lighten up. "Each of you will have a certain amount of freedom when you're not training. But you'll be expected to pitch in and help with chores. You'll be assigned to kitchen and latrine cleaning duty. I am required to tell you that there are two things you cannot do while on your own time. One is fishing for salmon in our burns. You call 'em rivers, we call 'em burns. Also, you cannot hunt deer. That's what I'm required to say." He winked.

The food arrived, and each plate contained a chunk of meat. For Bjørn and those at the table, their diets mostly lacked red meat since before the war. Not one of them set down their knife and fork before their plate was empty.

"That was good. What kind of meat was it?" one trainee asked.

"Venison," Robertson responded.

———

Bjørn's first weeks of training were as demanding as Lieutenant Robertson advertised. Every bit of his strength, stamina, and commitment was tested. Part of it had to do with the terrain. SOE established the training site in the Scottish Highlands because it gave trainees a formidable playground.

The terrain resembled Norway, with high plateaus of ever-present snow, dense forests with treacherous glacial rivers, rugged mountains with rocky faces, and sheer granite cliffs that plunged to the sea. The region contained four of the highest peaks in the United Kingdom. The unforgiving geography coupled with cold, blinding blizzards and frequent coastal rain even in summer provided an ideal proving ground.

Norwegian special forces planned and trained for the extreme. They weren't being trained to resist Nazis in the streets like in Paris or in flat, marshy landscapes like in the Netherlands. Norwegian commandos would be exposed to the harsh conditions of a northern arctic climate for prolonged periods of time with little or no support or resources.

Activities based out of Glenmore and two other old estates with mansion-like country homes—Forest Lodge and Drumintoul

Lodge—took full advantage of the rugged landscape. Every morning, Bjørn and the other men rose and rushed to get out the door to an adjacent grass-and-dirt field for calisthenics. That was followed by a heavy mix of classroom instruction, practical applications, and outdoor activities such as challenging runs through obstacle courses, both man-made and nature-created. The nature-made routes were designated by the trainers to be conquered under challenging and grueling conditions. Bjørn and the others frequently were forced to swim in glacial water with waterproof packs on their backs. He emerged from the water shivering in his wet clothes and feeling drained of energy, only to be ordered straight up a mountain with the others.

Then there was running. They were required to run everywhere at a steady clip. They ran to classes. They ran to the firing range. They ran to camps at the other estates several miles away. The only time they walked was when training was finished for the day. And long training days that stretched into night left little time for that.

Fatigue, soreness, and pain were Bjørn's constant companions during the first weeks of training, which focused on physical strength and endurance. But over time, he realized his body not only began to adjust but it seemed to thrive on the demanding regimen.

Instead of dreading morning reveille, Bjørn in later weeks treated it as embarking on just another day of hard work. His once-aching muscles, painful shins, and wheezy breathing eased. One day, he had been tested with a ten-mile run on a hilly road. When it had ended, he believed he had enough energy go another ten.

On the firing range at Glenmore, Bjørn handled almost every weapon commonly used by allies and enemies alike. Rifles such as the American M1, German Mauser, and British Enfields. Pistols such as a Colt .45 and German Luger. The Sten submachine gun was popular with commandos because of its compact, simple metal stock. The trainees took each of the weapons apart and reassembled them under timed testing to grow familiar with them.

Bjørn did particularly well on a timed test requiring that he draw, cock, and fire an automatic pistol through a two-foot-square open window. He hit the cutout target of a man's head and upper body five times in less than five seconds at ten paces.

His hands shook the first time he pulled the pin from a hand grenade and threw it over a reinforced wall, creating a deafening explosion. But tossing the oval-shaped explosive, which the trainees dubbed "live eggs," soon became almost second nature to him.

Mastering instruments of sabotage was a critical part of training. He tested everything from Molotov cocktails to mines and dynamite. Charges were laid in all sorts of places under many conditions. Bjørn was required to calculate how much explosive was needed for particular tasks. He strung wires, set fuses and timers, and used plungers to blow up makeshift facilities.

Beyond weaponry, the men of Kompani Linge learned close-in, hand-to-hand fighting and ways to kill silently. Bjørn was introduced to the ancient Japanese martial art of jujitsu, as well as boxing and the techniques of knife fighting. He simulated killing with choke holds, sudden head twists, and the so-called rabbit slip—a violent, quick hand chop to vulnerable body parts.

There was schooling in radio communications and wireless telegraphy. He learned Morse code and how to send, receive, decipher, encrypt, and disguise messages. Communicating with England and transcribing orders and instructions would be a critical part of Bjørn's mission.

He also was drilled in compass and map reading. One day, he climbed aboard a bus with other trainees. The vehicle's windows were closed by thick curtains so they could not see outside. After an hour-long ride, they were let out in mountainous terrain in groups of five. They were given navigation tools and the assignment to find their way back. Each group was required to work independently, treat the others as the enemy, and avoid being seen.

Another exercise tested Bjørn's skill at evading enemy pursuers. He found himself alone at night in the mountains. At one point, Bjørn descended a steep tree-and-brush-covered mountain. When he reached a river at the bottom of a ravine in the moonlight, gunshots suddenly rang out from behind where he had been. He splashed across the stream through shallow but frigid water. On the other side, he scrambled under a thicket of brush and stayed silent and hidden. Bjørn heard footsteps near him, but he was not discovered. Eventually, the voices of Robertson and another trainer called for him to come out, announcing the exercise was finished.

"You did well, Corporal," Robertson said. "You passed the test."

Four months into the training, Bjørn flourished in the art of war and resistance. He was in the best physical condition of his life. He felt as if he could take on the entire German army by himself.

CHAPTER 17

March 24, 1943

Bjørn stood tall on Hay's Dock in Lerwick's town harbor with a gunnysack full of gear in each hand. He scanned the narrow waterway between the town on the main island of Shetland and an island named Bressay on the east side of the channel. Bressay held the lighthouse that guided *Hildur VI* in during the harrowing North Sea crossing in September 1941. His feet felt the very dock where he had ended that journey. Awaiting him now was the return trip home.

The same boat that had delivered him would take him back over the same two hundred miles of ocean. There it sat, its side bumpers brushing gently against the dock. *Hildur VI* was stenciled in bold black capital letters over the white paint just under the bow's rail. *How ironic*, he thought. Bjørn hoped his return journey would be far more forgiving than the trip from Norway.

He turned and looked back at the town of Lerwick. He had seen so little of it when he'd arrived sick, wet, and tired in the dead of night eighteen months ago. Now he could see the quaintness of the town of about four thousand. Its buildings and homes gradually ascended a gentle hill sloping away from the harbor. A distinctive clock tower peered over the rooftops.

The town and the islands had more bustle now because of the war. More than twenty thousand British troops descended on them, and the islands had become a major platform for military operations to monitor and potentially attack anything moving on the North Sea. The fortified island chain also gave England a layer of protection over the northern reaches of the United Kingdom. The Royal Air Force had fighter bases in the north of the main island of Shetland, and the British Army camped northeast of Lerwick.

Even Kompani Linge's overseer, SOE, had installed a base here since Bjørn's last visit. It organized a fleet of private fishing boats to transport commandos and supplies to Norway, an operation commonly referred to as the Shetland Bus.

Bjørn stared at the boat rocking comfortably at the dock. He couldn't stop smiling. His military training in Scotland was behind him. He had graduated near the top of his class and was a newly installed Norwegian Army commando in Kompani Linge. He now wore a single silver star on the epaulets of his uniform. Upon graduation, his rank had been bumped to second lieutenant in the special forces unit. His mastery of training prompted First Lieutenant Ian Robertson to keep him in Scotland months longer to help train incoming recruits. Even though Bjørn was itching to get back to Norway, he'd agreed to stay on.

His uniform was tucked deep in one of the gunnysacks. As he prepared to board *Hildur VI*, Bjørn wore clothing fit for a coastal fisherman. He had on a thick gray wool pullover sweater, a blue wool cap that fit snugly over his head and ears, waterproof foul-weather gear, and sturdy rubber boots. The clothing would allow him to hide in plain sight when he reached Norway.

Only one item remained of clothing that had come with him across the North Sea in 1941. The military-style field coat he had disguised with black dye. The thick wool coat kept him warm and dry during many cold, snowy, and rainy nights, and he was not about to part with it.

His physical appearance was different, altered to make him less recognizable when he returned home. He grew a thick mustache that spread across his upper lip to almost the outer creases of his mouth. British stylists had added their touches in London. They trimmed and lightened his dark-bronze hair to light brown, almost blond, and styled it across his forehead instead of swept back. Form-fitted pads were stuffed inside his mouth, puffing out his slightly recessed cheeks. He had a pair of wire-rimmed glasses. Those who knew him still might be able to recognize him up close. But the intent was to make him less noticeable or at least create doubt from a short distance.

Bjørn had received a new identity. He carried a falsified identification paper identical to that the Germans required of all Norwegians. On it was a fictitious name. He had to choose the name quickly when the document was being prepared in London. He thought of Mons, a relatively common first name. Then the word for a birch tree popped into his head as a last name. So, his forged document read "Mons Bjørk."

He was assigned a commando code number that would be used to receive instructions from his handlers in England. Bjørn's number, eighty-three, carried importance, as did the numbers for all agents and spies operating behind enemy lines throughout Europe.

In Norway, an agent's number was part of a numerical code imbedded in regular BBC broadcasts of the nightly program "News of Norway." If Bjørn heard his number announced, he needed to write down subsequent numbers. Then he would refer to his assigned book, in his case, a thick, pocket-size Bible, to decipher the code. Each number read in the broadcast would direct him to specific Bible books, verses, and words, all of which formed phrases and sentences delivering information and instructions.

Finally, he got the code name Ram. He would use that to identify himself in telegraphed Morse coded messages sent to England
and when contacting other commandos and resistance fighters
in Norway. A wealth of operating instructions was crammed in
Bjørn's head for his return trip to Norway.

As he boarded *Hildur VI*, its skipper gave him a long look.
"Have you been on this boat before?"

Bjørn immediately recognized the captain, Anders Kongsgaard. He responded with a sly grin. "September 1941. It was
rough. A sudden storm. I was sick as hell."

The beefy captain tilted his head back. "*Ja*, I remember you
now. You do look a little different to me."

"Credit the people in London who create disguises."

Kongsgaard gave him a berth forward in the captain's quarters where a bunk was attached to each side of the bulkhead. For
this trip, he would be the only passenger joining the skipper and
an expanded three-member crew.

But accompanying him were four tons of weapons, explosives, equipment, and supplies stashed below. Upon his return,
one of Bjørn's first tasks was to find help to transport and hide
the cache in secure locations. Part of it would serve his needs, but
some would supply resistance operations in and around Bergen.

Bjørn was eager to get moving, but foul weather was keeping the trawler in port and delaying their departure. Rain soaked
Lerwick and a storm whipped up the sea. Over two stormy days,
Bjørn and Kongsgaard sat on their bunks and chatted late into
the evening. Bjørn brought the captain up to date about his experiences in London and training in Scotland. Kongsgaard, in turn,
told his passenger about joining the Shetland Bus. *Hildur VI* had
made four other trips to Norway since their last journey together.

"Three trips went well," Kongsgaard said. "We took a Kompani
Linge agent to an island south of Bergen, another farther north
near Aalesund, and another to an outer island near Sognefjord.

On each trip, we brought back people fleeing the country. Most of them were Jewish people the Germans would certainly have killed if they'd stayed."

Bjørn remembered he had not seen Hans Martensen, the crewman, and asked about him.

Kongsgaard dropped his head. "Hans is no longer with us. On one trip last year, we hit a storm coming back and almost didn't make it. Worse than you had it. Part of our bulwark was damaged, and sad to say, Hans was swept overboard. We limped to Shetland with twenty-one refugees."

His voice trailed off. "I took losing Hans hard. He was a good friend."

Bjørn nodded. He couldn't imagine how he would deal with the pain if he ever lost Jon.

Kongsgaard told Bjørn that several boats of the Shetland Bus had been lost at sea.

"German planes have attacked some boats. The Germans also have patrol boats out looking for us. We take our trips in the wintertime, since the fog and darkness can be our ally and help us avoid detection. But weather often is bad. It's getting better now. This will be my last trip until next winter."

The skipper pointed out that guns were added, enabling *Hildur VI* to defend itself if attacked. "You noticed oil drums bolted to the foredeck?"

Bjørn nodded.

"Inside them are American-made machine guns," Kongsgaard continued. "The lid comes off, and a spring-loaded mechanism brings up the guns. My crew is trained to use them. We also have a special mounting for another machine gun aft."

Bjørn had weaponry of his own. He carried a Sten gun and .45 Colt pistol as well as a pair of metal knuckles for his fists.

He was restless while the boat was stuck in Lerwick waiting for the weather to clear. Kongsgaard seemed to sleep like a baby.

His snoring was proof of that. Bjørn lay awake most of the nights. Part of it was excitement. His mind was on his mission once he reached his homeland. There was something else that weighed heavy and unnerved him. It was anticipating his initial contact after arriving. The contact was code-named The Monk.

His SOE handlers had briefed him on his mission before he'd left London. His territory of operation would be in a coastal area just over the mountains from his home. It was familiar territory and relatively close to his farm.

Once he reached Norway, he was directed to Bølgeland, a small coastal fishing village, where he was to contact The Monk. Bjørn was very familiar with the village. But when he heard the name of the place and The Monk's address, he had gasped. It was the home of Olav and Rita Sonnesen, parents of his former girlfriend, his first and only love.

———

Her name was Truni Sonnesen, and they had met at a community dance. She was seventeen and so was Bjørn. He remembered being captivated by the sparkle of her blue eyes. They were alluring. Her blond hair was short and shimmery straight. With her home just over a coastal mountain range and to the west of Erlikvåg, the distance that separated them was not terribly far. By car, it was roughly thirty miles through foothills and on a coastal road along parts of two fjords. Bjørn frequently grabbed a ride, borrowed a car, or hitchhiked his way to see her. Sometimes he would hike over the mountains, a four- to six-hour trek.

They had attended separate schools but spent as much time together as they could. When they were together, they took long walks either through town or on the winding road along the coast. Bjørn was more than an occasional guest at her family's dinner table and often spent the night. On those nights, Truni's mom, Rita, showed him to his separate bedroom. Mountains just to the east of Bølgeland were a favorite hiking area. Truni's family had a cabin high and isolated above the tree line. The *hytte* had been a frequent destination for them.

Olav Sonnesen, her father, owned a small pewter factory that made bowls, cups, ornamental spoons, candle holders, and the like, some for shops in Oslo and some for export. It earned the family a comfortable living. Truni worked at Sonnesen Tinn Fabrikk maintaining the books and accounts. Olav had offered Bjørn part-time work at the business. Although he had to turn it down due to the demands of the farm and schoolwork, it was one of many kind acts that made the family special to him.

Bjørn thought Truni was pretty and sweet. Petite, she stood almost five foot four, and had a shape that would make most boys look twice. She also was smart and practical. She was a top student throughout her school years and an accomplished knitter, learning the skills handed down by her grandmother and mother. Bjørn benefitted. One Christmas, she knitted him a sweater with a popular Norwegian design adorned with snowflakes. It was still stuffed in a drawer on his farm.

In their time together, Bjørn believed she could very well be the one he would spend the rest of his days with. The first one he loved also meant the first one he kissed with passion.

He remembered one of their lazy strolls near where she lived. They snuck into an old remote barn in a pasture along the road, climbed a rickety ladder to the loft, and lay down on a pile of soft, dry hay. Their kissing lasted longer than usual. Bjørn moved his hand under her shirt. It was new territory for him, and it was awkward. Truni moaned softly at his touch. When he sought to proceed further, she stopped him.

"I want to wait," she whispered. Bjørn backed away. She had set clear limits, and as difficult as it seemed at times, he respected them.

As they neared the end of their secondary school education, they began to grow apart. Bjørn saw his future working the family farm. He was used to it, he was good at it, and it was what his father wanted him to do.

Truni, meanwhile, had dreams and ambition beyond her town or living on a farm. She wanted urban life in Oslo and even beyond, setting her sights on London and Stockholm. She hoped her bookkeeping skills acquired at her father's factory and her school marks might provide a ticket to city life.

She loved Bjørn as much as he loved her, and they talked of marriage and raising a family together. But their contrary dreams meant something had to give.

Just past graduation from secondary school—both were nineteen by then—Truni was offered an opportunity to work as an accountant in her uncle's fish-processing business in Stavanger to the south of Bergen. It didn't fit precisely into her plans, but she believed it posed a stepping-stone. Her uncle's factory was a much larger operation than her family's business.

Truni was conflicted. Bjørn knew that in her heart she wanted to leave, and he stopped short of discouraging her. He hoped they could still remain together even from afar. But cracks formed in his own heart. He feared her leaving could spell the end of their relationship.

In the end, she accepted the job. They had promised each other they would write and visit whenever they could. But the visits didn't happen, and initial letters of love and commitment eventually waned and then stopped altogether. Ultimately, she sent him a Dear Bjørn letter concluding they both needed to move on.

Bjørn's heart suffered. He knew he had to get over his sadness and move on. Then came his father's death, and the hurt had worsened.

CHAPTER 18

March 28, 1943

Bjørn was on deck when the Norwegian coastline surfaced above the east horizon. He squinted. There wasn't much to see. The outer islands were barely visible in the distance. He widened his legs to sturdy himself on the gently rolling seas.

The trip across the North Sea had been smooth. No engine trouble, no storms, no German planes or boats. It was late in the afternoon after the day of departure. By Kongsgaard's calculation, they were eight to ten miles offshore. From Norway. From home.

Amid his excitement, Bjørn was captured by an odd feeling that he was returning as a foreigner to a country where he was born and raised. He was a native son, a citizen, who stood on mountain tops, dug his hands in the soil, and fished in its waters. He knew the language, the people, the culture and traditions.

But things were different now. With Nazis in control, it didn't feel like he was returning to his country. He would operate behind enemy lines. His freedom of movement would be restricted. He would have to avoid being seen by so many he knew. He would have to sneak into his own house in the dark of night. He had to exercise care in whom he trusted. He didn't look like the man who had left. He had to use an alias for required identification papers.

He had a code name and an agent number. Indeed, it felt odd. He thought that he might as well be entering China or Africa.

Kongsgaard decided to turn *Hildur VI* around and motor farther from shore. They were about four hours from dusk. Good weather and relatively mild waters had carried *Hildur VI* and its occupant and the three-member crew across the North Sea ahead of schedule. That blessing became a bit of a curse once they came within eyesight of Norway's west coast. They would be sitting ducks to enemy planes and patrol boats. But the skipper thought it safer to approach shore as nightfall set in.

"When it gets dark, we should see a little fog build," Kongsgaard told Bjørn. "Keep an eye out for German planes, and be prepared to fight it out."

They saw no sign of Nazi activities. When the late evening arrived, Kongsgaard opened the throttle and pushed *Hildur VI* toward shore at a low, steady chug.

The breeze was chilly, and a light fog gave them some cover. There was enough light to make out the approaching landmass. The nearer the boat got, the more remote this part of the shoreline seemed. Land with no lights, no structures, and no signs of civilization. It was perfect.

They navigated around islands and skerries, the protruding tiny rocky reefs typical of Norway's rugged coast. Kongsgaard pulled back the throttle, slowing the speed, minimizing the wake and limiting the sound of the engine's huff. No running lights. Enough moonlight filtered through the fog to make out land.

At last, they reached a long stretch of shoreline that was the mainland. They faced a long, high cliff of solid rock that seemed to reach the sky. The monstrous sheer face looked like it had been cut away with a sharp knife. It filled Bjørn's vision of the shore. They were close enough now to hear waves lapping against it.

He scrambled inside the wheelhouse. "How are we going to land on that rock?"

"Don't worry," Kongsgaard assured him. "There's a gap through there. Hard to find, but it's there. Just wide enough for the boat. Like threading a needle."

Bjørn trusted the skipper's knowledge and skill augmented by navigational equipment. He had no doubt Kongsgaard would find the channel through the rock.

Two crew members stood at the bow to help direct Kongsgaard. No talking. No smoking. They held flashlights and switched them on just long enough to illuminate the rock cliff and seek out the gap but not long enough to draw the attention of any German patrol boat that might be in the vicinity. They extended their arms to point right or left, directing the captain where to aim *Hildur VI*'s bow.

The cliff was less than fifty feet away. Every inch of rock looked the same to Bjørn, just a smooth, solid wall. Then his eye picked out an opening where the rock separated. It looked barely wide enough for a rowboat let alone a beamy trawler.

Kongsgaard seemed to know what Bjørn was thinking. "It's tight, but I've done it before. Water's deep, too. These cliffs plunge way down into the sea. Beyond the gap, there's a small cove and an abandoned *hytte*. It's got a dock. That's where we'll drop you."

They were barely making way now. Just when Bjørn thought the boat would strike the wall, Kongsgaard gingerly turned the wheel to the right and squeezed *Hildur VI* into the narrow channel. Bjørn took a deep breath.

If Bjørn were standing at a side rail, he thought he could easily have touched the rock. Calm waters helped Kongsgaard navigate his vessel through without even a slight nudge. They came out of the tunnel-like gap and entered the cove.

Light fog and weak moonlight made it difficult for Bjørn to see. But there was enough light for him to conclude the cove was small, perhaps no more than fifty yards across and a hundred yards deep. Shadows of trees surrounded it. The trees seemed to climb a steep hillside just beyond the water's edge.

One crew member on the bow aimed his flashlight and illuminated a dock. After more skillful maneuvering, Kongsgaard pushed the boat alongside the tiny dock, and the crew secured lines around end pilings.

Bjørn had the honor of stepping onto the dock first ahead of Kongsgaard. They advanced twenty or so feet down the slanting planks, and Bjørn made footprints on spongy Norwegian soil.

They found the *hytte* cuddled in trees on flat ground just twenty paces from the dock. Bjørn had his Sten gun ready, and Kongsgaard carried a pistol. But it was quiet and the *hytte* and its surroundings looked deserted.

"We're told it's been abandoned for some time," Kongsgaard said. "But it'll give you shelter. A good place to store the stuff we brought until you have to move it."

They pulled the handle and opened the front door. There was no lock. Isolation was the security. Kongsgaard set a lantern on a table, casting enough light to fill the room. It was primitive. No furnishings. No running water. No electrical fuse box. There was a fireplace, but it showed no sign of recent use. There were two uncovered windows with glass intact.

Kongsgaard and Bjørn joined the crew, which had already begun unloading. Within an hour, they were done. Boxes and barrels of weapons, equipment, and supplies filled more than half of the *hytte*'s main room.

"How far are we from where I need to be?" Bjørn asked Kongsgaard.

"We're north of Bergen, and your contact is not too far, I believe. Just north of here over the mountain."

Bjørn pulled a map out of his pocket, and in the lantern light, Kongsgaard pinpointed where they were. Bjørn now had a starting point. He figured he was a day's hike through forest and over a moderate-size mountain from the village of Bølgeland and the Sonnesen home.

"Well, we must leave you now," Kongsgaard said. "I want to get home to Hernar before daybreak and see my wife and daughter."

Bjørn remembered Hernar Island, the place he'd left on the *Hildur VI* for Shetland.

As they parted, Kongsgaard looked back. "I hope our paths cross again when this bloody war's over."

The *Hildur VI* motored out of the cove, leaving Bjørn on his own in the sparse confines of the cabin. It was close to midnight. He grabbed a sleeping bag from a gunnysack, wrapped himself in a layer of warmth on the hard floor, and tried to sleep. He would wait for the morning light to study the map, get his bearings, and chart his next course. For now, he enjoyed breathing Norwegian air.

CHAPTER 19

March 29, 1943

It was dead quiet when Bjørn awoke early in the *hytte* among stacks of equipment. He peered out the window to an eerie stillness. Nothing moved outside except a small flock of shorebirds floating in the flat, calm cove.

He first checked out the security of his surroundings. With his Sten gun at the ready, he crept through the forest around the cove and found no evidence of human activity, recent or past.

The rest of the day was spent in the *hytte* studying his map to plan his trek across the mountains to Bølgeland and looking through the crates and barrels. His handlers had reviewed the equipment and supplies with him before he'd left London and had provided a full written inventory. After making sure all the materials were there, his instructions were to destroy the list.

The cache was considerable. The large paint cans contained weaponry, including disassembled Sten guns, M1 carbines, nine-millimeter pistols, knives, and American-made grenades. Hansa beer crates held dynamite sticks, limpets, and other explosives, along with rolls of wires, fuses, and plungers. Fish barrels were chock-full of food, bandages, and first-aid supplies; American Camel cigarettes; and other personal items. The all-important radio transmission equipment was there, too, packed in a nonde-script suitcase any traveler would use.

Bjørn organized and separated the containers into two stores, including one for his use. He needed to transport and secure his share close to his base of operation. The other was destined for Bergen later. It would be handed off to a Kompani Linge agent there with the code name Hammer. He had been assured by his superiors that his primary contact, who he assumed to be Olav Sonnesen, would help him transport his supplies and arrange getting the rest to Hammer. For the time being, he would leave it all in the *hytte*.

For his immediate needs, Bjørn repacked his rucksack and put in food and essential items that he took from the cache. He also held out some of the cigarettes, which he thought might pro-vide inducements for soliciting help.

He left the *hytte* about noon the next day to set out for the Sonnesen home.

———

Hidden in the hillside forest, Bjørn looked down on the house, his first recognizable landmark since returning to Norway. A peeka-boo view through the trees was enough visibility to watch for any activity there. It was the Sonnesen home, a place he'd visited often before the war.

Different circumstances brought him here now. When his handlers in London had given him the location of his contact, Bjørn had pictured it immediately. When he had learned the con-tact's code name, The Monk, it struck him as odd. The Sonnesens were Lutherans, not Catholics. Whatever the name, Bjørn was ready to make contact.

It had taken him six hours to slog over a rugged moun-tain through an almost-steady rain and some snowflakes. His dull-green slicker had shed it well and kept his inner clothes dry. The thick wool cap was soaked on the surface but had kept his head and ears warm and dry.

Bjørn's fully packed rucksack weighed heavy on his back. A pair of snowshoes were strapped on top of that. An early-spring snowmelt that created a sopping mush had made for sluggish progress.

Bjørn waited for daylight to fade before approaching the house to avoid unwanted attention. The home was located at the upper end of the village, away from a cozy harbor and along the road that led out of town. There were other homes in the vicinity, but for the most part, the Sonnesens were set off by themselves.

It was a modest two-story structure with a small front porch, just a quick step above the ground. He remembered the inside as roomy with three bedrooms on the second floor. The room where he had spent many a night was in the back right corner. The kitchen was small, but Bjørn recalled the sumptuous meals that came out of it. Lutefisk, lamb stews, and Rita Sonnesen's specialty, *rømmegrøt* sour cream pudding.

Bjørn was nervous at the thought of seeing Truni's parents again under such different circumstances. As instructed, he would use his code name, Ram, to identify himself. He expected that to be short-lived. Even with his cosmetic alterations, they would certainly recognize him.

The Sonnesens were trustworthy people. Loyal people. Bjørn was not surprised Olav would be involved in resistance activity. It had been nearly four years since he had last seen Truni's parents. They could settle his curiosity about her. He had thought of her often and had wondered how she was faring in Stavanger at her uncle's factory. For all he knew, she might be married and have already started a family. He also had to face the likelihood she and her parents had put him out of their minds.

The evening grew darker, and it was quiet. During his vigil, no one had entered or left the house. Bjørn decided to make his move. He emerged from the trees toward the house. With black-out requirements and a likely curfew, the house seemed dark and more buttoned up than he remembered.

He worried that the sight of a stranger in a dark-shaded slicker on an unlighted porch at night might scare them. For Norwegians living under Nazi tyranny, an unexpected knock on the door was greeted with uncertainty and fear. But Bjørn pressed ahead. It couldn't be helped. He walked quietly up to the door and tapped it with his knuckles.

There was a long pause. To him, it seemed an eternity. Eventually the door opened and the inside light illuminated him. It wasn't Olav or Rita Sonnesen who answered. It was Truni.

———

With a cautious blank expression, Truni held the door just wide enough to size up the stranger.

"*Ja?*" she said.

Bjørn stood on the porch with his mouth open and eyes wide. He blurted out his reaction. "Truni?"

He couldn't disguise his voice. Whatever cover he had was blown. And for the moment, code name Ram and alias Mons Bjørk meant nothing.

Truni's weary eyes widened and softened at the same time. They traded bewildered stares. She broke into a broad smile. "Bjørn? Bjørn? Is it really you?"

He nodded and saw her eyes began to well up. His eyes also filled, and he hoped she wouldn't notice.

Her hand went over her mouth. She stood motionless. Then Truni pushed the door open, moved forward, and thrust her arms around him, ignoring his wet slicker and the pack and snowshoes slung over his back.

Bjørn extended his right arm around her and kept the left dangling at his side. He could no longer remain stoic, and a tear tumbled down his cheek.

"I wasn't expecting you," he said.

Her lips pursed and she stepped back. "Who did you expect?"

At that instant, Olav appeared in the hallway and trudged toward the entryway.

"Who is it?"

"Father, it's Bjørn," she said.

"Erliksen?" He opened the door a touch wider and looked out at Bjørn in the doorway.

Seeing Olav, Bjørn-the-commando fulfilled his instructions. "Ram has arrived," he said.

Olav raised his eyebrows. He looked at Truni. She peered out the doorway, looking left, then right, then tugged on Bjørn's coat sleeve and pulled him into the house.

It wasn't Olav who spoke next. It was Truni. "I'm The Monk."

———

Their reunion was stretching late into the night. The gathering had started around the dining room table with a meal, one much sparser than Bjørn had enjoyed there in the past. Among the four of them, they divided up two potatoes, three carrots, and a small piece of cod that Olav obtained from a fisherman back from the sea. Bjørn had dipped into his rations and contributed a can of mixed meat and vegetables. It wasn't particularly tasty, but it contained hard-to-get protein.

They had a lot to cover. Bjørn hadn't seen any of them since his and Truni's relationship broke off. Much had changed in their country. Nazi Germany's occupation of Norway had just passed its third year. Over dinner, the talk had centered on other family members, mutual friends, and the hardships brought on by the war.

With dinner over and the table cleared, they stayed put, seated where they had been throughout the meal. Bjørn and Truni were directly across from each other, and her parents were at each end. Bjørn's gaze stayed where it had been much of the evening, fixed on Truni.

He was still shaking off the shock not only of Truni's presence, but also her revelation that she was his contact. She looked older and, he thought, life under the Nazis had worn her. Dark, sallow circles had formed beneath her blue eyes. Her once-neat short hair flowed over her shoulders. Her facial features had thinned. Her lips were missing the red lipstick she frequently wore when they dated. Eying her now-dull, fleshy pink lips, Bjørn still remembered how he loved to kiss them. To him, she remained through it all a beautiful creature.

He remembered how somber he had been when they parted ways, and her final letter. The sadness had consumed him for some time. He had believed he might never see her again. Now, there she sat little more than an arm's length away.

Olav and Rita were gaunter than he remembered them. But their smiles and friendly tone left him feeling that they were enjoying the evening and were genuinely happy to see him.

He was dressed better for the occasion than when he arrived. Bjørn had shed his wet outer layer and boots and changed into a second set of clothing—a green-and-brown plaid shirt and black pants—pulled from his rucksack.

It was Olav who turned the conversation around to Bjørn's life. "We're eager to learn what you have been doing since we saw you last. What we hear, we will keep to ourselves. We will speak nothing of Bjørn Erliksen."

He felt a close kinship to the family but selected his words carefully. Truni knew who he was now, and her parents had to assume some things. But he could share nothing of his military training or mission. The less said, the better. So, Bjørn stuck to his experience from the time the Germans invaded, the short-lived war, his journey across the North Sea. And that's where he ended it.

Olav and Rita Sonnesen seemed to understand his reluctance to talk about his time away and reasons for his return. They asked no questions, leaving it to him whether to tell them or not.

When he finished, Olav only said, "You've had quite the adventure."

Bjørn stared across the table at Truni. "What have you been doing?"

She returned a gaze with soft eyes. "Where do I begin? There's so much that's happened . . . that's brought us together."

Bjørn directed his reply at Truni in a hushed tone. "*Ja*, sitting here with you and your parents, it's like I'm dreaming. I never could have imagined that the war would bring me back to this table."

He sat quietly with his hands folded in his lap as Truni touched on her time working in Stavanger for her uncle. She had lived with him and his family.

"When the Germans invaded, Stavanger was a main point of attack, particularly from the air," she said. "I heard so many booming explosions, some far, some near. It was frightening. Soon, German soldiers were all over the city.

"In the beginning, I continued to work at my uncle's fish oil factory. Aside from Germans being around, life went on as usual. Then one day, they came to the factory and said they were taking seventy-five percent of the fish oil. They demanded records showing how much we produced. I protested and told them it was none of their business. But this Nazi officer threatened me with arrest, and I showed him the records.

"A few weeks later, they demanded ninety percent of our production. The other ten percent was designated for rationing. They paid for it, but at well below the cost of producing it.

"Things became difficult," she went on. "The workers' wages were cut, and they didn't like working for the Germans. They talked about striking. But when Nazis heard about the threats, they brought troops to the factory and said they would shoot anyone who didn't show up for work."

She said her uncle could no longer afford to pay her, but she continued to work at his factory without a salary for a time.

"It also got uncomfortable for me. I couldn't go anywhere without soldiers trying to talk to me and get me together with them. They spoke to me in German, a little English, and even some Norwegian they must have picked up. I ignored them at first. Then I got angry and started talking back and telling them what they could do with themselves. I know how to defend myself, but my anger was getting the best of me. They didn't take it very well."

She straightened up and rested her forearms on the table. "Eventually, I thought it best to come home."

Truni turned to her father. "Bjørn should know what's happened to your business."

Olav nodded and let out a burst of air. "My factory's supply of tin, antimony, and copper dwindled in the weeks after the German invasion and eventually stopped altogether. I could not make pewter products and had to close the factory and lay off my employees.

"Then the Germans ordered me to start the factory up again. Not our products. They gave me drawings and specifications to make aluminum parts for the rear rudders of their airplanes. I resisted doing that, but they made it clear I had no choice."

Bjørn dropped his head and frowned.

Olav let out a long sigh. "I know, Bjørn, there are times I feel like a traitor. But it was either that or prison. I had no choice. I reopened. I was glad my employees could come back to work. For them, it puts some food on the table. But for what we're paid, we don't earn much money."

Olav said the Germans assigned a Norwegian Nazi sympathizer to monitor production and report to German authorities. "He has no skills. He doesn't know what we're doing. He stays out of our way, so that's good.

"My employees and I agreed to keep production as low as we could by creating machinery breakdowns. We're able to interrupt production from time to time. We have a saying. 'Six hours for the king, two hours for the Germans.'

"I've been under pressure to increase production. But so far, we've been able to keep output below what we really could produce."

It got late, and they all decided to turn in for the night. Bjørn passed up more comfortable quarters, insisting on sleeping in the back room. Staying near the back door gave him a feeling of security and a speedy exit if necessary. He slept in his clothes on top of his sleeping bag.

He and Truni had agreed to devote the next day to get him settled so he could begin his commando operations. She had an idea about where he would stay, and she promised to help move and secure his share of the weapons and stores he had brought with him.

Bjørn didn't tell her, but he had other priorities, too. He wanted to see his family.

CHAPTER 20

March 30, 1943

Just after daybreak, Bjørn and Truni left the Sonnesens' house and made their way up steep mountain terrain. She already had solved one of Bjørn's priorities, finding a secluded place to stay central to his base of operation. They headed to her family's *hytte* on the mountain plateau. They had hiked and skied to it many times when they were together. The *hytte* was remote, and it had been an ideal place for them to be alone. Now, the place where fond memories were created would make a good hideout for Bjørn.

No trail or well-carved pathway directed them to his new living quarters. They had to climb thirteen hundred feet of steep, rugged mountainside through thick trees and around rock outcroppings. Truni knew the least treacherous way, and Bjørn followed her lead. Her healthy pace reminded him of her stamina and strength. She always had been physically fit, a complement to her adventurous spirit. Bjørn thanked his months of training and conditioning for enabling him to keep up with her.

He remembered that the *hytte* was built by her late grandfather, who had purchased a large parcel on the plateau and built the *hytte* for his use while grazing sheep there in the summer.

They were only a short way into their journey when he asked her the question foremost on his mind: "I didn't want to bring this up at dinner, but how did you become my contact?"

"It would have been all right to ask in front of my parents," she said. "They know."

Truni pulled in a deep breath of air and released it. "For me, it started when people showed up in Bølgeland desperate to leave the country. Jewish people. Entire families. They said their lives were in danger. They had money and were willing to pay any price to go across the sea. They were asking around to hire fishing boats to take them.

"A small circle of my friends decided to help them and arrange transportation. We found a fishing-boat captain willing to take them to the Shetland Islands. I think they paid the fisherman. We took no money from them. One of my friends knew the district sheriff's family. The sheriff was loyal to the king and sympathetic. He agreed to provide additional ration documents for fuel so the boat could make the trip."

Truni smiled at Bjørn. "You remember the old barn in that field outside of town?"

Bjørn contorted his mouth into a wry grin. "How could I forget?"

"That's where we hid them until they left," she said. "We fed them. There were four families, eleven people in all. One was a six-month-old child.

"Other trips were arranged as more people looked for a way out," she said. "But the Nazis must have gotten suspicious. They came around and began asking questions. They were not Germans. Not Gestapo. They were Norwegian. The State Police. We had to lay low for a while.

"Later, a Bergen man came to visit me. He used his code name, Hammer. I think he's like you. Back from training in England. He had heard about my group, and he wanted us to help him. So now we monitor what German troops are doing in the area and where patrol boats go and when.

"That's when I got the code name The Monk. He told me an agent from England would be coming here and asked me to help him. I agreed. He gave me your code name . . . and here you are."

Truni told Bjørn that she arranged the place where he had arrived by boat two nights before. "The owner no longer uses the *hytte*, and it just sits empty. He doesn't know we're using it, so we won't keep your supplies there for long. But it's perfect for bringing in people and weapons. It's out of the way and difficult to get to."

"I need to contact Hammer," Bjørn said. "Some of the supplies are for him."

Truni responded without hesitation. "I'll take care of that."

Besides shuttling part of the cache of weapons and equipment to Hammer, she agreed to connect Bjørn with him. She also had a hiding place in mind for Bjørn's share of the material left in the *hytte* on the cove. She proposed a hidden cellar in an old barn in Tøkla, a lightly populated farming community north of Bølgeland. Truni pledged that trustworthy members of her group would transport it there.

He knew he could trust her. Already, he was finding her a quick-thinking, organized resistance leader. And after a broken heart when their relationship ended, Bjørn found it beginning to beat again.

———

Bjørn and Truni had reached the plateau surrounding her family's *hytte* in a little more than two hours. It was barren, desolate, and isolated, and was dressed mostly in white. They wore snowshoes to cross the plateau to where the *hytte* sat alone in the middle with snow piled around the lower half of the sides. Remnants of winter left a lone door partially obstructed. Truni dug out two shovels from an adjacent woodshed, and they attacked the hard snow, shovelful by shovelful, clearing their way to the door.

"You remember this?" said Truni, extending her arms to show him his new quarters when they entered.

Bjørn combined a grin with a nod.

The inside showed no ill effects from being encased in snow during the dead of winter. There was no electricity or plumbing. But it was comfortable. The only enclosed space was a small bedroom with two narrow beds. A cot against the wall in the main room provided another place to sleep. A table and four chairs flanked the open room, and a woodstove anchored one wall with a stack going straight up through the crest of the steeply pitched roof.

Truni breathed in deeply and smiled. She'd known the musty but inviting smell since she was small. Her eyes then locked onto his.

"Time has gone by quickly, and so much has happened. I wish the times we live in now were different," she said. "Mother and Father don't want me to do what I'm doing. I'm their only child, as you know, and they worry about me. They fear what will happen to me if I'm caught."

Bjørn shifted his weight. "They're right to be concerned. It's dangerous work. I can't help but worry about you, too."

She grabbed his hand. He sensed she had something weighing on her mind.

"Bjørn, I'm sorry," she said. "That last letter I wrote you, I must explain it."

"There's nothing to—"

She cut him off. "Please. There are things I need to say. When I went to Stavanger, I didn't see myself returning to Bølgeland. I had my dreams and knew they were not your dreams. I had to follow mine. I just had to. When my uncle offered me the job, I had to take it.

"While I was in Stavanger living and working, I realized that it wasn't fair for you to remain committed to me. My mind was so troubled. That's why I wrote you. The letter was very difficult for me to write. Because I loved you. And I still do."

Bjørn's thumbs gently moved across the top of her hands.

"After a while, I realized city life was not any better than my life here," she said. "I missed you . . . and hated myself for writing the letter. Then the Nazis came and everything changed anyway. I came back home.

"Several months ago, I went to Erlikvåg hoping to see you. Åsta told me you'd gone. She had received a message and knew you were safe. I was worried I might never see you again."

Tears trickled down her cheek. "Then there you were at the front door. I know things are not the same. You're here under different circumstances. You have a purpose, and so do I. I don't expect anything from you. I simply want you to know my feelings. I never stopped loving you."

When she finished, Bjørn continued to look into her eyes. They still gripped each other's hands. He hesitated to speak. His thoughts raced. He faced a woman he believed he still loved. But he was reluctant to admit it to her. Things were different. He'd been back less than a day. He had a job to do. His own organization to build. Operations to plan. Dangerous missions to carry out. He needed to focus on what he'd come back to do. Already, he was concluding that a working relationship with Truni could be useful. A romantic one would complicate their work.

Truni could take the silence no longer. "Please say something."

He kept his eyes on her. His smile was tender. "There is nothing to be sorry for. That was a long time ago. Yes, I was heartbroken at the time. You moved, and then my father passed away. It was a difficult time for me. But I understood why you left."

Bjørn's touch was gentle when he wiped a teardrop from her cheek. "I still have feelings for you. Seeing you after all this time reminded me of those feelings. But now we have an enemy to fight. We both have responsibilities. We're putting our lives at risk. We must put ourselves into what we have to do and then see what our futures hold. I hope you understand what I say."

"I understand." Her eyes drifted down. "You're probably right. For now, it has to be like this."

They left it at that. Soon after, Truni was on her way home. Bjørn was on his way to his farm. Carrying a light load on his back, he pushed himself at an accelerated pace. His thoughts swung back and forth between seeing Åsta and his home and his conversation with Truni.

She had caught him off guard. He hadn't been prepared to answer her. He was uncertain whether she wanted to rekindle their relationship. She didn't say it directly, but she did say she loved him. Bjørn admitted to himself he still loved her and had never stopped. He knew it when she had first appeared in the doorway. An arrow. A lightning bolt. Or something else struck him. He felt it.

But he doubted that she was expecting they could simply pick up where they'd left off before she moved to Stavanger. And right now, he didn't want that. His mission would put him in harm's way every minute—awake or sleeping. She faced her own danger. He needed her help at least in the beginning, but he could control how much he involved her. Becoming lovers would only subject her to more danger.

Bjørn pushed those thoughts aside and focused on getting to the farm. His contacts in London knew he would see his family. They didn't object, but admonished him to limit the visits home, avoid being seen by anyone else, and not to talk about his activities. He understood the risks. But how could he not see Åsta? Before the day was out, he would be home.

———

It was late afternoon, and the sun was out, a rare day during the transition between winter and spring. Like the day before when he'd watched the Sonnesen home from afar, Bjørn was concealed in trees spying on another house. His own.

The farm appeared no different to him than before. One exception. He saw no sign of animals in the pasture. But the garden looked fully tended, likely with potatoes, rutabagas, and other root vegetables in the ground. The chimney emitted a stream of smoke.

He waited until dusk. Bjørn could not be seen by a neighbor, a passerby, anyone. He had to be certain Åsta had no visitors. One sighting and recognition of him, and the whole town would know of his return.

Bjørn shifted his weight from foot to foot. He took turns sticking his hands in his coat pocket and folding and unfolding his arms across his chest. A piece of him wanted to bury his caution in the good earth and rush to the house, open the door, and throw himself in Åsta's arms. But his training told him not to, and he waited.

He decided to stay put until the sun dipped behind the mountains. Bjørn closed his eyes, anticipating the feel of his own bed during his intended overnight stay. His thoughts returned to Truni and something else that troubled him. It was Olav Sonnesen's manufacturing business now feeding the German war machine. It didn't matter that Olav was finding ways to reduce production. As part of his mission, Bjørn had pledged to identify and report such activities. If instructed, he had a responsibility to destroy the factory. He faced the dilemma of whether to report it.

As daylight faded, Bjørn finally left his hiding place and scurried down the hill to the house. He delivered a light rap on the door, opened it, and called out, "Sister. It's me, I'm back." He had been imagining this homecoming for months.

Her shriek reached him from another room. Åsta appeared from the kitchen with a hand over her mouth. She rushed to him and collapsed in his arms. Åsta seemed weightless, as if she could not stand. He held her up and wondered if she'd fainted. As he slowly lowered both of them to their knees, Bjørn had trouble keeping his eyes dry.

They stayed on the floor in the back entry, holding each other without speaking. At last, Åsta backed away from the embrace and took a long look at her brother. "You've changed," she said, smiling through sniffles. "That mustache. I've never seen you in one before."

Bjørn wiped the wetness left by Åsta's tears. "I had to grow it and make other changes to my looks. But it's still me."

The pounding of footsteps from the stairway behind him jolted Bjørn to his feet.

CHAPTER 21

March 31, 1943

Three sets of eyes on smiling faces stared back at him while Bjørn struggled to catch his breath. Brother Arne moved in for a quick hug. Arne's wife, Inga, beamed, and little Kristi bounced up and down in excitement. It wasn't the quiet homecoming Bjørn had expected with his sister. No, he thought as he turned on a broad smile, this had the makings of a security disaster.

Åsta explained, "They came to live with me a few months ago. Isn't it wonderful?"

Bjørn nodded in agreement. He felt his stomach tighten.

"Of course, you'll stay for dinner and overnight?" Åsta said. "Your bedroom has been unused and waiting for you."

Bjørn privately had been weighing the answer to that question since the moment Arne's family appeared. Should he cut short his longed-for sleep in his own bed? He felt confident Åsta could be trusted to keep quiet about his visit. But the risk of a damaging slip of the tongue had been multiplied by three. How many times had he been cautioned by his English handlers to avoid just such exposure? Yet, he reasoned to himself, the larger group was unexpected. Yes, he slipped up by not figuring out that Åsta wasn't alone. But surely if anyone could be trusted to keep his visit quiet, it was Arne, given his law enforcement background and his family.

"You bet," Bjørn said.

Åsta made quick work of putting dinner together with Inga's help. The table was arrayed with plenty of vegetables, and even a special treat of cured lamb Åsta brought up from the cellar. Bjørn's gift, honey he carried across the North Sea from a Scottish beekeeper, was a hit. Sugar was scarce under Nazi rule.

At the dinner table, Bjørn still wrestled with feelings of guilt while trying to keep up with the happy conversation. Maybe he had been too caught up in the moment as a result of the rare hug from Arne. Åsta's cover story for him had been that he was away fishing in the north, and that's the way it had to stay to keep them all safe. He planned to emphasize that point with the adults before he left.

After bread and honey, Inga rose from the table. "Say good night to everyone," Inga told Kristi.

"Good night, Uncle Bjørn," Kristi said.

Bjørn tried to mask his cringe with a smile. The girl had just turned seven when he'd left eighteen months ago. But she remembered him well enough to call him Uncle Bjørn.

He blew a kiss to Kristi as she was led away. He realized that, at eight years old, she was old enough to understand some of their conversations. Sweet Kristi probably represented the biggest risk to him and his future covert operations, Bjørn concluded. Every word picked up and innocently repeated at the wrong time would place them all at risk. At the sight of Kristi disappearing upstairs, Bjørn felt his nerves ease a little.

Åsta, Arne, and Inga could hardly wait to hear from Bjørn. They peppered him with questions, and they sucked in stories of his experiences like thirsty lambs—his experiences across the North Sea and London. He stopped short of specifics on who he now was and why he was back. They avoided questions about it. That was a relief to him.

Bjørn had no doubt they knew he was a resistance fighter of some sort. The less they knew, the safer they'd all be, he reminded himself.

Åsta told him about Truni's visit to the farm to look for him. "You have a large place in her heart," his sister said.

Bjørn nodded and asked about Truni, hoping his face wouldn't show his guilt about concealing that he'd already seen her.

Arne passed along a warning that sucked air out of the room. The Germans had decreed that any agent or commando reentering the country from England would be interrogated and executed within twenty-four hours after being caught, he said. There would be no exceptions.

Bjørn was already aware of the decree. He answered with a few quick nods. "No one else can know about my return. I will limit my visits here and be careful not to be seen. Those around us must believe I'm still fishing up north."

He abruptly changed the subject. "I saw no animals in the pasture."

Åsta moved forward in her chair. "The Germans have taken all our animals except for one milking cow and five chickens. Our pigs, cattle, sheep. All gone."

She tapped her fists on the table. "We still have to give them most of the produce from the garden. But we're able to get by."

Arne was subdued and appeared distracted. Bjørn took it as a sign that times remained difficult in his police work.

Bjørn set his elbows on the table and rested his chin on his thumbs. "Arne, you've got things eating at you."

Inga flinched but said nothing. She glanced at her husband, who looked down and took a deep breath. He aimed his eyes at Bjørn.

"It's been very stressful. When I go to work, I feel like I'm on top of a volcano that's getting ready to erupt."

He said he was reassigned from his longtime foot patrol in a northern neighborhood of Bergen near his home. He now patrolled in a car and had to be available to respond to calls throughout the city. The assignment was fine, he said, since he had a driver's license and many of his fellow officers didn't. But his work shifts—four hours on and four off—for days at a time separated him from his family.

"We decided to give up our home in the city and have Inga and Kristi stay here. It's safer for them. I come here when I can. But mostly I'm working. It's rare to even get a day off. Now I've had two days off, and I have to go back tomorrow."

He leaned back and folded his arms. "It continues to be difficult to know whom to trust. Many police officers have joined the Nasjonal Samling for fear of losing their jobs. They were offered promotions, pay raises, and better assignments if they did. We also had two officers fired because they refused to return a 'heil Hitler' salute.

"I'm asked constantly about my political views," he continued, "and I've had offers of promotion if I become a Nazi. I try to brush it off. I usually say I have a job to do and a duty to be neutral. I tell them I don't worry about what side I'm on. That's not an acceptable answer to my superiors."

Arne told of one incident in which he'd responded to a report of a fight near the university. It involved a small group of Hird Youth, the Norwegian version of the Hitler Youth.

"The Hird are the devil's children," Arne said. "They're mostly illiterate school dropouts and young criminals. With the Nazis in control of the country, they have power. I don't think the Germans try to control them. They just let these boys roam around making trouble."

He said he'd arrived to find four Hird Youth boys dressed in brown shirts beating up another young kid.

"He was a university student who wore a paper clip in his lapel. Since it's a symbol of support for the king, it must have angered these young Nazis."

When Arne got out of his patrol car, three Hird members ran away, he said. But the fourth one kept punching the student lying on the ground. Arne said he rushed over and pulled the Hird Youth off the victim.

"He began taking swings at me, and caught me on the ear," Arne said. "I took him to the ground, handcuffed and arrested him, then took him to the station. But in no time, he was released. Then I got called into the office of my supervisor, who scolded me for making the arrest. He questioned my loyalty and warned me not to harass those boys again."

Arne said some of his fellow officers left the Bergen Police Department and joined the Statspolitiet, the Norwegian State Police.

"It's called Stapo for short," he said. "The traitors who join it are the worst among us. They work with the Gestapo to crack down on resistance groups and investigate sabotage and crimes against the state."

"*Ja*, I know of the Stapo," Bjørn said. "I heard them called Quisling's goon squad."

Arne thrust his hands out. "It's true. Do you remember me telling you about Amund Hoggemann, the fascist?"

Bjørn nodded.

"He joined Stapo, and now the Germans really like him," Arne continued. "He's a traitorous bastard who has been very successful at breaking up resistance organizations. His work led to arrests and executions. If you are who I think you are, Bjørn, you must be careful of him."

Arne paused and glanced down. He then looked back at Bjørn. "Did you hear about Telavåg?"

"*Ja*, a little bit. I learned of it while training in Scot—" Bjørn caught himself. He frowned. With a few words, he'd revealed too much. "Forget I said that."

Åsta spoke up. "Don't worry, we'll never speak of it. We will not speak of you being here. We know why you went to England. So how can we not know that you're back to do some good?"

Bjørn's mouth formed a smile. "We shouted the phrase 'Remember Telavåg' for motivation."

———

Arne filled in details about the small village and Amund Hoggemann's role in it.

Telavåg had been a small but thriving coastal fishing community of four hundred people on the island of Sotra about twenty-five miles southwest of Bergen. It had become a jumping-off point for Kompani Linge agents, and weapons and supplies arriving on the Shetland Bus.

German authorities became suspicious and in April 1942 sent Hoggemann to investigate. He posed as a Bible salesman and circulated through the community knocking on doors. He declared he wished to go to England as he sought to sell Bibles under false pretenses.

Eventually, he found a sympathetic ear and was directed to a house in the village. He was told that men who had just arrived from England by boat were there. Hoggemann alerted the Germans. Sturmbannführer Gerhard Behrens, regional commander of the German Schutzstaffel, the feared SS, personally led a contingent of nine SS and Stapo officers to the village.

The Nazis stormed the house, and in an ensuing gun battle, Behrens and his second-in-command were killed along with one

Kompani Linge commando. A third German officer and another commando were wounded. The wounded commando along with the homeowner were seized, later tortured, and ultimately executed.

Subsequently, at the hour of the funerals of the dead regional SS commander and his assistant, the Germans took eighteen Norwegian inmates from the Grini prison camp near Oslo to nearby Transdum Forest, and a firing squad shot them. Their bodies were dumped in a mass grave.

The German retribution didn't stop there. The week after the shoot-out, German troops arrived in Telavåg with rifles at the ready. They ordered every villager out of their homes and lined them up. Reichskommissar Terboven soon arrived and ordered the village destroyed. With the villagers looking on, all homes and buildings were torched. Fishing boats were destroyed or confiscated. Horses and cattle were hauled away for German use. Terboven also ordered all men between sixteen and seventy-five sent to the Sachsenhausen concentration camp in Germany, and all women and children and older men interned in concentration camps in Norway. The village ceased to exist.

The scale of such revenge sent shock waves through the Norwegian underground and put organizations on edge.

———

Arne's listeners greeted his description with silence. Bjørn had known bits and pieces about the atrocity. But Arne's complete picture made him feel like he'd been punched in the stomach. From what he saw, the others felt the same.

Åsta spoke first. "What makes the Germans do what they do?"

"Their desire for power and their thirst to destroy anything that gets in their way," Bjørn said.

"Whatever you do, we'll worry about you, but we'll support you," she said. "And we will die before telling anyone about you."

Arne and Inga nodded their heads. Bjørn saw in his family's eyes that they shared his determination to right the wrongs the Nazis were inflicting on Norway.

Åsta shifted backward in her chair and turned the conversation. "Jon comes to visit every so often. He always asks if we've heard from you."

"Just tell him you heard from me and that I am safe," Bjørn said.

He avoided telling them that his best friend's farm was his next stop.

CHAPTER 22

April 1, 1943

Bjørn spotted Jon through the trees as he descended a hillside behind his friend's farm. Jon was behind his weathered red barn cutting grass with a scythe. Bjørn felt a rush of excitement at seeing him again. But he approached with caution to avoid being noticed by Jon's wife and son. The fewer people who saw him, the better. He was glad the barn screened him from the house.

When Jon caught sight of Bjørn, he dropped the tool and stood motionless. He looked away briefly with a furrowed brow, then redirected his gaze to Bjørn.

Like Bjørn, Jon was known for his reserved demeanor. Not this morning. He rushed toward his friend and gripped him in a hearty bear hug.

"I thought my eyes were playing a trick on me," he said. "But here you are in the flesh."

Jon squinted. "What's with the mustache?"

Bjørn shrugged his shoulders. "No one can know I'm here."

Jon acknowledged this with a nod. "Let's talk in the barn."

In Erlikvåg, like other farming communities, barns served as good places for private conversations away from others in houses. Inside the barn, Jon pulled out a bottle of homemade liquor tucked away in a storage box. He grabbed a couple of worn wooden chairs from the corner and handed the bottle to his visitor.

"*Skål!*" Bjørn said before sipping directly from the bottle.

They traded swallows of the potent liquor and started catching up. Jon wasted no time before venting about the struggles to maintain his farm under Nazi rule.

"The Germans have taken most everything," he said. "A cow and two sheep are all I have left. Almost all my hay goes to the Germans now. You know what I'm talking about, but it got worse after you left. We're fortunate to have a healthy garden, but we even have to give up some of that."

Bjørn's tone was dour. "Is that traitor, Jens Grutermann, still hanging around?"

Jon grimaced. "He shows up sometimes to check on what everyone's doing so he can report to his Nazi sheriff. The sheriff himself doesn't come around. Doesn't need to. He's got Grutermann as his snitch."

Bjørn grabbed the bottle and took a swig. "I've got to remember to watch my step."

He turned the subject and delivered news he knew Jon would want to know. "Brittvik's alive."

Jon's jaw dropped. He took a hard gulp of alcohol. "*Så du det?*"

"*Ja*, in England." Bjørn then told Jon about meeting their old unit commander. Jon kept shaking his head.

Bjørn stopped short of saying anything about joining Kompani Linge, his training in Scotland, and the reunion with Truni. He leaned back in his chair and swept his hand through his hair. "You probably wonder what I came back to do."

"I have my suspicions."

"It's better that I don't say much about it. You understand?"

"*Ja*, I understand." Jon smiled. "But I am curious."

Bjørn cast his eyes at his friend. "I might need your help with some things."

Jon folded his arms across his chest. "Whatever you need. I'll help."

Bjørn leaned forward again and rested his arms on his knees. "Good. We can team up against the Germans."

Jon took his eyes off Bjørn and pointed them to the ceiling. "I'm already involved in something. With Jonas and a few others. We've got a group of young men hidden in the mountains."

He described how the Quisling government required all men in their late teens and early twenties to register for trades and labor-oriented jobs. Vidkun Quisling claimed the decree was intended to match men with industrial jobs they were qualified to do.

"Well, we all smelled a rat," Jon went on. "These guys are of military age. Their parents panicked. They feared it would lead to their sons being sent to fight for Germany."

He said many of these men fled major cities, where they were most likely to be picked out and forced to register. Some arrived in Erlikvåg and neighboring communities to stay with relatives and friends.

"Others just showed up," Jon said. "No place to go. We found them *hyttes* in the mountains. It's been difficult finding food and supplies for them. But so far, we're managing."

Bjørn retrieved the liquor for another swallow. "How many are up there?"

"Eleven. We call them *gutter på fjellet* (boys in the mountains)."

Bjørn released a quick burst of air. "That's a lot of mouths to feed."

An idea popped into his head about how he could help Jon with that.

"I think I know where we can get some pork."

—

Outwardly, Jens Grutermann was like everyone else in these rural reaches. He farmed acreage in the nearby community of Nestad, raising pigs and cows and growing hay. Politically, he was woefully out of step. Bjørn had struggled to understand what caused Grutermann to subscribe to the precepts of fascism and join the Nasjonal Samling party. But somehow it had reached the man's bloodstream.

The Nazi sheriff had handed Grutermann responsibilities that harmed Bjørn's and other farmers' livelihoods. It had made Bjørn's blood boil. A farm community that once tolerated Grutermann now hated him. They feared him, too, with his newfound power under Nazi control.

Bjørn also knew there was resentment because Grutermann was allowed to keep most of his livestock. So before Bjørn left Jon's farm, they hatched a plan for the Nazi farmer to contribute more for a common good. Jon agreed to scope out Grutermann's property over the next few nights. Bjørn would return the following week to carry out their agreed-upon mission.

It didn't take a trained commando to steal a pig. Bjørn's rigorous Kompani Linge training was intended for much larger jobs. But the idea of stealing from a stealer fulfilled him in a way that nothing had since taking on bullies in school. He convinced himself it could be done quickly without taking away from his bigger mission. It also gave him a chance to help Jon, who had promised to help him.

Taking a pig from this particular farmer, however, did come with extra risk and required planning. With Grutermann's connections to the sheriff and other Nazis, Bjørn and Jon faced serious consequences if they were caught. Bjørn's cover could be blown and he could face death. They still wanted to do it, reasoning that a pig theft was too small of an offense to attract the Gestapo's interest. And Bjørn and Jon planned to leave no traceable evidence.

———

The following week found Jon and Bjørn together at dusk in a small cluster of large oak trees directly behind Grutermann's pigsty. Jon described the layout and his observations during the three previous nights. He pointed through the trees to where four female pigs were penned in a large enclosure with an equal number of piglets. A single boar was held in a smaller, sectioned-off area. Jon estimated the boar's weight at about three hundred pounds.

Bjørn's eyes widened. "Hefty. That would keep your boys fed with cured pork for some time. Tough to haul out, but I'd like to go for the boar. You?"

Jon nodded. "The boar it is."

Since pigs spent most of their hours sleeping—when they weren't eating—Jon's advice was the two men open the pen, swiftly kill the boar, drag it out, and cover their tracks.

Bjørn cautioned, "The other pigs will make a big ruckus. Our biggest risk is being discovered early. But the house looks to be a good seventy yards away. If we act fast, we can make it out of there before the squeals draw Grutermann outside."

In the fading light, Bjørn was able to make out the structures on the property. The pen was simple and a decent size. It didn't look like much, a crude, four-foot-high fence of weathered boards nailed haphazardly to well-set posts. A flat shingled roof supported by eight-foot-high posts covered part of the enclosure. It was across a grassy pasture from the house.

Grutermann's home was a modest two-story place painted white with a mildly pitched slate roof. The road from the farm led to the heart of Nestad.

"We've got another two hours until the lights go out," Jon said. "It's been the same every night. He doesn't venture out after seven, and it's lights out at ten or ten thirty."

As they waited to make their move, Bjørn kept his eyes on the house. He felt relieved when he saw the lights go off just as Jon predicted.

———

It was after midnight when they made their move under threatening skies and a light intermittent rain. Bjørn had only a knife to take the pig's life. It was a British-made Fairbairn-Sykes fighting knife he got during training in Scotland. Its seven-inch blade was designed primarily for stabbing, but the razor-sharp steel could easily slash a boar's throat.

Bjørn was confident in his ability to handle a knife. He had slaughtered many pigs at his farm, and commando training added to his skills. His intent was to kill the boar as quickly as he could, not only to limit squealing but also to minimize pain and suffering.

They had no firearms. If Grutermann caught them in the act, the last thing they wanted to do was shoot it out with him. Reports of gunfire and a dead quisling would certainly draw the Gestapo to the community.

The Kompani Linge commando crouched low in soft darkness with Jon close at his heels. The rain had stopped. His boots left a slight imprint in the spongy dirt. A low squeak sounded when he lifted his feet from the divots. Not enough noise to cause the pigs to stir, Bjørn prayed. They would smell him soon enough.

The gate to the pen was broad enough for both men to enter side by side. It was fastened by wire looped over a gatepost and curled off. Secure but easy to open.

Bjørn paused to look across the pasture to the house. Nothing stirred. The house was dark. He lifted the wire, and both men entered the pen. He spotted the boar a few feet away and went right for it. He made quick work with his knife. But he had to contend with a struggling animal. Before taking its final breath, the boar's squeals were loud and sharp.

Not my best work, he thought. He'd done it many times before more efficiently. He wanted this particular kill to be done quicker and more humanely. The boar had suffered. It was a job he never liked on his farm, and now he hated it.

By now, the other pigs were dashing around their enclosure squealing at the top of their lungs. It sounded like a riot. There was no way Grutermann would be able to sleep through that kind of noise. At any second, Bjørn expected the lights to come on in the house.

They dragged the boar to the side of the pen farthest from the house. The fenced enclosure next to them rose nearly to their shoulders. They exchanged quick glances and drew some deep breaths before grabbing both ends of the animal and hoisting it over the fence.

Bjørn scrambled over the fence, and Jon went up and over right after him. They ducked down behind the fence alongside the now-lifeless boar. Bjørn peeked over the fence and kept his eyes fixed on the house.

Light flooded the back porch as the door opened and a head poked out. A man emerged from the doorway, stood on the porch, and aimed a flashlight toward the pigpen. The light fell a few feet short of where they were. Distance and limited visibility above the fence prevented him from identifying the figure, but it had to be Grutermann. Bjørn crouched back down with Jon behind the enclosure with their prize catch wedged between them.

A rifle shot rang out from the direction of the house followed by another one a few seconds later. Bjørn and Jon froze in place.

Bjørn hoped the firing wasn't at a specific target and was intended only to scare off whomever or whatever was out there. He worried that the Nazi would move toward them armed. In that case, they would need to make a quick getaway without the boar.

Bjørn raised his head again and peered over the fence. Grutermann stayed on the porch, making no moves toward them. The pigs were still squealing when he disappeared inside. Bjørn and Jon sprang up and each grabbed a side of the dead boar. They huffed and puffed out loud, dragging the animal into the trees.

Bjørn hoped Grutermann wouldn't reemerge soon to inspect his pigs. He'd undoubtedly have his rifle. The saying "never bring a knife to a gunfight" flashed through his mind.

Jon snuck back by the pen to brush away their footprints into the trees, watch the house, and alert Bjørn should Grutermann head in their direction. Bjørn, meanwhile, pulled the carcass deeper in the woods. With a firm grip on the hind legs, he tugged the boar across the ground in short bursts until he reached a small, wheeled cart they had stashed.

Looking behind him, Bjørn realized the boar had left its own scented, bloody trail straight to where he was. He wrapped the still-bleeding animal in heavy canvas and secured it on the cart with a rope. He then placed leather slings attached to the cart handle over his shoulder like a rucksack and slogged up a hill with the cart trailing behind him.

Before long, Jon caught up with him, carrying the fir bough he used to erase their footprints and bloody drag prints. He reported seeing no sign of Grutermann.

Bjørn began to think the Nazi might venture out as far as the pigpen, but would likely go no farther. Even with his rifle, there was no telling who could be waiting for him. Grutermann had many enemies to worry about if he ventured into a dark forest.

The men took turns pulling and pushing the getaway cart. A gentle hillside behind Grutermann's farm allowed them to make steady progress. Much of the terrain was covered in thick mountain grass, which swallowed their footprints and hopefully would frustrate any attempt to track them.

After two hours they reached Jon's place. They took the pig to his work shed where they dressed it, cut the meat into pieces, and salted it. A few steaks were set aside for themselves, but almost all of the meat was destined for the young men.

Jon planned to ask for Jonas Seversen's brother, Anton, to take the pork along with other supplies to the mountain hideaways in a horse-pulled wagon. He vowed not to tell Anton where it came from.

After they finished, Bjørn hiked to his mountain hideout that Truni provided for him. He went to bed in the early-morning hours. He was exhausted. Before drifting off, he thought taking one pig didn't settle the score with Grutermann, but it was a start.

CHAPTER 23

June 1943

Approaching headlights illuminated the road in front of Bjørn. Hidden in the shadows, he watched a vehicle speeding from the city bouncing on uneven pavement. Its headlight beams danced in the twilight. He stood, shifting his weight from his left leg to his right, and leaned forward. Two mailboxes nailed to sturdy posts concealed him just off the highway.

He expected that the oncoming vehicle's driver was his commando contact and his ride to their joint mission. His mind painted a worst-case scenario that the vehicle could be German or Stapo. But Bjørn tried to dismiss that possibility. During his already half-hour wait, not one car had gone by. This had to be the agent code-named Hammer, like him, a Kompani Linge commando.

The time, the date, and the location had been arranged by his London handlers, who'd sent him a coded message via a BBC broadcast.

Bjørn wished for less light. In his work, darkness was his friend. In early summer, days were long and the black of the night never really came. Dusk arrived late and stayed that way until early morning when the sun rose. It provided good visibility for him to navigate his way. But in the Land of the Midnight Sun, he found it difficult to stay completely hidden.

The vehicle slowed as it neared, and a dark-colored sedan pulled up in front of the mailboxes. Bjørn cautiously emerged from obscurity. He brought no weapons with him. He had to trust that this was the car. Reaching toward the door handle, he stepped next to the sedan and pulled open the front passenger-side door.

Bjørn attempted to size up the man in the driver's seat. But dusky light made the figure less visible. "I see that the moon is out tonight," he said.

"Yes, it is almost full," came a quick reply.

Their words confirmed the connection was made between Ram and Hammer. Bjørn jumped into the passenger seat. The men shook hands, and they were on their way. The car roared up the road as Hammer pressed hard on the accelerator.

Bjørn's eyes held steady on Hammer, who focused straight ahead. "Where are we off to?"

"The mountains," Hammer said. "We've got a plane coming ... dropping weapons and supplies. We've got to prepare the drop zone tonight and retrieve the stuff. Not the perfect time of year for an airlift. Darker is better. But at least we'll be able to see where the parachutes land. And we still need to light up the landing area to guide the plane in."

"Anything up there?"

"I've got a *hytte* next to the drop zone. There's a meadow with a shallow lake. It's open and big enough to get supplies in there. Remote, too. It's a good place to hide everything."

They were alone on the road, headed in a southeasterly direction away from Bergen. An ancient forest abutted the road with a wall of high trees and overhanging branches providing a canopy, which further subdued the dimness.

Beyond briefly talking about their mission, both men said little and avoided telling about themselves. The less said, the better, in the event the Gestapo seized and interrogated them, Bjørn thought.

Hammer revved the engine to push the car up a healthy grade. Bjørn could see in the moonlight they had reached an elevation where long winters stunted tree growth. They turned off the main highway onto a steep and winding dirt road. The sedan bounced through the ruts. The going was slow. Headlights splashed off trees along both sides and found curves ahead.

As they climbed higher, patches of snow appeared on the road. The sedan sloshed around when it hit them. Hammer maintained the car's speed and maneuvered it through ruts and around divots. At times, the car's bottom panel scraped the road's center between the ruts. The car came to a stop where the road ended on level ground. Outside, alpine firs stood scattered throughout a patchwork of exposed, low-growing meadow grass.

Hammer switched off the ignition. "We'll walk the rest of the way. It's not far."

The air was crisp. Bjørn pulled up the collar of his jacket. He followed Hammer across sometimes-crunchy, sometimes-slushy ground. There was enough light to easily make out their way.

Before long, the forest opened into a large stretch of open, plateau-like meadow. Bjørn estimated it at about a mile across. He could make out a lake in the middle. The surrounding meadow was thick with clumps of grass among scattered sections of snow. To the left on the edge of the meadow, Bjørn spotted what looked like a *hytte*.

Bjørn breathed in a dose of fresh mountain air. "It's beautiful here."

"Very quiet and peaceful. I use it sometimes in the summer. There's no one else around except for sheep that find the meadow. It's perfect for what we're doing."

They entered the *hytte*, and Hammer lit a kerosene lantern that filled the cabin's front open area with a warm glow. Bjørn made a quick check of the space. It was modest but cozy with a stone fireplace, a couple of chairs, and a sofa. The kitchen was open to the main space with a wood cooking stove. Doors on each side of the fireplace likely led to bedrooms.

Hammer turned toward a shelf in the corner. "Now we have to create the drop zone."

He pulled off the shelf a neatly arranged group of lanterns and set them on the floor. Bjørn counted eight. Hammer reached for a can of kerosene and filled each lantern.

"You take four, I'll take four," he said. "When we're in the meadow, you go left and I go right. We'll set these out evenly spaced across from each other. Watch where I put mine. The plane will be here before long."

The overnight air was dry, clear, and chilly. Visibility remained decent. Bjørn did as instructed. On the other side of the lake from Hammer, he arranged the lanterns in a straight row directly across from where Hammer put his. It became a well-marked, lighted outline for the drop.

When they finished, they headed back to the *hytte*. Hammer glanced at Bjørn. "The pilots know these mountains. We've had a couple of drops here. Lanterns direct the planes. The chutes come down right where they should. You'll see. C'mon, let's make some coffee while we wait. I'll get a fire going in the stove."

———

The whine of an airplane broke the silence of the early-morning hours. It was unmistakable and loud enough to hear even indoors and with the plane still in the distance. Bjørn peeked at his watch: 3:05. Both men set down their coffee cups and crossed over to the window. Bjørn looked at Hammer. "British plane?"

"Probably. Could be American. They've been using American planes, too, from what I've heard."

The men stepped out of the *hytte* and waited. The lanterns remained positioned and lit, showing a clear pattern. In minutes, the aircraft engine whine transformed into a roar. Bjørn stuck fingers in his ears. Suddenly, the aircraft cut a shadow across the sky and flew over the zone. Bjørn saw no running lights, just the encroaching shape fast and low.

It happened quickly. No sooner was the aircraft there than it disappeared, leaving white fluffs trailing long, thin objects drifting down on the meadow. Fortunately, there was no breeze. As the parachutes neared the earth, their speed seemed to increase and their attached cargo hit with thuds. One sailed slightly beyond the meadow in trees on the far side. A couple landed near the *hytte*. Two splashed in the lake, and their trailing chutes collapsed over the water.

Hammer pointed at the lake. "We'll be able to get them. It's shallow. The water's cold, though. I'll grab a pair of rubber boots." He squinted at Bjørn. "Our work begins."

Bjørn counted seven parachutes of white fabric anchored down by their cargo scattered across the meadow. He saw another in the trees.

Hammer lifted a wooden skirt attached to the *hytte* and removed a long, sleek wooden sled. A wagon-like structure with low sides was mounted on a skid base. It appeared handmade but sturdy. Grabbing crude rope handles, he dragged the wagon behind him as they moved toward their treasure.

Bjørn approached the first parachute and saw a metal cylindrical container about six feet long at the end of the chute. A pan-shaped cover was attached to the bottom, and he assumed it was there to cushion the landing. He lifted one and gritted his teeth. The container probably weighed almost as much as he did.

He and Hammer worked together, fitting only one container at a time on the sled and securing it with heavy rope. With Hammer pulling and Bjørn pushing, they were able to glide the sled across the snow. The skids frequently got hung up in the exposed grass and bare dirt. When the sled got caught, Bjørn lifted the back of the carrier just enough to free it. Repeated trips to the *hytte* cleared the meadow.

Next came the containers in the lake. Hammer waded into frigid water to grab each chute. He half stepped, half stumbled backward, tugging on the chute by its cords to get the cargo to shore. Bjørn advanced a step or two into the water to help muscle the load onto land. In no time, his boots were waterlogged, and his teeth chattered from the water's icy bite. Hammer also began to shiver after lake water overflowed into his rubber boots.

They were fortunate the container that fell in the trees reached the ground around low-growing alpine fir.

After little more than an hour, they had the loads piled in front of the *hytte*. They then doused and retrieved the lanterns and returned them to the shelf. As the morning light surfaced, the meadow took on its normal, picturesque appearance, as if nothing had occurred during the night.

Back inside to thaw out, Bjørn removed his soaked leather boots and set them by the stove to dry. Hammer had done the same. They slid chairs next to the stove and warmed their wet, sock-covered feet.

The two commandos worked the rest of the early morning opening the cylinders and inspecting the contents. Bjørn discovered six of the eight containers actually were five smaller pieces hinged together, making it possible to separate them for easier handling and storage. They held Argentinean-made Ballester-Molina .45 pistols, Tommy submachine guns, Sten guns, grenades, limpets and other explosive material, full gas cans, heavy clothing, and canned food rations.

The two single-piece cylinders held American-issued M1 carbine rifles, weapons packed with a slick, waxy glaze of Cosmoline to preserve them.

"Where's this stuff going?" Bjørn said.

Hammer continued to paw through the material. "We'll store it here for a while, but eventually much of it will go south to organizations in Stavanger and Kristiansand. We'll use some in Bergen, too."

He pulled out several round metal petrol gas cans that had fit perfectly in the containers. "I need these for the car. Take what you need from the rest of the supplies."

Bjørn kept some food rations, coffee, and flour, stuffing them in his rucksack. He shoehorned them in, requiring every square inch of his pack. He also set aside a .45-caliber pistol and a silencer that screwed on the end. Hammer kept a large-caliber revolver with a snub nose.

Under the rug in the kitchen, a trapdoor with ladderlike steps led to a large carved-out space under the floor. The size of a small bedroom, it was lined with wood boards and had a planked floor. Once cold storage for meat and vegetables, the space now served as a hiding place for military weapons, supplies, and equipment.

Returning to the car, Bjørn was weighted down with a five-gallon can of petrol in each hand, along with the rucksack strapped on his back. Hammer, who carried his own supplies to his sedan, opened a rear door and lifted the back seat by tilting it forward. Underneath was a hidden storage compartment across the length of the seat. He put the petrol cans, supplies, and ammunition there to conceal them. Backpacks went in the trunk, minus the supplies from the drop.

Fully loaded pistols were tucked under the front seat. While they hoped to avoid any trouble on the way back, they had to be prepared.

———

The return trip gave Bjørn a daylight glimpse of new scenery. Hammer did not drive back toward the city. When they reached the highway, he wheeled left and continued up the roadway in the opposite direction from the way they had come the night before. Then he turned left on a road and followed a circuitous route around the mountain that eventually would put them east of Bergen. Hammer intended to take Bjørn back by skirting Bergen, driving along the east side of Osterfjord and dropping him off at a place called Flodgrund. From there, Bjørn needed only to take a ferry across the fjord and then hike back to his hideout.

Hammer explained to Bjørn that he preferred less-traveled backroads. This route would enable Bjørn to get his newly requisitioned weapon and supplies home without going through the security checkpoint at the Bergen ferry terminal.

They had been on the road for a little more than an hour when they neared a bridge over Jøfjord. At 150 yards long, the bridge spanned the fjord's narrowest section. As they rounded a corner to approach the bridge, Hammer suddenly lifted his foot from the accelerator.

Two Nazis waited in the road a short distance ahead, one in a German uniform with a short-barreled submachine gun slung over his shoulder and the other wearing a Stapo uniform with a sidearm in a holster on his hip. Their military sedan with an Iron Cross stamped on the side was parked nearby.

A deep frown creased Bjørn's forehead. "Just our luck," he mumbled to his partner. "A Nazi checkpoint."

"Hope they're just checking documents," Hammer said. "Only two of them. If they were looking for somebody, there'd be more."

Bjørn inched forward, repositioning the pistol that he had stashed under his seat for rapid retrieval. Hammer stopped the sedan next to the soldiers. The German stepped toward the driver's side window. The Norwegian Stapo officer stayed a couple of steps back. Hammer rolled down his window.

The German soldier thrust out his hand. *"Papiere!"*

Both commandos pulled out their identification documents and handed them over. Bjørn's false ID carried the name Mons Bjørk. He assumed Hammer's was falsified, too. The German turned toward the Norwegian officer, and they reviewed the documents and conferred. The Norwegian helped with the interpretation. His pistol stayed holstered.

Now it was the Norwegian Nazi who returned to the driver's side window, with the German behind him.

"Where are your papers for the car?"

Hammer motioned to Bjørn to get his Nazi-issued permit to operate the sedan. Bjørn slowly lowered the glove box and pulled out the document. As he did, the Norwegian Nazi moved his hand down near his sidearm. Bjørn gave the permit to Hammer, who slid it into the Norwegian's hand.

"What were you doing on this road?"

Hammer did the talking. "I have a *hytte* in the mountains, and we've been up there. We're coming back."

"Where is that?"

"Near Jaarstuen."

"Why were you there?"

"Needed to check it. Haven't been up there since before winter."

"Who's he?" The quisling officer pointed at Bjørn, who tensed slightly. He felt a rush of adrenaline.

"My friend," Hammer replied. "He came along to keep me company."

The German said something in a low tone to the Norwegian, which prompted him to say, "I want to look at the trunk."

Hammer pulled the keys from the ignition and grabbed the door handle to exit the car.

"Stay in the car," the Norwegian commanded.

Hammer handed him the keys, and the Nazis went to the rear and unlocked the trunk. All they found were two backpacks containing warm clothing and little else. They conversed in German.

The Norwegian came back to the window. "You're not carrying much for a trip to the mountains."

Hammer smiled slightly. His right hand was at his side balled into a fist clenched tight. Bjørn felt as though the exchange was taking place in slow motion. He was prepared to grab his weapon if anything went sideways.

"We didn't need much for this trip," Hammer explained. His outward demeanor remained calm. "Just wanted to make sure the roof was still on."

With an air of authority, the Norwegian Nazi looked over both men inside the car. Then he handed the keys and their documents back without another word and waved them on.

Bjørn waited until they were over the bridge and well past it to let out a deep sigh.

Hammer clenched down on his teeth. "I wanted to tell those Nazis to go fuck themselves."

Bjørn nodded. He felt his nerves just beginning to settle down.

CHAPTER 24

August 1943

The midday sun baked Bjørn's face as he stood just outside the door to his mountain hideout. He spotted a figure coming toward him in the distance. He had no doubt who it was. Truni.

He anticipated her reason for coming. She had begun feeding him reports of German ship and troop movements observed by her network along the coast. Before, Truni had been reporting enemy activities to Hammer. But with Bjørn in place near her and having radio equipment, it was more efficient for him to transmit her information to SOE. Hammer had agreed to the switch. Bjørn's stash of weapons and equipment included four pairs of high-powered binoculars, and he gave three of them to her group. She now made weekly trips to her family's *hytte* that served as his refuge.

Truni made her way toward him with energetic strides. This time of year, the going was easy. Bright sun and heat had erased the deep snow they had crossed on snowshoes five months earlier just after Bjørn returned to Norway. Now shades of pale-green and yellow meadow grass showed on the plateau's uneven, rolling contour formed from flat slabs of granite. Truni had to wind her way around huge boulders sculpted over time by nature and two small lakes that captured winter's snowmelt.

Bjørn enjoyed working with Truni and looked forward to her visits. Without the war, he yearned for a romantic relationship as it used to be. But times were different. He still held on to the belief that his mission and her own activities came first.

Bjørn also believed Hammer would never approve a relationship on grounds that close connections between agents created more exposure and a greater risk of being uncovered by the Gestapo. Hammer knew nothing about Bjørn and Truni's past romance, and Bjørn wanted to keep it that way. That knowledge might jeopardize his and Hammer's collaboration on future operations. But try as he might to keep his budding romantic feelings for her from blossoming, his resistance was weakening. Bjørn realized it.

When Truni reached him, she greeted him with a quick peck on the cheek as she brushed past him into the *hytte*. Bjørn followed her, displaying a hint of a grin.

She dropped into a chair at the table while Bjørn poured them tea from a kettle sitting on the still-warm woodstove.

"I have something important for you," Truni said.

He spun his head away from the stove and directed his eyes toward her.

"The Germans are installing big guns on a cliff overlooking the sea at the end of Siklefjord. It's at a place called Novabår. We weren't able to get close enough to see it ourselves. We also don't know how far along they are. But we saw trucks with materials coming and going—"

Bjørn jumped in. "How do you know that's what it is?"

Truni thrust her hand out. "I'm getting to that. A group of soldiers was in Bølgeland, and one of my people overheard them. They apparently are stationed there to guard it. They said the emplacement has seventy-five-millimeter cannons the Germans took from the Maginot Line when they took over France."

He carried the tea across the room and joined her at the table.

"Good work," he said. "England needs to know about this. I'll report it tonight."

"My people have good eyes and ears." Truni's smile soon vanished. "There's something else."

He leaned toward her, his arms resting on the table. "You have my ears."

"The Germans have a base for patrol boats on Tommeløy Island," she said. "Also, what looks like a fuel depot. Do you know about it?"

"I've only heard of the island, nothing else."

"Someone in my group heard that the Germans took over the island and put a base there. I went there in a small boat to see for myself. I also noticed two tanks on top of a hill on the island. I could only see their tops, but they looked big. There were large pipes coming down the hill to a dock with boats next to a patrol station. I assume the tanks are petroleum."

Bjørn's mind filled with questions. He took a long stare at Truni. "How big is the island? And what does it look like?"

"It looks long and a little narrow," she said. "Sits in an inlet with maybe about a quarter mile across to the shore on each side. I saw a ferryboat going from the end of the island to the mainland."

Bjørn sprang to his feet and began pacing the room. He turned back to her. "What's security like? Is it being guarded?"

"Didn't see any. But couldn't see the top of the hill."

His hand went to his chin. The thought struck him that this day had turned perfect. What he heard was a job made for him. A job he was trained for. "This may give us a way to damage the Germans."

Something else lifted his spirits. It was Truni who had gathered the intelligence and brought it to him. He always knew she was smart. Now he could count on her to determine relevant information. He took another look at her. All he could think of was that he wanted to kiss her, to fold her in his arms.

She had her back turned to him. Bjørn began to move toward her, then stopped in midstride. The temptation of having her within arm's reach was hurting them both. He told himself he would need to do better at keeping his distance.

He returned to business. "We'll need to investigate more. Wonder what Hammer would think."

———

Every evening he could, Bjørn listened to BBC "News of Norway" broadcasts. He had to be religious about it. On any given night, he might hear a coded message meant for him. Radio presenters almost nightly read a series of numbers at various intervals of the program. To most of the Norwegians who risked penalties by listening to broadcasts with outlawed radios, the numbers had no meaning. But they knew the numbers meant something to those fighting for their freedom.

Bjørn tuned in using a small pocket-size radio receiver dubbed the Sweetheart. The radio had just been developed by SOE for clandestine use, and he was one of the first to get it. Small enough to fit in his coat pocket, it required little power and had a built-in antenna strong enough to get reception even in areas with weak signals. A separate battery pack that lasted up to two hundred hours came with the Sweetheart. There was no knob on the device to switch it off. That was done by disconnecting wires from the battery pack. It also came with a set of small crystal earphones hidden in a circular tobacco tin.

Keeping up on the war was a side benefit of his required listenership. By the fall of 1943, the news was encouraging. The tide of war had turned in the Allies' favor. They had driven German forces completely out of North Africa. An American general named Patton had invaded Sicily with his forces, routing the Germans and capturing thousands of Italian troops fighting for fascist leader Benito Mussolini. The British and American troops subsequently were advancing rapidly up Italy's mainland boot. Italian forces crumbled, and the Germans rushed in more troops there to stop Allied progress.

Elsewhere, Russian troops retook chunks of their homeland, and the Germans continued to fall back. Nazi Germany's own borders were no longer immune from attack. Unrelenting Allied bombing raids were well underway, pounding German industrial centers and crippling the enemy's war production.

As word spread in Norway that the once-omnipotent German war machine was on the ropes, hope intensified that life soon would return to normal. The intimidation and fear of living under Nazi rule deepened Norwegian citizens' resentment and anger.

That gave rise to a greater will to resist. Underground groups sprouted up throughout Norway, some with clear focus and others with ragtag disorganization. A flurry of resistance organizations kept the Gestapo and Stapo busy. With more ordinary Norwegians willing to serve, a greater risk of mistakes and recklessness emerged. Tongues slipped, and the Nazis became more effective at infiltrating resistance groups. Arrests became more frequent, followed by greater numbers of executions. Existing concentration camps expanded, and new ones were established throughout Norway.

Bjørn's own efforts to build a secret citizens' army were made easier by the heightened desire to push back against the Nazis. By the fall, eighteen men and four women from around the area had joined. He had known none of them before. They only knew him by his code name, Ram. He dipped into his hidden weapons cache and assigned them Sten guns, a few M1 rifles, and pistols. He taught the recruits how to use them, even though firing was only simulated to prevent unwanted attention from gunshots and

Gestapo suspicion. Trainees were limited to cleaning their weapons, sighting targets, and practicing positions for shooting. The kinds of large-scale exercises and drills he learned in Scotland gave way to confined maneuvers in a ramshackle barn.

Beyond training his own small-scale army, he held a strong desire to deliver a crippling blow to the Nazis. Bjørn's thoughts returned often to the Nazi-run petroleum tanks and boat station reported by Truni.

CHAPTER 25

October 1943

He trained a pair of British-made, high-powered Ross binoculars on the potential targets. Two large petroleum tanks were perched on top of a long hill at the western end of Tommeløy Island. Bjørn avoided blinking to keep a steady focus on them. He squatted behind thick brush halfway up a hillside on the mainland across from the island. It provided a good vantage point to see the hilltop holding the tanks.

Tommeløy Island was a mile long and fit neatly inside a V-shaped inlet along a stretch of Norwegian coastline northwest of his hideout. An open flattop ferry only large enough for several vehicles connected the island to the mainland at the end of the inlet right at the V's notch. From the ferry dock, a lone dirt road led to three small farms scattered on mostly flat pastureland at Tommeløy's eastern end. From the farms, the island sloped steeply up to the hilltop at the western end where the tanks stood.

He peered through the binoculars' 7x50-power prisms, sizing up the tanks. They were big. He estimated each at more than two stories high and beamy in circumference, perhaps twelve to fourteen feet in diameter. These monoliths could hold thousands upon thousands of gallons. Each sat on a thick concrete slab. A fence encircled them made of strung wire, which he hoped was not electrified. But with the right kind of cutting tool, Bjørn thought, it was penetrable.

This was his third visit to the shoreline across a narrow channel to observe the comings and goings on and off the island. He moved with care around the inlet, which contained a smattering of scattered homes, farms, and boathouses. He found an unlocked boathouse sitting by itself with a fourteen-foot rowboat inside. It was a quarter mile from the island's northwest shore. Bjørn considered this find potentially useful to the operation.

His surveillance revealed a steady stream of fuel trucks crossing on the ferry day and night to make deliveries. On the southwest side of the island, he observed a small contingent of German Navy seamen at the patrol boat station. As Truni had described, two aboveground pipes were strung down the slope feeding petrol from the tanks to three pumps on the dock. During Bjørn's vigil, he saw as many as four boats at the dock at one time filling up or waiting. He concluded the facility was a major refueling station for patrol boats covering a long stretch of the coast.

He had identified something else that raised the risks of a sabotage mission. A garrison of German troops had taken over the farms on the eastern end and built a makeshift barracks to use along with the homes, barns, and outbuildings. It was difficult for him to be certain, but he guessed the troop strength at company sized between eighty and one hundred men.

Bjørn got a look at a guardhouse on the south side of the tanks with two sentries. They seemed to work in six-hour shifts before changing guards. Almost like clockwork, one armed guard regularly patrolled the fenced perimeter around the tanks on what looked like a dirt path.

Taking everything into account, he realized that any operation to damage or destroy the tanks was fraught with risk. Every aspect of an attack would need to be timed, particularly around a sentry's patrol of the perimeter. But given the opportunity to disrupt German boat patrols, he still deemed it a risk worth taking.

Bjørn needed experienced help. For that, he decided to turn to Hammer.

———

They met in the old barn at Tøkla at the northern foot of the mountain plateau where Bjørn had his hideout, only an hour's hike away.

Hammer took the *rutebåt* from Bergen to a nearby community and made his way to the barn, following Bjørn's instructions.

The barn showed its years of neglect and abandonment. Set in the corner of an unused, overgrown pasture, the structure still stood, and its roof remained sufficient to keep the inside dry. But its paint was worn off from the weathered wood siding, which now had turned to shades of dark brown and black.

Inside, it was airy and empty. There were no animals, farm implements, or hay in the sagging loft. Not even a table and chairs for the meeting. Just a thin layer of old straw on the dirt ground. Unseen under the straw in the corner was a thick wooden hatch leading to a wood-lined cellar carved out of the earth. It was where Bjørn's cache of supplies and weapons was stowed. Bjørn kept the hiding place secret, even from Hammer.

The two commandos stretched out on the ground in the middle of the barn, and Bjørn laid out a map with the section of coastline showing Tommeløy Island. Over the map, he placed his crude drawing of the island with notations of the locations of the tanks, the guardhouse, boat station, and garrisoned German troops. He described his plan for the mission.

"It's risky, but it can be done," Bjørn told his companion when he finished. "We could really disrupt the Germans' ability to patrol the coast."

Hammer kept his eyes on the drawing. "You really scoped it out."

"There was a lot to see."

Hammer put on a weak smile but did not look up. Bjørn sensed Hammer's reaction to the proposed mission did not match his enthusiasm.

Hammer brought his head up. "I can see the merits of this. The tanks would be a worthy target. But is it worth the risk?

"If we succeeded, the Nazis would certainly retaliate," he went on. "More torture, more executions, more destruction. And for what? The interruption would only be temporary. The Germans probably would make up for the lost fuel by taking rations from the fishing fleet. They'd repair the tanks and would be back patrolling as if nothing happened."

Bjørn felt his stomach go numb. He said nothing.

"One mistake, only one, and it could be disastrous for us," Hammer added. "Let's not do this."

Bjørn shook his head. He had listened respectfully long enough. "Isn't this what we signed up to do? Isn't this our mission? Our duty? To make life difficult for them? I'm not talking about killing Germans. And we know they'll keep killing Norwegians no matter what we do. There will be more Telavågs."

"Think of the bigger picture," Hammer said. "The Germans are retreating everywhere. Who knows how long the war will last. There are rumors of a big Allied invasion somewhere, maybe in France, maybe here. We should be preparing to fight the Germans if they try to destroy things as they leave Norway. What difference do two fuel tanks make?"

Bjørn released a deep sigh. "For us, there's still a war. The Germans are occupying us, stealing from us, starving us. No one's helping us. We have to do it ourselves."

Hammer put his hands up. "Please agree with me, we will not do this."

Bjørn cocked his head. "All right. Let's not."

Hammer stared at him, studying Bjørn's face and posture. "I said no, Ram."

"And I agreed, we won't do this."

"All right, then. Good. It's settled."

The meeting adjourned. They left the barn and went their separate ways. Bjørn returned to the *hytte*, recognizing he'd agreed to something. But he didn't think it was the right decision.

———

What happened to Hammer? The question filled Bjørn's mind as he paced the tight space of the *hytte*. He was heavy in thought. His fellow commando had turned cautious. Bjørn didn't know why. Maybe he was right. Maybe this sabotage mission was too risky. But as Kompani Linge commandos, they were trained to take risks. If not this one, they needed each other for future missions. Now Bjørn wondered whether he could rely on Hammer.

He still believed sabotage of the fuel tanks should be done. But how? With Hammer out of the picture, his ability to carry out the mission was impacted. Bjørn thought about what he'd agreed to. They wouldn't do it jointly. But what would prevent him from carrying it out without Hammer? He didn't agree not to act on his own. He didn't need Hammer's permission. He had reported the tanks to England and received a thumbs-up to sabotage them.

He settled on a decision just before Truni arrived for a visit. The sabotage mission was fresh on his mind, so he wasted no time getting to his request of her.

"I'm considering an operation and I need your help."

Truni's response was quick, and it wasn't a question. "The fuel tanks." She sniffed it out.

"*Ja*, the fuel tanks. You have two men in your group who were in the army. Would they be willing to join me for this mission?"

"Is Hammer involved?"

"*Nei*, he doesn't think we should do it. And he shouldn't know I'm going ahead with it."

Her eyebrows lifted, and she let his request hang in the air before speaking. "I'll ask them. I'll see if I can get one. I'll be the other."

Bjørn took a step back. "No, Truni, no. It's too dangerous."

Her eyes widened and focused hard on him. "I'm willing to take that risk."

"I can't put you in harm's way."

She stiffened. "What do you think I do every day? I'm at risk now. And I can do as good a job as anyone. I can shoot, and I can take care of myself. Don't you think I'm capable?"

Bjørn pulled in a deep breath and slowly released it. "That's not it. I just don't want you involved. I care about your safety."

The volume of Truni's voice lifted. "Don't I have a say in this? And shouldn't I care about the risk you face?"

"But I've trained for this." Bjørn knew she was pinning him in a corner. She was cagey and quick thinking. When they were together in earlier years, he often wondered what someone as smart and beautiful as her saw in him.

"OK. But you do what I tell you to do, no questions asked."

"Agreed." Truni stepped toward him and pulled him close. Bjørn felt a surge of electricity. Their faces were inches apart. Their eyes locked on each other. Bjørn could no longer resist the urge. Their lips met and stayed that way. Lasting and passionate. Like before.

Then Bjørn pulled away. "I'm sorry. It can't be like this."

"Why not?" Truni's glow dimmed. "Life's too short. Neither one of us knows what tomorrow will bring."

Her eyes pierced through him. Then, in a firm tone, she said, "I want you to admit it. I can see it in your eyes. I felt it in your kiss."

"I don't know what you want me to say." Bjørn's tone was soft.

"Yes, you do. Say it."

He nodded. "I love you, Truni. I never stopped. You've always been in my heart. But"—his throat grew tight—"but we can't be together like this. Now."

Bjørn read a blend of love and disappointment in her eyes.

Truni formed a slight smile. "You can be quite stubborn, you know."

She shrugged. "I guess I'll be on my way."

CHAPTER 26

November 1943

The oars gently lifted from the calm water, and momentum carried the rowboat softly to shore. Four saboteurs, all dressed in black, faced the four- to five-foot-high rock face of Tommeløy Island. Bjørn felt the nighttime chill on his face and neck, not knowing whether his shivers were from the cold or nerves.

The dark, overcast sky and a hint of foggy air had helped conceal them while they had rowed across the channel in a boat borrowed from an isolated boathouse. As they closed in on the shore, Bjørn leaned over the bow with outstretched arms to press against the rock and cushion any noises caused by the boat bumping against it. He leaped off the rowboat and scrambled over a ledge before securing the boat's rope around a protrusion in the granite.

Bjørn squatted low and looked up toward the top of the hill. The fuel tanks, the saboteurs' targets, were invisible in the darkness.

Jon followed Bjørn out of the boat. Truni scrambled from the boat next, followed by one of her men, a guy she introduced as Tomas. He had served in the regular army's Fourth Division and had been in hard fighting against German forces near Voss.

Jon and Tomas were armed with American-made Thompson submachine guns from Bjørn's hidden weapons stockpile.

Thirty-round box magazines were shoved in the guns' undercarriages. Truni held a Sten gun, which Bjørn had trained her to use. She and Tomas were assigned to wait at the boat and prepare for a quick getaway. They also would provide backup if shooting started.

Bjørn was armed with his weapon of choice, the paratrooper Sten gun with a folding metal stock. It was unfolded and ready. The Fairbairn-Sykes fighting knife was sheathed to his ankle. Despite the weaponry, Bjørn hoped they all could slip in and out without firing a shot. If they engaged Germans in a shoot-out, the odds were against them to escape alive.

Bjørn's small backpack carried one British-made limpet mine. Jon had the same explosive in his rucksack as well as a few other needed items. The limpets had been designed to magnetically attach to ship hulls below the waterline. Activated by a delayed timer, the device could be set to blow holes and disable or sink the vessels when they were at sea. This night, the mines, potent enough to blast sizable holes in the petroleum tanks, would be used above water.

Bjørn and Jon began their ascent up the gradual hill toward their target. Bjørn led, dipping his body and making long, low strides to reduce his silhouette. He held his Sten gun prepared to use it, magazine in place and his finger alongside the trigger just outside the trigger guard. He looked back and found Jon two paces behind. When Bjørn gave him a thumbs-up, Jon returned the gesture.

They crept without making a sound. As Bjørn approached the crest of the hill, the shadowed shapes of the large twin tanks loomed ahead, partially shrouded by a surrounding fog. A few scattered light poles pierced the darkness. Bjørn sighed. He didn't like exposure, even if the area was only dimly lit. Staying low to the ground, the two moved over the flat earth on the hilltop to reach the wire fence.

Both men halted to scan their surroundings. All was quiet. Eerily so. Bjørn checked his watch. If his previous monitoring of the guards held up, he and Jon had just forty minutes to penetrate the fence, place and set the timers on the charges, and sneak away.

With Bjørn as lookout, Jon pulled a pair of heavy wire-cutting shears from his pack. Six strands of dense wires made up the six-foot-high fence. Sharp razor wire curled across the top. Holding the wire were metal posts pounded into the ground at about ten-foot intervals. To test the wire, Bjørn flicked his finger against the top strand. He let out a sigh of relief. The fence was not electrified. Jon started with the bottom wire a foot above the ground and worked his way up, snapping the lower three. It required strength, patience, and a steady hand to cut each wire. With each clip, a dull pop sounded. Bjørn held his breath, hoping the noise wouldn't attract attention from the guardhouse hidden from view on the opposite side of the tanks.

The cutting stopped, and Jon motioned for Bjørn to crawl through. The opening was just big enough for them to go under one at a time. Bjørn shimmied through the gap, followed by Jon. Side by side, both men galloped toward the tanks about fifty feet ahead across grass and dirt.

The tanks stood about eight feet apart on concrete pads. When they reached them, Bjørn headed to the tank on the left, and Jon veered right. At the base of the tank, Bjørn knelt motionless with his weapon ready, listening for footsteps. Satisfied that no guards were coming, he removed his pack and retrieved the round eighteen-inch-diameter mine weighing twelve pounds. Jon was doing the same.

The magnetic force kicked in and pulled the mine in Bjørn's hands toward the metal tank. His mind flashed back to the first limpet he had set in military training on a thick slab of iron. After the explosion, he had gone back and found a mangled mess and a hole almost big enough to put his head through. Now, he faced the real thing. He firmly gripped the explosive to keep it from attaching with enough force to shatter the silence with a loud clang.

Bjørn placed the mine with a barely audible clink about two feet above the tank's base. He set the timer for thirty-five minutes, and hoped it was enough time for his team to get away. Jon signaled with a thumbs-up that he was done, and they made their getaway together back to the fence.

Bjørn part shimmied, part crawled through the fence opening and served as lookout while Jon came through. They stopped long enough to straighten the bent wires so the cuts would be less obvious to patrolling guards.

As they sprinted back to the hillside, Bjørn heard footsteps. A crunch of boots on the gravel path. Jon must have heard it, too. In unison, they dived over the edge of the hill, hugged the ground, and stayed motionless. Bjørn glanced at his watch. The timing was off. He thought they had more time between patrols. He worried they had been heard.

As they lay flat, the two positioned their weapons at the ready. Bjørn hoped the fog combined with darkness had worked in their favor and that they hadn't been seen before they lunged over the hilltop. He pressed the side of his head tight to the damp wild grass on the side of the hill and, with one eye, peered over the top. He caught a glimpse of a patrolling German soldier walking the perimeter at an unhurried gait. The guard approached where they cut through the fence.

Bjørn and Jon lay side by side, close to each other. Bjørn shimmied his body closer to Jon and pressed his mouth against his friend's right ear.

His whisper was barely audible. "You go. Back to boat. You three leave. I'll take the guard. Meet at the boathouse."

Bjørn didn't intend to use his gun. It would make him more vulnerable, but he had his knife. And he anticipated a cold swim. "Take my gun and watch. Go. Row fast."

He then nudged Jon's back with his arm. Jon's head moved in a slight nod. He started a gradual slide backward down the hill, inches at a time. As Jon began his ever-so-slow descent, he grabbed Bjørn's Sten gun and watch. Bjørn kept his eye on the guard, who seemed not to pick up on their presence, and then watched Jon get far enough away to safely pick himself up and make a beeline to the waiting rowboat.

Bjørn lifted his head again just enough to see the guard, who by now had stopped at where they had gone through the fence. The sentry had unslung his rifle. He looked back at the edge of the hill, then focused again on the cut fence.

The guard knelt down, his face level with the fence opening. Bjørn made his move. He rose and sprinted the short distance to the sentry, who looked up just before Bjørn was on him. By the time the guard started to turn, Bjørn wrapped his right arm around the German's neck. He jerked the guard up and back. As the soldier began struggling from the sleeper choke hold, Bjørn swayed him back and forth to keep him off-balance and limit his ability to fight back. The guard let out a slight grunt before collapsing in Bjørn's arms.

The Norwegian commando eased him to the ground in a heap. He pulled out his knife and struck the guard's skull with the lead ball at the end of the handle. It was hard enough to keep him unconscious and allow Bjørn time to escape.

Bjørn glanced in the direction of the guard shack. No one else was in sight. He hoped the other guard stayed holed up in the warmth of the shack and hadn't heard the scuffle. He sprinted over to the top of the hill and raced to a point at the water's edge that seemed the shortest distance to the boathouse across the fjord. He picked up a faint sound of the splashing of oars pulling a boat across the water.

He waded into the chilly water and pulled in several puffs of oxygen from the deep recesses of his lungs. He then pushed off and began stroking toward the boathouse. The frigid water encased him. His clothes weighed him down. But Bjørn summoned all his strength to cup the water and pull it behind him in rapid movements.

Bjørn knew he was in a race against time and the chilling cold. The biting cold would zap his energy as much as his movements. Each pull of his arms had to be quick and efficient. He put the distance to the boathouse at about 250 yards.

If only Arne could see him now, he thought. In a boyhood scuffle, Arne had thrown him in the lake below the farm. At the time, Bjørn didn't know how to swim and had struggled in water over his head. Arne had to rescue him, telling Bjørn, "I should have let you drown." The humiliation caused him to excel at swimming. He had vowed never to let that happen again. When he turned sixteen, he swam the one-mile length across Osterfjord and, after a brief rest, swam back.

As Bjørn made his way across the channel, he was forced to stop and try to spot the boathouse in the darkness. He drew nearer to shore and held up again to look for the moorage. He spotted it maybe only fifty yards away. It was then that a thunderous boom rang out and brightened the sky. Another came seconds later. Bjørn figured the limpets must have gorged huge holes in the tanks.

The sound of a siren and alarm floated across the water to him. Was it a call to arms for the German unit? Bjørn felt a rush of adrenaline. But muscle fatigue and the effects of frigid water set in and slowed him down until he again visualized Arne's early taunts and picked up a little speed in his stroke.

He swam through the open door of the boathouse a few minutes later at a sluggish pace. His three fellow saboteurs waited on
the planked platform alongside the rowboat floating in its slip.
Jon and Tomas tugged on his soaked clothes and hoisted him out
of the water. Bjørn was as limp as a sopping-wet towel.

"We've got to get moving, and fast," Truni said to him. Bjørn's
nod was feeble.

Jon spoke. "You must have taken out the guard."

Bjørn nodded again. "Just knocked him out."

He slowly got up on his feet and rubbed his legs and arms.
Truni wrapped him in a foul-weather slicker she'd found in the
boathouse, and they were off.

The group set off into dense brush near the shoreline and
soon disappeared into thick forest up a steep embankment. Bjørn
struggled with the climb. His breathing came in gasps. But he
soon regained strength and picked up his pace.

The morning light had just arrived when they were far enough
to be safe. Jon and Tomas peeled off to go their separate ways.
And Bjørn and Truni had another hour or so to reach the *hytte*.

———

Bjørn arrived at the cabin soaked, cold, and dead tired. He put on
dry clothes. Even then, he still shivered. Truni set a blaze in the
fireplace, fired up the woodstove, and brewed tea, pouring him a
hot mugful.

They didn't talk much, and he fought to keep his eyes open. "I'll
report our work to England tomorrow. We'll see what Hammer
thinks of it."

Her tone was reassuring. "He'll be all right with it. We were
successful."

"Ja" was all he said before Bjørn nodded off. He woke up in the afternoon in his bed under heavy covers. He remembers nothing of how he landed in bed. Truni had left.

CHAPTER 27

January 1944

The encrypted message contained in the BBC broadcast was meant for him. Bjørn heard the first number, "eighty-three," and scrambled for a notepad and pencil to record the rest. He hastily scribbled the numbers. When the announcer finished, Bjørn retrieved his Bible; applied the numbers to passages, words, and letters; and decoded the message.

When he finished, it took several seconds for him to grasp the meaning. He leaned back in his chair in the *hytte* and processed what he had been ordered to do. He brought his eyes back to his decoding and stared at the scribbles.

The powers that be in England directed him to team with Hammer and eliminate the dangerous Stapo policeman, Amund Hoggemann. An assassination. His gut instinct told him it would be murder. He didn't like or want such an assignment.

But Bjørn thought further. Norway was at war. Hoggemann was Norwegian and a Nazi. He was no longer a fellow countryman. He was the enemy. Arne had described how the Nazi's undercover work rooting out resistance groups had been lethal, leading to dozens of arrests and executions.

Hoggemann's name had surfaced during Bjørn's briefings by his handlers in England. At the time, he was only suspected of leading the Nazis to Telavåg and helping cause the deaths of Kompani Linge commandos and the subsequent destruction of the village. The Norwegian government in exile and the British must have confirmed it, Bjørn reasoned. Hoggemann had the blood of Norwegians on his hands as if he'd pulled the trigger himself. So, SOE ordered his assassination.

If he and Hammer succeeded, one less Nazi—a dangerous Stapo officer at that—would walk the earth. That was what mattered most, he convinced himself.

—

Planning the hit on Hoggemann began late in the shivery month of January 1944 when snow covered the ground most days. As soon as Bjørn entered Hammer's Bergen hideaway in the basement of an abandoned business, he found tension in the room.

"Someone blew up those fuel tanks after all," Hammer said before even greeting his fellow commando. "Glad you weren't involved."

Bjørn picked up a cynical tone in Hammer's voice. "I was involved. It was you who wasn't."

"You agreed not to do it!"

"*Nei.* I agreed we would not do it." Bjørn showed a wry grin. "I didn't break our agreement. I did it with my own people. We left no clues of who it might be. And listen, Hammer, the mission was a success."

"You'd feel differently if you knew Norwegian lives were put in front of a German firing squad because of it."

Bjørn put out his hands. "We need to move past this. We've got another operation to plan."

"You're right," Hammer replied in a quieter tone. "And I'll admit it. You did a good job on those tanks. I heard it made a mess of things on that island and did cripple boat patrols for a while. We picked up no signs that the Nazis can point to anyone in the resistance for doing it, either."

Bjørn's grin widened and then vanished. "Now, we've got a tough assignment coming up. It's not an isolated island out in the sea. This one's in the middle of Bergen."

———

Snow fell heavy and wet outside the *hytte* as Bjørn sat by a crackling blaze in the fireplace and weighed a decision he needed to make. It related to Truni. As if she had been reading his mind, she showed up.

Truni unhooked her snowshoe bindings and shook snow off her heavy coat before coming inside. She removed the coat and boots, pulled a knit cap from her head, and went right for the fireplace.

"It's coming down out there," she said. "I was knee deep climbing the mountain."

"Didn't expect you," he replied. "I thought the conditions would keep you off the mountain. But I'm glad to see you."

She turned away from the fire and smiled at him.

Her visits had become more frequent. Bjørn had to admit to himself he welcomed seeing her more often. He missed her when she wasn't there.

Winter conditions had made it more difficult for both of them to get around. His return from meeting Hammer in Bergen three days earlier had been long and arduous. From the *rutebåt* stop near Tøkla, he had trudged back through a snowstorm.

Truni held her hands out toward the fire. "This feels good."

That broke through Bjørn's serious focus. He smiled. "I'll keep it fed, then, if it makes you want to come here."

Bjørn had been deliberating whether to use her for the Hoggemann operation. He had agreed to supply two people for the hit, and the Bergen-based commando committed to assembling the rest. They hadn't settled yet on how many were needed.

Bjørn already had talked to Jon about joining the team, and he was in. Based on trust alone, Truni was a logical choice for the other. But Bjørn had to confront his same old dilemma. He was reluctant to put her at grave risk. His love for her got in the way.

He had raised her name with Hammer, who liked the idea of using her. He was well acquainted with Truni and was aware of her abilities leading her own organization.

While many courageous women participated in resistance activities, Hammer believed Nazi authorities still tended to dismiss women's involvement. That would make her even more valuable in a mission like this, he and Bjørn agreed.

Bjørn had pointed out Truni's other attributes. She had an innocent look, but beneath her exterior were courage and toughness. She was decisive, able to think on her feet, and could talk her way out of most anything. He stopped short of telling Hammer about their past relationship and his current feelings for her.

By the time Truni had arrived at the *hytte*, Bjørn knew what he would do.

"I met with Hammer a few days ago in Bergen," he said.

"Oh. Is everything all right between you two?"

"*Ja.* He admitted he was glad we took out the fuel tanks. It was easy for him to say that. We succeeded."

Bjørn's smile disappeared. "Besides, we will need each other. We have a new assignment. From England. And it's much bigger."

"What?"

"An assassination."

Truni's mouth formed an oval. "Who?"

Bjørn cleared his throat. "A man named Amund Hoggemann."

"I know of that name." She tilted her head up. "*Ja,* isn't he a policeman?"

"Telavåg!"

"*Ja*, now I remember. A Norwegian. But an evil Nazi."

Bjørn nodded and mentally prepared for his question. It was still difficult for him. But he had to face up to it. He felt himself tighten. "I have an important question for you."

Truni was already a step ahead of him. "I know what you're going to ask. My answer is yes."

Bjørn let out a deep breath. "Good. Thank you. We can use you. We still haven't worked out all the details."

He had been thinking of something else just before she arrived. That Truni was right when she told him life was short. And there was no doubt his love for her was deep.

Bjørn probed her blue eyes and she held his stare.

She offered a curious smile. "What?"

He stayed silent a few seconds more. Then it came out. "Would you stay with me tonight?"

She leaned toward him. "Are you sure?"

"*Ja*, I'm sure."

"I'd like that."

Truni eased her way forward into Bjørn's outstretched arms.

———

May 10, 1944

Dawn ushered in a picture-perfect day. The morning sun beamed down on the city. The air was dry and comfortable. Warm enough to produce sweat among those who waited to kill.

At precisely seven thirty, a red door swung open, and Amund Hoggemann exited the front door of his house on Kristiangård Gate. He stepped down the six steps to ground level, turned left on the cement sidewalk, and began his regular stroll to work.

His face appeared freshly shaved, his jet-black hair combed smooth left to right across his scalp. In his early forties, Hoggemann was average height, about five foot ten, and was heavier than what would be considered a good physique. But he walked as if he were twice his height. Wearing a neatly pressed black Stapo uniform and a holstered sidearm strapped around his waist, he held a black briefcase and a stubby-billed police hat in his left hand.

His home in the city was about a mile from Stapo headquarters. Someone of his reputation certainly could command a car or an alternative form of transportation to work. But the way he carried himself showed he preferred parading his authority. People moved aside and gave him the sidewalk when he passed.

Seven attackers were lying in wait, including Bjørn and Hammer. Hammer provided three of his group to supplement Bjørn's recruits, Jon and Truni. They all were armed with pistols. They would follow a detailed script, improvising only if necessary. If cornered in a worst-case scenario, they all vowed to shoot it out. Arrest was not an option. It would only delay an inevitable execution. Imprisonment, interrogation, and torture surely would come first.

Their plan was to take out Hoggemann at an unexpected time, the light of day, in the unlikeliest spot, downtown Bergen near Stapo headquarters. Such boldness had been precisely what convinced them the plan would work.

They had taken every detail they could think of into account, from specific assignments to escape routes. They did not believe witnesses would be a problem. Who would want to stick around to answer Nazi police or Gestapo questions? The possibility of fellow Stapo officers milling around had created anxiety for Bjørn and the others. So the group of assassins had factored in the potential of calling the whole thing off if anything appeared suspicious.

Truni and one of Hammer's men waited on a side street for Hoggemann to pass. They posed as a couple on their own way to work, Truni in a dress and light jacket and her partner in a suit.

Hoggemann crossed the street in front of them, and they began to follow. Their assignment was to tail him and alert the others immediately if he deviated from his regular route.

But the Nazi continued down the sidewalk on his usual way as if he were marching to a drumroll. His body erect, left arm with the briefcase and cap stiffly clinging to his side, and his right arm swinging in rhythm with his stride.

Police training drilled into officers the need to be alert and aware of surroundings. If Hoggemann suspected Truni and her partner were following him, he didn't show it. He maintained his commanding presence and focused only straight ahead.

When he made a right turn onto Allehelgens Gate as expected, Truni and her partner broke off and rushed ahead using adjacent corridors to get into position and prepare to provide added help and firepower should it be required.

Two other group members emerged from a narrow street behind him and picked up the trail. Only a handful of people were on the streets, but enough to help his pursuers blend in. Hoggemann still gave no outward sign of noticing them.

Bjørn was posted in a doorway just off Christian Michelsens Gate on a side street. His doorway was deep enough to keep him in shadow and out of sight. It put him slightly more than a block from Christian Michelsens Gate 4, Stapo headquarters.

He was decked out in a dark-navy suit with a red tie. The fit was suitable but far from a tailored look. He didn't know where Hammer had gotten it. But the outfit gave him a business look appropriate for a workday in a business district. It was uncomfortable. But in the city, it served as a form of camouflage.

Bjørn repeatedly shifted his weight from foot to foot. He rubbed his hands to ease their trembling. He willed himself into a state of calm. But his gut would not obey.

He peered around the corner of the recessed doorway. Looking left, he saw Hammer standing across Christian Michelsens Gate outside a shop as if he were waiting for someone. Bjørn's head poked out of the doorway just enough for him to keep his eyes on Hammer.

At last, Hammer pulled out a cigarette and lit up, the signal that Hoggemann was coming. The wait was over. It was time. Bjørn stiffened. He steeled himself for the job, gritting his teeth and inhaling deeply through his nostrils.

Bjørn stepped backward into the shadows of his hiding place. He fixed his eyes on the main street where the Nazi would pass and held still. His vantage point was no wider than the blink of an eye. Then a silhouette of a man in a black uniform swept by.

Bjørn stepped smartly out of the dark onto the side street, the rubber-clad heels of his dress shoes quiet on the sidewalk's stone pavers. Nerves were no longer an issue. He focused on his job. He'd been trained for such a moment. He held a folded newspaper tucked under his left armpit. Inside the fold was a .22 pistol with a silencer screwed to the barrel. His arm squeezed the paper and gun tight against his side.

He rounded the corner onto the sidewalk of Christian Michelsens Gate and fell in line four feet behind Hoggemann, whose head stayed fixed straight ahead.

Despite Hoggemann's steady clip, Bjørn's step was quicker. He closed the gap to three feet. He caught himself in midstride. Adrenaline had pushed him faster than he wanted to go. Too early, and Hoggemann might be on to him. Bjørn slowed.

Then another figure emerged from the doorway of a pastry shop down the street and approached the target head-on. It was Jon.

Jon called out to Hoggemann. "Herre Hoggemann?"

The Nazi seemed surprised and slowed his pace, approaching this stranger with a hint of caution. "Yes."

A planned distraction. It focused Hoggemann's attention in front of him and confirmed that this officer was, indeed, their man.

Bjørn had a few words he planned to say to the Nazi. He closed the gap and drew the pistol from the newspaper. "This is a gift from our king," he said.

His voice drew Hoggemann to turn his head and pivot his upper torso toward Bjørn. Hoggemann's eyes grew wide when he spotted the gun, but he had no time to react. Bjørn fired one shot, aiming right at the heart.

Hoggemann recoiled, stumbling back two steps. His shocked, wide eyes foretold his fate. Bjørn knew where to aim the gun for a second shot, slightly higher. He squeezed the trigger. Hoggemann dropped to the pavement.

Bjørn knew he had been successful and didn't wait for any aftermath. He was gone, as were the rest of the group. They melted away, vanishing in separate directions down alleyways and other avenues of flight.

Bjørn burst around the corner onto the side street where he had waited earlier and hurried along the pavement. He stuffed the gun in the newspaper and glanced back to make sure he was not being chased. Farther down the block, he picked up a long, light raincoat he had stashed earlier and put it on over his suit. He topped his head with a broad-brimmed hat. With those alterations, his clothing no longer matched any descriptions a witness to the shooting might give.

Bjørn didn't know if there were witnesses. He remembered a few people being around, but he had been too focused on Hoggemann. As he fled, he avoided looking directly at anyone he passed. His planned exit route turned corners and followed side streets and alleyways, zigzagging through the city. He checked over his shoulder for signs of pursuers. So far, he was in the clear.

Only when he reached a park a mile away from the shooting did his quick stride become more leisurely. Bjørn came to a halt alongside a wide and deep pond in the middle of the park. He noticed a few people in the vicinity. A woman who seemed to have her hands full with two young boys in the distance. An elderly man walking away from him supported by a cane. A young man and woman conversing with heads close together almost hidden by a tree. None paid attention to him. He unwrapped the newspaper, flung the pistol into the pond, then deposited the paper in a nearby trash bin.

As Bjørn left the park, he saw a police car speeding by in the direction of Christian Michelsens Gate with siren at full blare. He continued on a wide, circuitous route to Hammer's hideout, frequently tugging at the front brim of his hat and checking behind him.

As he approached Hammer's hideout, he stopped and leaned against a tree. He began to feel relief that he had gotten away. He wondered if the others had, too. Bjørn had been so focused on doing his job and escaping that only then did the gravity of taking another human life sink in. He doubled over and retched.

CHAPTER 28

June 1944

Bjørn feared he was being followed. The snap of a twig. The rustling of brush or a tree. Sounds usually heard in a forest. But tweaked in a certain way, they raised his sensory antenna. He was hiking through forest on his way to see his family in Erlikvåg. As Bjørn quickened his pace, he plotted how he might find out.

Ahead was a large rock outcropping. When he reached it, he tucked into a thin gap between two jagged boulders and waited in silence. He had a pistol out and ready.

Minutes passed. He heard and saw nothing suspicious.

Ten minutes.

Nothing.

Twenty minutes.

Still nothing.

Bjørn was not far from his farm. Instead of pressing on, he doubled back, convinced someone was stalking him.

He hiked high up the hillside and moved quietly and carefully, ducking at times behind trees or thickets to observe and listen. Nothing stirred, and he began to question his instincts. He rubbed his stubbled cheeks. No question he had heard something, stealthy movement at the edge of his perception. It could have been an animal, a dropping branch, or wind moving through trees. He wondered whether he was becoming paranoid. Even so, in the weeks since the assassination of Amund Hoggemann, Bjørn had become jumpy. He had heard nothing from Hammer, who'd promised to contact him if danger surfaced.

Everyone involved in the killing had made it back to Hammer's hideout. But Bjørn had dreaded the possibility that Nazi retaliation and an expanded Gestapo dragnet could snare resistance fighters. No news was good news, he wanted to believe. But no news made him uneasy. Anxious enough to suspect a hunter when none was there.

———

Bjørn completed the trip to his farm without hearing more unnerving sounds. He hid among the trees and conducted his usual visual sweep of the farm and surrounding environment. Prepared to stay concealed for a stretch, he lowered himself to the ground and sat at a good vantage point.

He thought it surreal that he needed to remain out of sight at his own place. And he couldn't see his friends and fellow villagers except for Jon, who was helping him. But such were the times under German occupation and the danger he faced. There would be no escape from death for a captured Kompani Linge commando. Only Jon, Truni, and his family knew he had returned. Everyone else he worked with knew him only as Ram. Bjørn had considered eliciting Jonas's help, but decided against it to keep the list of his contacts short.

The farm was a bit different now. There were no animals. No cows. No sheep. No goats or pigs. All the chickens were gone. The Nazis had seized them all. His family subsisted on potatoes and other vegetables from the garden and occasionally got their hands on pieces of fish caught in the fjord.

Bjørn's visits to his farm had increased in recent weeks. He looked forward to seeing Åsta and Arne's family and spending the night in his own bed. It gave him a sense of normalcy. The stays were usually timed to when Arne would be there on his infrequent days off.

Satisfied it was safe, Bjørn hurried across the pasture to the farmhouse's back door. As soon as he opened it to enter, he could tell that things were not right. Inga appeared from the kitchen, her face drained of color. Tears rolled down her cheeks. Åsta trailed her, her own eyes bloodshot and wet. No smiles, just a look of dread.

"What is it?" Bjørn asked as he rushed inside.

Inga stumbled getting words out. "Arne. They took him. Arrested."

Åsta breathed deeply at seeing Bjørn and interjected. "One of Arne's police friends called. The Statspolitiet took him and six others."

Bjørn's jaw fell. "Stapo! Why?"

"They all refused to sign a loyalty oath the Nazis were forcing on them."

Bjørn closed his eyes. "Did the friend say where they took him?"

"He just said, 'Arne won't be coming home,'" Åsta responded. "The friend said they were sending him to an education camp to learn how to be a good Nazi. We were told we could pick up some of his things at the police station."

Silence took over for a brief moment. Bjørn stared at the ceiling. His mind raced. The Nazis had struck close to home. Taking their farm animals and their livelihood was bad enough. Now their grasp extended to a member of his family.

He shifted his eyes between Åsta and Inga. "When I hear education camp, it means concentration camp."

More tears trickled down Inga's cheeks.

Bjørn tried to be positive and suppress the gloom. "It doesn't mean prison," he said. "Prison would be worse. Maybe it won't be long before he's released."

With a shaky finger, Inga wiped away the wetness under her eyes. "One day last week, Arne did say he was worried something would happen to him. But he was more worried about losing his job. Not being arrested."

Åsta glanced at Bjørn. "Is there anything we can do?"

"We just have to wait." It was all Bjørn could offer. "When will you go to pick up his things?"

Inga sniffled and spoke quickly. "Tomorrow."

"When you go to the police station, ask if you can see him or contact him. And ask where he is. They probably will not let you see him. But they may tell you where he is or where he's going."

Bjørn released a long stretch of air. "Other than that, I just don't know."

CHAPTER 29

August 1944

How did they find out? The question filled Bjørn's thoughts as he stared at the piece of paper with a scribbled, decoded message. Orders from Kompani Linge headquarters in England. It had felt like his heart plunged to the pit of his stomach as he was converting the numbers relayed by the BBC newscast into letters that formed the words.

The fingernail of his right index finger repeatedly tapped the paper. The message was simple and direct. "Bølgeland airplane factory. Destroy."

Bjørn hunched forward in his chair, planting his elbows on the table. His orders were to blow up Olav Sonnesen's plant, which was making airplane parts for the German Luftwaffe.

Like the ache of a slow-healing canker sore, the issue had gnawed at him since Olav had first told him nearly a year and a half ago what the Nazis were forcing him to do. As part of Bjørn's mission, a business feeding the German war machine should have been among his prime targets for destruction. But he had balked. Despite a sworn duty to his country, he'd turned a blind eye to destroying the factory.

Bjørn knew of Olav's steadfast loyalty to the king, of his disdain for being forced to help build Germany's military, and of his efforts to slow and interrupt production. Bjørn's relationship with Truni tempered his resolve. He had not reported the factory to his superiors in London.

Now the business was in their sights. It didn't take him long to figure out who'd likely told them. Hammer. Who else could it be? Bjørn had let slip word of the Sonnesen plant when he and his fellow commando had retrieved the supply drop. What he hadn't told Hammer was that Truni's father owned the factory. Bjørn had explained the production slowdowns to show the owner's loyalty. And he had disclosed its location in the town of Bølgeland.

Why had he told Hammer? Perhaps it was to make a good impression and show his new commando contact he was capable of fulfilling his mission. Bjørn felt no ill will toward Hammer. But why didn't his colleague leave it to him to decide whether to notify England? The factory was within his operational territory.

Bjørn was left with a monumental decision. Should he disobey orders, allow the factory to continue making airplane parts, and live with the consequences? Or should he carry out a sabotage mission that was sure to cost him the woman he loved? Truni would know he did it and would not forgive him.

On this warm summer night, Bjørn stayed inside his hideout and faced the conundrum. He slumped over the table. It was as though a heavy anvil rested on his shoulder blades.

He had almost missed the message for him embedded in the BBC broadcast. He had been absorbed in the news. Throughout Europe, Allied troops continued to advance. British and American forces had reached the outskirts of Paris. French resistance forces had staged an uprising in the city and attacked German forces preparing to evacuate. In Italy, after liberating Rome, the Allies had driven the Nazis from Florence and had advanced to a German line of heavy fortifications in Northern Italy. The Russian Red Army, meanwhile, had launched an offensive in

Axis-aligned Romania. Unrelenting Allied bombing of German cities continued.

The once unstoppable German Wehrmacht was crumbling everywhere. Nazi Germany's defeat was inevitable. It was just a matter of time, Bjørn thought. What difference would one small airplane factory make?

He weighed deeper risks. The sabotage certainly would bring the Gestapo to Bølgeland and to the Sonnesens' front door. The Nazis' brutal methods of interrogation could elicit confessions. There was grave risk of someone talking and pointing the Nazis to Truni and to him.

But orders were orders. He felt duty bound to follow them, regardless of the circumstances and distaste of carrying them out. Who was he to question them? Wasn't it what he'd committed to?

He recalled what one of his contacts in England had told him: "We need to break apart the Nazis little by little, piece by piece. Eventually the whole pie will be gone."

The soft glow of a single kerosene lantern cast Bjørn's shadow against the *hytte*'s wall. He studied the shadow, fixated on the distorted dark figure. All he saw was the silhouette of a pathetic man who was shirking his duty. Bjørn picked up a tin mug from the table and heaved it at his shadow. The mug ricocheted off the wall with a ping. He flinched. At that moment, Bjørn caved into his conscience. He owed it to his country to blow up the Sonnesen factory.

—

Dusk approached as Bjørn embarked on his four-hour journey to Sonnesen Tinn Fabrikk. He trekked under a not-quite-full moon and clear skies with a comfortable temperature. The mountainous terrain was rugged, but it had become his natural habitat.

Bjørn's legs, feet, and lungs were strong, and he was more than prepared for the hike. The distance had become routine.

His rucksack was stuffed with sticks of dynamite. Each stick was a tightly packed cylinder of sawdust, cellulose, and nitroglycerin. His training had taught him that just one could do considerable damage. He kept the sticks separated except for one pair that he taped together. Long wires were attached to a blasting cap at the end of each stick. To defend himself if he encountered trouble, Bjørn carried his .22-caliber pistol with the silencer and his Sten gun.

Even though he tried to maintain his focus on his mission, thoughts of Truni seeped into his mind. The previous evening, she had visited him and spent the night. When she had arrived, he had already collected the explosives and stored them in the cellar beneath the floor where she stood.

His eyes had avoided hers, and she had noticed.

"What is it? You've got something weighing on your mind."

"Nothing, really," he had replied with a faint smile and wrinkled forehead. "Got a lot of things to think about."

Truni had known better than to ask about his activities unless he raised them. So, she dropped it.

At night, Bjørn had wrapped her in an embrace but made no move beyond that. They held each other until sleep claimed her. Bjørn lay awake much longer. His mind wrestled with thoughts about her and the deed he was about to do. He did love her so. But he was committed now. This night, he had thought, could well be the last time she would be in his arms.

As he progressed up the mountain toward his target, Bjørn continued to rationalize the mission. War was ugly. There was tragedy and heartbreak in it. Treachery. Sometimes brother against brother and neighbor against neighbor. Friends often became foes. War had to be stopped. In doing so, it often required actions that on their face seemed like betrayal. But the actions were necessary to keep enemies from building armies and to deny them materials to equip those armies. He had to fulfill his mission.

Bjørn had made two key decisions. First, he would act alone. No help from Hammer or Jon. The fewer people involved, the fewer people at risk. He would face any consequences by himself.

Second, the operation required thorough reconnaissance outside and inside the factory. The equipment and assembly layout would determine what kind of explosives to use and how much. The perimeter would reveal security measures, such as sentries, fencing, and trip wires, as well as how easily he could slip inside.

During his scouting, Bjørn had found no fencing or security of any kind. The building was deserted at night. The small and simple back door had been locked, and the windows secured from the inside. But the front was vulnerable. Large sliding barn-like doors were secured by a heavy chain connected to hooks on each door. However, no padlocks prevented entry. To gain access, he needed only to unhook the chain and slide the doors open.

On his recon, Bjørn had done exactly that. Moonlight seeping through the uncovered windows had allowed him to move around the factory's innards. He had come away with a good idea of the assembly line, worktables, and storage of raw materials.

He had found security was nonexistent for a plant making vital war-related parts. The Germans must have believed the facility was safe given the building's small works and remote location, Bjørn had reasoned. Now that he was approaching the building loaded with explosives, he would take advantage of Nazi complacency.

Bjørn felt his fingers grow jittery. Not from fear. From the strange feeling of being at a building where he'd briefly worked and being just a short mile up the road from Truni's home. He was an intruder in a place he used to frequent. And he was charged with destroying it.

The manufacturing facility was barely larger than a typical barn but without the round-cascading roof and not as tall. The single-story plant was rectangular with a gently pitched roof and a series of large windows running down each side. Weathered wood planks painted white covered its sides. Plain and industrial, it was typical of a family-owned manufacturing business in a small coastal community. The building was connected to the village by its own dirt road, which went no farther than a loading yard outside the factory. It was set off by itself, and the forest around it made for a clean getaway.

Despite his belief it would be easy pickings, Bjørn moved with caution. He couldn't afford to be complacent. He stayed hidden in the brush and trees, drew his pistol, and crept through the forested landscape. He covered a wide swath of ground surrounding the plant, stopping at frequent intervals and tilting his head to listen.

When Bjørn was satisfied no one was around, he emerged from the trees and checked the back door first. It remained locked, just as it had been on his scouting trip. The windows were secured. He found the front sliding door hooked by the chain but unlocked as before. Bjørn slid it open, and once inside, he pushed it nearly shut, leaving the door open just a crack. He hid kneeling behind a table near the front with his pistol ready. Bjørn remained in that position for a minute, watching and listening for any movement or breathing from inside. It was quiet.

Even with a little moonlight leaking through uncurtained windows, the factory was nearly pitch black. Dark shadows of machinery hunched in the gloom. Bjørn paused to let his eyes adjust from the dark outside to the darker-yet inside. He pulled out his flashlight, intending to use it only for quick peeks.

The room appeared just as it had on the earlier evening of his reconnaissance. He could make out the outlines of the many tables positioned as assembly stations. Assorted tools lay scattered on them. A bulky apparatus stood near the back door. Large sheets of metal were stacked next to it. He had concluded it was a machine that cut thin strips of aluminum.

Bjørn stepped back to the front and peeked out the window in the direction of the road. It remained peaceful outside. As he backed away from the window, he bumped into a stack of odd-shaped pieces of aluminum leaned against the wall, setting off a low clang. A quick aim of his flashlight illuminated what appeared to be finished airplane pieces ready for shipment.

He unshouldered his rucksack and peeled off his light coat, which he used to cover the flashlight. Bjørn then tucked his head under the jacket so he could work without the light being seen from outside. He started near the entrance and gradually made his way around the room toward the back, placing single sticks of explosives strategically under the assembly stations, at stacks of finished products, and on raw materials.

As Bjørn inched his way backward, he cut strings of wire from a spool, spliced them together, and attached them to the dynamite sticks. The two pieces of dynamite taped together were saved for the large cutting machine. It seemed critical to production, and he thought it might need an extra blast for full destruction.

Under the subdued glare of the jacket-covered flashlight, he worked with precision. He knew how and where to set the explosives. Occasional thoughts of regret entered his head. But he worked through them, focusing on bringing the factory to a pyrotechnic end.

A little more than an hour had elapsed when he reached the back, having created a network of wired explosives. He unlocked the back door and went out, unrolling a single main wire from the spool as he distanced himself from the manufacturing plant and entered the forest.

At about two hundred feet away, he pulled out an electrical box with a plunger and connected the wire. All that was left was to press the plunger down, and Sonnesen Tinn Fabrikk, a family-owned business that had made simple but elegant pewter cups, spoons, and decorative plates before it was forced to make aluminum aircraft parts for the Nazis, would be no more. The thought gave him no joy.

The plunger was on the ground beside him, all hooked up and ready as Bjørn shielded himself from the blast behind a massive hump of rock. He stuffed cotton in his ears and wrapped a heavy scarf around his head to hold the cotton in tight. The explosion would be heard for miles. He put on his jacket, shouldered his pack, and got ready for a quick getaway on the exact route he had mapped out in detail beforehand.

Bjørn lay prone to the ground, tucked and protected behind the boulder. Taking a deep breath, he closed his eyes tightly and girded himself. He hesitated a few seconds. Then he pushed out all other thoughts and did what he'd set out to do. He pushed down hard on the device's T-shaped handle.

An electromagnetic current rushed through the wires and set off the blasting caps in the dynamite sticks, exploding the nitroglycerin. It all was instantaneous.

The explosion shook the earth and bounced Bjørn off the ground. At one point, no part of his body touched the earth. But the rock he hid behind protected him from flying debris. The earplugs only slightly muted the roar of the blast, which sent building sprinters and pieces of equipment raking the forest, slamming into trees, snapping trunks and branches and hurtling them down. Smoke and dust permeated the air.

He yanked out the wires still connected to the plunger and stuffed everything in his rucksack. He was gone within a minute of the blast. His body still quivered from the shock as he raced through the forest. He coughed through the smoky, dusty air. His sole focus now was getting away without stumbling or tripping.

In three hours, he was back at the hideout, exhausted both physically and mentally. But he couldn't rest just yet. He unpacked the materials he'd carried back with him and gathered the left-over sticks of dynamite and other unused items. He wrapped them up well, took them away from the house, and buried them in the ground. All evidence that might connect him to the sabotage was gone.

———

Four days later, he still hadn't heard from Truni. Bjørn knew that was not a good sign. She would have no doubt he was the saboteur. He had fallen from grace.

Guilt and worry captured his psyche. Bjørn still believed destroying the factory was right. He had to believe that now. But he grew more concerned about the potential consequences. The act placed Truni and her organization at risk, and that could lead to him. Gestapo agents likely were already circulating through Bølgeland questioning anyone and everyone.

Truni showed up on the fifth day. Bjørn greeted her with wariness. He couldn't help letting his discomfort show on his face. No smile. Just a blank expression.

Her eyes closed in on him. "I know it was you. You don't need to say anything. I know you won't admit it. I want you to listen to what I say."

Her look was cold and her voice was flat. There were no tears.

"You took advantage of my parents and me. You ruined our lives. You didn't think at all about our struggle to survive. My father is not a Nazi conspirator. The Germans forced him to reopen and make those parts. He was doing all he could to limit production. All he tried to do was provide for us and for the people who worked for him."

Bjørn tried to speak. "Truni, I—"

"Stop," she demanded, shaking her head stiffly and rapidly side to side. "Only listen. You betrayed me. You broke my heart. I will never forgive you. And you need to leave this *hytte*."

She turned to leave, and Bjørn rushed to get words out. "You must stay out of the village and lay low."

Truni showed no indication she'd heard him. She was gone.

CHAPTER 30

October 22, 1944

A boot kick to his bed jostled Bjørn awake. His eyes opened to face the blinding brightness of a flashlight. He raised his arm to shield his bleary eyes.

Behind the light stood two murky figures in his otherwise darkened upstairs bedroom at Erlikvåg. In a stout tone, one called his name.

"Bjørn Erliksen. Do not try anything or we will shoot you and kill you. Do you understand?"

He was groggy. His nod meek.

One of the intruders found the small box of matches on the dresser and fired up the oil lamp. The room illuminated, and the channeled shine of the flashlights went black.

His eyes adjusted to the light. More clearly, he saw two men in uniform standing at the foot of the bed. Their short-barrel weapons with long straps slung over their shoulders were pointed directly at him. He recognized the weaponry—Schmeisser MP 40 submachine guns.

One man wore the dark-green uniform and patch of the SS. His tight trousers flared out at the hips, and he wore a stubby-billed cap with a gold swastika pin. He was Gestapo. The other was big and brawny and fit clumsily in the black uniform of the Norwegian Nazi State Police, the Stapo.

Bjørn's head cleared. Reality set in. He had no means of escape. His training screamed at him to fight back. But his enemies had caught him by surprise. His guard was down. How could he have slept through their intrusion?

"You know why we've come?" the Norwegian Stapo agent said. His tone made it a half question, half statement.

Bjørn feigned ignorance and innocence. "*Nei*, I have no idea. You have put my brother in a concentration camp. Have you come to tell me something happened to him?"

The Stapo agent chuckled. "*Nei*, that's not it. Our purpose is different. We think you know why we're here. Now, put clothes on. We're taking you with us. And I warn you again, do not do anything to resist or we'll shoot you."

Bjørn sighed in resignation, pushed his bedcovers over, and sat up on the edge of the bed. Steams of anger with himself built inside him. How could he have been so complacent and let the enemy get the better of him? How did he not hear them come?

In the months after the factory bombing, he had moved out of the Sonnesen family *hytte* on Truni's orders and had been sleeping on the cold ground inside the barn at Tøkla where he had secured the cache of weapons, supplies, and equipment. He had been visiting his farm with increased frequency, joining Åsta; sister-in-law, Inga; and niece, Kristi, for dinner and spending the night in his own bed. During these visits, Bjørn had continued to exercise care to ensure he was not seen by neighbors entering and leaving his home. The comfort of being in his own house had given him a false sense of safety, he now realized.

Bjørn's lips curved down. He grabbed for his woolen trousers sitting next to the bed. As he dressed, he was under the constant eyes of his captors. The Stapo agent pointed at a Bible on his nightstand.

"I see you're a religious man," he said.

"*Ja*, I am," Bjørn replied softly, his voice barely audible.

"That's good. You'll need more than forgiveness from heaven for what you're facing."

The Gestapo agent stood silent, keeping his submachine gun steadied at Bjørn.

The reference to the book set Bjørn's nerves on edge. It was the Bible he used to decipher messages from England. Notes on codes to send and receive messages were scribbled on pages. At least he had the presence of mind the evening before to stash his telegraph equipment under a pile of potatoes in the cellar. But leaving his Bible on the nightstand was another sign of complacency. Carelessness. Bjørn turned his eyes away from the book.

His hands turned clammy. He had another piece of incriminating evidence at an arm's reach. His .22-caliber pistol with the silencer was tucked under his pillow. A simple toss of the pillow would find the gun, and he had no doubt that its discovery would bring grave consequences.

He had put it there to defend himself in situations like this. His instinct was to reach for it and kill the Nazis. But that would be senseless. They had the draw on him. His only option was to dress as quickly as he could, comply with every instruction, and get out of his bedroom. The longer he took, the more time his captors had to get snoopy.

He also thought of his family. If he tried to resist, their safety and the security of his farm could be in jeopardy. He had to follow their orders and get out of the house.

After Bjørn buttoned his heavy work shirt and laced up his boots, the Nazis handcuffed him with his arms behind his back. Bjørn left the room and descended the stairs to the ground floor. He felt his captors' breaths on the back of his neck. He assumed their weapons were pointed at his back.

Åsta and Inga waited at the bottom of the stairs in bathrobes and slippers. The Nazi intrusion had rousted them from their beds.

His sister-in-law stood in silence with tears rolling down her cheeks. Seeing Bjørn in handcuffs seemed to have rekindled the horror of Arne's arrest and set off her fragile emotional state all over again, he thought.

Åsta appeared outwardly calm, giving a blank stare with raised eyes. But she couldn't hold back. "Oh dear God, please don't take him."

Bjørn made quick eye contact with her as he moved by and whispered, "It's OK." Words of comfort that he knew weren't true.

The Nazis brushed by without speaking or looking directly at the two distressed women.

He motioned with his head toward his coat hanging on a hook by the door—the former army coat he had colored black. The SS soldier gave him a suspicious look. He stepped back and pointed his gun at Bjørn. With a slight nod of his head, he motioned to the Stapo officer to remove the handcuffs. With hands free, Bjørn entertained the idea of rushing his captors. Foolish, with a bad ending, he decided. He put on his coat, yielded again to hand-cuffs, and went out the door with the Nazis.

As they passed an old oak tree that stood by the road on the edge of his property, he looked down the hill at Erlikvåg and the shadows of the farmhouses below. It was a little before five, the appointed time when many farmers rose to face a day of work. Darkness still filled the air. Nothing stirred. He wondered if any-one was aware of the Nazis' arrival.

Damp air moistened Bjørn's face. The cool bite of a breeze coming off the fjord reddened his cheeks. They walked down the road at a steady clip. He knew the road well, but he still stumbled at times from unsteadiness caused by cuffed hands behind him and occasional shoves.

All the while, he kept mentally beating himself up. The words "stupid" and "reckless" surfaced in his thoughts. He had violated tenets of commando training. His heartbeat quickened as he focused on what could happen next. Intense interrogation? Beatings? Torture?

Perhaps, he thought, it was good they had found him at home. Who knew what the Gestapo would have done had he not been there. The Nazis were capable of anything. They may have taken Åsta, Inga, and even Kristi into custody and sent them to a concentration camp.

As he passed through the heart of the village, he saw no one. He noticed windows on farmhouses were still dark. No one was out. Had some villagers seen him, they likely would have been shocked. Would he ever see Erlikvåg again?

As they made their way past Jonas Seversen's general store, Bjørn knew he had to mentally prepare for what was to come. He had to steel himself against revealing his activities and the names of others even in the face of death.

Another question crossed his mind. Who else had they seized?

———

A sleek gray-hulled military boat bumped gently against the wooden pilings of the community dock as Bjørn boarded it. It looked speedy, much bigger than *Lensmann*, the boat Bjørn shared with his siblings and had to leave in Bolstad. But it was smaller than the *rutebåt* ferry. Although shorter than being a warship, a lone machine gun was mounted on the front.

He saw two men through the window of the swept back–style wheelhouse, one who looked like the boat's pilot. His escorts pushed him through an open hatch and down steps to belowdecks.

As he set foot on the planked floor below, Bjørn saw others in custody. He knew two of them. Storekeeper Jonas Seversen and his brother, Anton, as well as two other men he didn't recognize were hunched on the floor with their hands handcuffed behind their backs. They were under the watchful eye of another eight Gestapo and Norwegian Stapo agents who, like his captors, held submachine guns.

The Seversens showed no acknowledgment of Bjørn, though he detected Jonas's eyes widening slightly. They had no idea he'd returned from England. But they all behaved as if none of them knew each other. Their blank faces disguised any emotion. No fear, no stoic pride, no resentment. Their eyes were cast downward. Bjørn's escorts gave him a hearty shove toward the captives.

"No talking among you," came a firm Gestapo command.

Bjørn was relieved that he knew little of his fellow captives' activities. It meant less information for the Gestapo to pry out of him.

The boat stayed docked at its mooring. It told Bjørn there must be others being sought. Jon? Who else? As those fears tumbled in his head, Bjørn grew concerned for Truni. Was there a roundup afoot to ensnare her, too?

Something puzzled him. The arresting Nazis had called him by his real name, not his alias, Mons Bjørk. Did they suspect him for what he did or was it something else? Did they know he was a Kompani Linge commando? Or did they merely assume he was tied to the Seversens' activities? Was the Gestapo intent on arresting Bjørn Erliksen the farmer, not the resistance fighter code-named Ram?

—

Bjørn and the four other prisoners huddled on the floor of the boat's underbelly for maybe an hour. Time crept at the speed of a snail. He and the Seversens traded no words or glances. They were good friends who had known each other a long time. They usually had each other's back. But under these circumstances, each kept to himself.

Finally, Bjørn heard others come aboard speaking in angry tones. Three uniformed men he hadn't seen before descended the steps below deck. One wore what appeared to be a senior officer's uniform with bars, stripes, metals, and an SS patch. He was the tallest of the three, and he carried himself as the officer in charge of the operation. He was red-faced, and the mouths of all three formed deep curves downward.

The officer shouted directly at Anton in German. He took off a black glove from one hand, grabbed Anton by the hair, and pulled the prisoner up toward him. The Nazi officer released Anton's curly hair and then slapped him sharply with the back of the other still-gloved hand.

His shouts were translated by one of the men who wore a Norwegian Stapo uniform. The translation carried the sting of the officer's taunt.

"You gave us the wrong house," the translator said. "There was a Jon there, but it wasn't Jon Møland. You lied to us."

Now Bjørn knew that Jon had also been targeted.

"I didn't lie," Anton pleaded. "I gave you the right house. I can show you. Please."

One of the agents pulled out a piece of paper with a crude hand-drawn map. The SS officer seized the map and opened it.

With his hands handcuffed, Anton twisted his body and pointed awkwardly to a spot on the map. "That's my mark," Anton said. "I gave you the right place. It's Jon's house."

More words and angry looks were exchanged between the German officer and Norwegian Stapo men. The officer looked at one of the Norwegians and asked a question. The Stapo agent moved a couple of steps backward and answered in German, *"Nein."*

The senior officer's reddened face turned even brighter. He shoved Anton back with the others and waved his arms in frustration. Bjørn fought to swallow a slight relieved grin, realizing the agents had gone to the wrong house. At least Jon had avoided arrest.

The officer then nodded toward some of the German Gestapo and Norwegian Stapo men and pointed at large hooks across the ceiling. With a quick turn, he stomped up the stairs to the deck with his two-man hunting squad.

"Stand up," one guard yelled at Bjørn and the other prisoners. The Nazis cinched ropes around the prisoners' handcuffed hands and flipped the ropes around the ceiling hooks. They hoisted the prisoners one by one off the floor, leaving them hanging with their arms behind their backs.

Searing pain coursed through Bjørn's shoulder joints. He felt as though his arms would be ripped from their sockets. This was a taste of what he anticipated and dreaded in the Gestapo's hands. Even the boat's gentle rocking at the dock created enough bounce to intensify the pain. Jonas and Anton gritted their teeth and winced. But no one cried out in pain. Bjørn was determined not to show the Nazis his suffering.

Minute by agonizing minute passed. For Bjørn, every minute was too long. From what he saw, it looked that way for the others, too.

Finally, footsteps came up the gangway and onto the boat. Bjørn heard voices on deck speaking in German. He didn't need to understand the words to know they were heated.

When no one appeared belowdecks after several minutes, someone on deck yelled something to the Nazis below, and they untied the three prisoners before shoving them in a heap along the inside walls of the hull. The boat fired up and sped away in a thunderous roar. Bjørn concluded that a second attempt to arrest Jon had also failed.

Bjørn's arms felt dead. Pain lingered. But he found comfort in the fact that Jon appeared, for now, to have evaded arrest.

CHAPTER 31

October 23, 1944

The ringing clang of muscular steel doors echoed down the cement-encased cellblock of the Kregfengsel, Bergen's city jail. Lying on his thin, bone-numbing mattress, Bjørn straightened up and pressed his back against a cold concrete wall. His eyes grew wide, and he listened. The stomping sound of guards' jackboots in an almost-synchronized cadence got closer. He was overcome with dread, suspecting that his Gestapo interrogation was at hand.

It was dark in his box of a cell. Only several slivers of subdued light came through slits in the center of the solid cell door. He was alone.

He, the Seversen brothers and the two other men had been delivered by car at the city jail directly following their arrival by boat at Bergen harbor. It took only about an hour for the boat to cover the distance down Osterfjord from Erlikvåg to a harbor dock. By midday of their arrest, Bjørn was dumped into a cell by himself. He assumed the others were in individual cells and, like him, on pins and needles waiting for their own interrogations.

Bjørn didn't know how long he'd been here. But it had been a while, perhaps a day, maybe less. He was left to stew over his fate.

He didn't sleep, and he wasn't fed. He was tired and hungry, and his body still ached from his rough treatment on the boat.

In the handful of seconds he listened to the guard's menacing march, Bjørn held out hope they might pass by his cell and take away someone else. He dismissed that thought. He was convinced his number was up. The Nazis wanted a crack at him.

He glanced up at the slits in the door. The heavy footsteps stopped directly in front and dull rays of light coming through went dark. After a rattle of keys, the door opened.

The flood of light blinded him briefly. But he made out their outlines. Two of them. The guard who spoke was blunt.

"We've come for you. Get up. Don't try to resist in any way or you'll force us to hurt you."

Bjørn struggled to get to his feet. The effort must have been too slow for the impatient guards in their custodial gray uniforms. They moved forward, grabbed him firmly under the arms, and pulled him up, one on each side of him. Ignoring his wince, they handcuffed him, then dragged him out of his cell and down the corridor. He attempted to gain footing. But they were quick and strong, and his legs and feet were not in control. One guard was tall, slender, and muscular, the other shorter but broad and thick.

They were Norwegian, but the rough treatment convinced him they were Nazi sympathizers. Bjørn had heard that some jailers had remained loyal to King Haakon VII and went through the motions to serve Nazi authority only to keep a job. They showed their loyalty by smuggling messages in and out of jail for resistance gangs and finding ways to help inmates. These guards acted like they would have none of that.

They hurried him out of the jail and onto the darkened street to a waiting sedan, which had its motor running but no lights on. Two men stood by the car. Bjørn knew right away what they were. Gestapo. They both wore long plain-clothed overcoats and fedoras. Dressed up for the occasion, he thought.

The chilling dampness of the night air refreshed Bjørn from the stale cellblock and soothed his aches. He had no idea of the hour. The dormancy of his windowless cell had disoriented him. This time of the year in Norway was unpredictable. When winter approached, sunset arrived early and dawn slept in. It rained often and was known to snow in October.

He had learned that the Gestapo relished the dark of the night. It was prime time for their evil. The short daylight of fall gave them plenty of time to work.

The agents tossed their prisoner in the back seat. With his cuffed hands behind him, Bjørn sat awkwardly and uncomfortably. One agent, the bulkier of the pair, got in the back seat next to him, and the other drove.

The car rumbled down deserted streets, and Bjørn could only anticipate where they were taking him. Surely Gestapo headquarters. His only uncertainty was whether he would live through the night.

No one spoke. He was left in the quiet of the car to ponder what was to come. Now twenty-four, he thought himself too young to die. He should have so much life ahead. But many young Norwegian men had been in the same predicament he now faced and had died at Nazi hands.

Questions raced in his head. How long could he hold out? Could he keep his tongue in check? Bjørn had been well briefed about Gestapo methods during commando training. Yet, those mock interrogation sessions probably were nothing like the real thing. He expected the physical abuse to be tormenting and unbearable.

It was time for courage. He had to keep his vow to not tell them anything useful and try to stay alive. Brave thinking, but Bjørn knew his fate was out of his hands.

—

The sedan pulled in front of a single four-story building. The agents hauled him out of the car. With one on each side, they grabbed his arms and tugged him toward the door. Unlike the jail guards, they allowed him to move under his own power. Bjørn felt his side brush against one agent's holster packed with a pistol. The gun was so close. He wished he could snatch it, shoot them both, and sprint away into the night. But handcuffs and the Gestapo agents' firm grips left him helpless.

His Gestapo transporters hustled Bjørn down a flight of stairs to the basement and deposited him in a room. It looked like it may have been an office at one time. It was sparse and now appointed purely for Gestapo purposes. Walls were painted a dull gray. The only furniture was a desk and three metal chairs, one behind the desk, one in front, and the other beside a chalk blackboard to the side of the desk. The blackboard was erased clean.

He found the basement location fitting for the Gestapo's evil. Belowground was closer to hell than heaven.

Two men waited for him in the room. One wore a suit and was short enough to have a Napoleon complex. But he appeared to carry a solid, stocky physique, and Bjørn sensed he could hold his own against bigger bullies. The other stood at about Bjørn's height, and also seemed hardened and tough. He wore a form-fitting SS uniform, black and snappy, as if the devil himself had dressed him. They both had ominous smiles and looked at him with cold, hard eyes.

Bjørn's heart pumped faster. His legs felt weak and shaky. He braced himself, and his face went blank. His mouth was flat with neither a smile nor a frown.

The Gestapo men who transported Bjørn from the city jail shoved him in the chair in front of the desk before leaving. The two men remaining in the room with him took positions on each side of the blackboard. The SS officer, who appeared to be German, spoke Norwegian and introduced the plainclothes man as Wolter. Bjørn had no doubt that he was Gestapo. Wolter targeted his cold eyes on him and spoke with German words he didn't understand. But the translation from the SS man was clear.

"The first time you are caught in a lie, your eyes will be taken out," the translator said.

He repeated the refrain differently. "If you tell us a lie, we will pull out your eyes, and your ears will be taken off so you can't see or hear anymore. Do you understand what will happen if you lie to us?"

Bjørn mumbled a barely audible acknowledgment.

"Was ist das?" Wolter shouted. His words and tone needed no translation.

The prisoner raised his voice. *"Ja,* I understand."

Questions came at him rapid fire. What was the name of his resistance organization? What was his role? How many were in it? Who were they? Wolter wanted names. That's what he was really after, Bjørn surmised. More people to arrest and torment.

At Bjørn's repeated denials, Wolter acted without hesitation. The German grabbed a blackjack club from the tray at the base of the blackboard and rushed toward the prisoner.

Bjørn knew what was coming. With his hands still handcuffed behind his back, he grabbed his shirttail and squeezed. He tensed. He had studied this Nazi instrument designed to punish the human body. The club was encased in dark rubber with lead at the end. Hard and smooth.

Wolter brought the club down on the top of his knees. Bjørn folded forward in the chair at the blow, and Wolter then slapped it across his back. Streaks of pain raced through his body.

Wolter muttered something, and the other goon translated. "Would you like more of this? We'll give you more if you don't answer us."

Questions continued. His organization. Its structure. Wolter tossed out names. Did he know this person? Did he know that person? So far, none of the interrogation focused on specific acts or crimes against the Nazis, or anything about who he was and what he did.

Bjørn stayed doubled over in the chair, exposing his back. He had not heard of or knew any of them, and he declared his innocence. Each "no" answer brought another stroke of the club on his back, causing an upward jolt. He winced in pain and released moans.

They asked him if he knew a person named Skistad.

It sounded familiar. Bjørn wondered whether if Skistad belonged to Hammer's group. His answer was meek. "*Nei*, I don't know the name."

This time, Wolter slammed the blackjack against his side, nearly knocking him out of the chair. But he regained his huddled position.

"I don't know him," Bjørn said in a louder tone, his contorted face squinting in pain.

The translator grabbed his shoulders to sit him straight up in the chair. Wolter then used his fist in a gloved right hand and belted him just below his left cheek. The blow flung him out of the chair to the floor. His jaw felt whiplashed and blood dripped from his nose.

Wolter said something menacing, again in German. It wasn't translated. As Bjørn curled up on the floor to protect himself, Wolter delivered another blow to his back with the club. The interrogator said something else to the translator, who played it back in the same stern tone the German delivered it. It was another name that Bjørn did not recognize.

"Nei," was all he answered as he girded for another strike, which arrived quickly in the same location.

And so it went. More names. More blows all over his body. His nose was bloodied and his jaw seemed out of whack, but his tormentors held back from striking his head with the club. That might have proved fatal. It seemed they wanted to keep him alive, at least for a while.

After the next several more hits, he stopped answering verbally and simply stayed curled on the linoleum floor.

Wolter and the translator pulled him up and positioned him upright in the chair. Then the interrogation took a slight turn. The names the questioners posed changed to code names.

"Who is the person known as Cheese?" At the question, Wolter shot a glance at the prisoner and studied the reaction.

Bjørn's tone was subdued. "I don't know."

"You lie, you lie," the translator yelled at him.

"Who is the person called Hammer?"

Bjørn felt himself flinch, but hoped his expressionless face was stiff enough for them not to notice. He shook his head and said nothing.

"Who is Ram?"

Again, he had no words and tried to keep his face firm, even though he felt exposed. They knew his code name but still seemed not to know it was him. Bjørn answered with only a shake of his head.

There were two more code names that he didn't know. The Monk, Truni's code name, was not mentioned.

At getting nothing out of the prisoner, Wolter grew hot. He kicked Bjørn in his sides and legs and rolled him over on his back. The Nazi landed several blows on his chest, then poked the butt end of the billy club into Bjørn's stomach.

He yelled, and the Norwegian translator transmitted it in the same tone. "All you do is deny, deny, deny. Tell us what we want to know, and you can save yourself."

Bjørn's voice was barely audible to the translator, who leaned over him to hear. "I belong to no organization. I'm just a farmer. Nothing more."

"Ahhhh," Wolter reacted after learning of Bjørn's words. He flashed a warped grin, dropped his right arm holding the club, and again spoke in German to the translator, who relayed it to Bjørn.

"Then why were you gone from your farm for a long time? Tell us where you've been."

So, they knew something about him. They knew of his year-and-a-half absence from Erlikvåg. Through his pain, Bjørn concluded the information about him must have come from one man—Jens Grutermann. But did they know what he'd become and what he'd done since his return?

He had prepared an answer while he was in Scotland should a question about his absence come. A verifiable answer, but a lie.

The abuse made him struggle to get the words out. "I went to fish. Had to feed my family."

"Where?"

"Lofoten."

"Who did you fish for?"

"Dagmar Holstein. Took me on as crew."

A fishing boat skipper by that name, indeed, lived and fished out of the Lofoten Islands. He had been a friend of Bjørn's father. From Scotland, Bjørn had sent word to Holstein that he might need his help corroborating an alibi someday.

"How long were you there?"

"Year and a half."

"Why did you come back?"

"Didn't need me anymore."

Hearing from the translator, Wolter pursed his lips. He stood stationary while considering the explanation.

He shook his head and spoke to the translator. The translation came back.

"If you're lying, we told you what we'd do," the translator said, matching Wolter's heightened voice and spraying sputum into the air.

With a motion of his club-filled hand, Wolter ordered Bjørn to get up. The translator removed his handcuffs and spoke. "Lower your pants! Lower them!" Bjørn struggled to comply, and the translator muscled him to his feet. They ordered him to lay over the chair, exposing his bare buttocks. The translator then took the club from Wolter and pounded his backside until the translator's breath was heavy. With each blow, the pain grew more intense. Bjørn tried to show no emotion, but he couldn't hold back the agony and released a few groans.

When the beating stopped, he was ordered to stand. He struggled and had to tightly grip the chair. He awkwardly tried to pull up his pants. But he was off-balance, causing him to fall. The translator grabbed him firmly and pulled him upright.

"Stand." The order was stout.

Bjørn managed to get his pants up and cinch his belt. The two Gestapo men seized him, one on each side, keeping him upright with tight, painful grips. They pulled him down the hall. He lacked the strength and willpower to walk. The men shoved him inside a holding cell with open metal bars across the front and locked it. The force of their shove sent him slamming against the back wall. He crumpled on the floor of the cell.

Time passed before Wolter and his interpreter returned. Bjørn didn't know how long. He might have lost consciousness. He looked up. They were with another prisoner. Someone Bjørn knew.

———

In Bjørn's weakened condition, it took every effort to keep him from responding with emotion.

Truni. She stood right outside his cell. A Nazi captive. They had her and made her look at his sorry state.

She gasped. Her wide, watery eyes expressed fear.

The translator's question of Truni was to the point: "Do you know him?"

She gave a slight shake of her head. *"Nei."*

"You've never seen him?"

"Nei."

Bjørn was an unsightly mess. Bloody signs of torment showed. From what Bjørn could see, Truni herself showed no signs of abuse. He assumed her interrogation was yet to come, and he was anguished by her plight.

She had reacted as any prisoner would seeing someone in Bjørn's worked-over form. He didn't think her initial reaction gave up anything. She now stiffened and showed no emotion or empathy. The way she needed to. The Gestapo men were looking for signs that she knew Bjørn.

His native impulses made him desperate to defend his love and rush the two goons. How could he overpower them now? He was powerless. He was on the inside behind steel bars looking out. His body useless. It was a struggle to stand, let alone raise his arms above his shoulders. Bjørn was relieved she failed to show she knew him, but heartsick she was in custody.

The two men led her away, returned, and hustled him back to the interrogation room in the same rough manner that they had dragged him to the holding cell.

Another man waited for them in the room. Bjørn knew the look. He sized the man up quickly. Another Gestapo thug through and through. Short and squat but thick. His face was hard and his eyes were beady and set back in dark shadows. Bjørn thought his blood must run cold.

He wore a suit, not a uniform, and greeted them with a devious smile. The smile a playground bully would display before sucker punching another kid from behind.

Bjørn wondered if he was there to strike the fatal blow. Was Bjørn minutes or an hour from the end of his life? So far, he had revealed nothing. Would they give up on him, end it here and discard him in an unmarked grave?

"This is Herre Gartner," Wolter said, this time in Norwegian. He emphasized it as if he wanted Bjørn to remember his abusers' names.

Gartner removed his suit coat and hung it over the back of the chair near the blackboard. He moved forward, leaned in close to Bjørn, and said, in perfect Norwegian, "Are you ready to talk?"

Bjørn said nothing.

Gartner backstepped and then cracked the left side of the prisoner's mouth with his fist. The punch split Bjørn's lip, which spurted blood, and loosened a front tooth. He felt woozy and thought he might fall. But he kept his footing.

"Wipe the blood from your mouth," Gartner demanded. Even that required effort, but Bjørn complied.

Gartner seized the club from Wolter, and he slammed it across Bjørn's chest with a loud thwack. He dropped to the floor.

"Get up." Gartner's voice was harsh and unforgiving.

Wolter and the translator interceded, pulling Bjørn up as he struggled. Gartner then whipped the baton back and forth high on Bjørn's shoulder. The prisoner fell again. The pain was sharp and excruciating.

The scene repeated itself. No more questioning. Pure brutality. Bjørn dropped and was pulled back up. Finally, he stayed down.

As Bjørn lay on the floor semi-curled up, Gartner used the club to beat him everywhere on the torso and extremities. Nothing seemed spared. He drifted in and out of consciousness. Then he was out cold. He felt the splash of water being poured on him.

When Bjørn came to, he was surprised to find the pain had subsided. He felt numb all over. Perhaps it was shock and his body's defense mechanisms taking over. He saw blood splashed around him, evidence that they had done serious damage. He ran his tongue around his mouth to check for missing teeth. A couple seemed loosened.

"You have been very foolish," Wolter said in Norwegian and in a tone more subdued than previously. "In time, you will tell us what you've done and what you know."

Bjørn could claim satisfaction that he said nothing. After what he'd endured, it was little consolation. But it was something.

———

He was transported back to his cell at the Bergen Kregfengsel by the same two agents who'd brought him to Gestapo head-quarters. In his cell, the pain returned. He shunned his cot. He couldn't lay or sit on it comfortably. He just lay still on the cold cell floor where he was deposited by guards. He could feel pain in his abdominal area. Kidneys? Liver? He didn't know which, but he wondered about the damage.

A heavyset jailer opened his door, and peeked in. "All right," he said. "We need to get you cleaned up."

He lifted Bjørn off the floor and cradled the inmate in his arms. The guard carried him down the cellblock corridor and then a flight of stairs. It was painful to be carried. Bjørn was limp and unable to move on his own.

This jailer's touch was gentle. He exercised care like he had seen the abuse before. He helped Bjørn out of his clothes and sponged him off with a cold, wet cloth. As he did, he whispered, "The Germans are no good. Hitler will fall. They're all cowards. You are the brave one." He repeated it again.

"Your name?" Bjørn's tone was thin.

"Knut."

He decided to risk the possibility that the guard was loyal to the king. "Is there a woman, Truni, here?"

The jailer shrugged his shoulders.

"If you see her, tell her I'm sorry. And I love her."

CHAPTER 32

Early November 1944

The German military lorry pulled to a stop along a narrow street somewhere in Oslo. Bjørn craned his neck, hoping to see his surroundings out the back. The truck had transported him and twenty-one other prisoners from the city's train station, but he had no idea where he was now. A dark-gray canopy covering the bed of the vehicle narrowed his view.

He was able to see a handful of armed German soldiers standing near the truck. One of them with a rifle slung over his shoulder approached the back and dropped the wooden rear gate.

"Out, get out, get out," he shouted.

Bjørn and his fellow prisoners scrambled out. Like the other inmates, his hands were handcuffed in front of him. For Bjørn, it should have been a simple four-foot hop down to the pavement. But in his weakened, abused condition, he faltered when his feet absorbed the shock of hitting the ground. He collapsed to his knees and gritted his teeth at the pain. He felt bruises all over his body. He thought a rib or two were broken. And some teeth had been loosened by the Gestapo beatings in Bergen.

He awkwardly levered himself upright and looked around. A handful of soldiers holding rifles and ready to aim formed a three-quarter circle around the truck. There was no escaping this formation.

"Velkommen til Møllergata 19," the soldier who issued the "get out" order shouted in Norwegian.

Bjørn winced. Hearing the notorious address, Møllergata 19, struck him with dread. He knew of this place. He'd been told all about it. Now Bjørn wondered whether it might be the last place he'd ever see.

A light rain mixed with a few snowflakes greeted him. Given his now-constant throbbing pain from the repeated beatings, the cold air numbed his bruises and cuts. He embraced shivering.

Bjørn glanced up at a large block building before him. The prison structure was like the weather, dreary and cold. Four stories of featureless stone and concrete. Each story was lined with small windows, just big enough for daylight to seep in. There was nothing distinct about the building. It was a purely institutional design. An ideal setting for Nazi torment, he thought.

For three-quarters of a century, Møllergata 19 had been a respectable address, serving as Oslo's city jail. It was connected to a stately structure that once was home to the city police and municipal court system. The Germans had converted it to house their dreaded security police, Sicherheitspolizei. SiPo, as it was called, was the umbrella organization overseeing the Gestapo.

The Germans converted the municipal jail into a prison for individuals whom the Nazis considered the most serious threats to their rule. Møllergata 19 now carried the reputation of a dungeon. From Bjørn's military briefings in England, he had learned that many Norwegians held here were never heard from again.

Bjørn's arrival at the prison had marked the end of a miserable overnight trip. He had been rousted from his jail cell in Bergen the night before and bused with a few other inmates he didn't know to the central train station. They had boarded a railcar, joining a larger group. He then was among twenty-one inmates headed to a destination unknown to them.

The overnight rail trip had wreaked havoc on his pained body with every jolt and jostle of the train. He and the others had only hard wooden benches to sit on. He hadn't been able to get comfortable, let alone sleep.

Bjørn hadn't talked to any other prisoners, and they hadn't talked to him. Few words were exchanged by anyone. He wondered if everyone's thoughts were the same as his. His focus had been concerns for himself and others as well as the uncertainty of what came next.

He had wondered what happened to Jonas and Anton Seversen. Why weren't they on the train with him? They must have faced the same questioning under the same Gestapo methods he'd endured. Did they survive it?

Bjørn had worried about Truni. He hated to think about the horrors she must have faced. As the train had rolled on, he had bowed his head and said a short prayer. "Please, Lord, let her live to see the future."

Surely, he had thought, the Gestapo had pushed Truni hard, attempting to have her give him up. The evil goons must have suspected some connection between them. Why would they bring her to his cell? But so far, there was no indication she had talked. Then again, he hadn't been sure about anything. Everything had posed a question mark.

In the morning hours, as the train had slowed to a stop, Bjørn had seen a sign for Oslo station. Only then did he realize his destination, the capital city. Now here he was, outside the infamous Nazi prison. As Bjørn waited to enter, he was certain about one thing. He faced more interrogations and suffering.

In Bergen, after the first interrogation and torture session by Wolter and Gartner, Bjørn had been delivered from the city jail to Gestapo headquarters repeatedly to face those same tormentors.

He had lost count of how many subsequent rounds of questioning and beatings he had suffered through. They all seemed to blur together. He could only guess at how long he had been in the Bergen city jail. *At least a week,* he thought, *maybe two.* Through all the kicks, punches, and strikes with a blackjack, Bjørn had revealed nothing of his activities and had not implicated others. He had stayed true to himself.

Now that he was in Oslo, he feared that the Gestapo here had found out who he was and what he had done. If they suspected him as a Kompani Linge commando code-named Ram, surely torture would get worse than the Bergen beatings. And he certainly would die.

———

There were three of them in a cramped cell on the prison's third floor. Bjørn and two others were jammed into a space slightly bigger than a closet. The cell was encased within pale-gray concrete ceiling and walls. The cell door's small frame of steel bars was the only opening. A tiny window on the back wall provided the only indication of night or day. Screened with tight checkered metal bars, it was too high to give them a view of the world outside.

Two-tiered metal bunk beds with thin mattresses stood flush against two sides of the cell, leaving a narrow space in the middle and minimal room to move around. There were no chairs or furniture of any kind. No sink to wash up, nor any plumbing. They shared a bucket to defecate. It got replaced every couple of days.

Bjørn's inmate number, 1338, was ink-printed on a flimsy piece of cloth that was sewn on the right chest of his prison garb, white coveralls with blue stripes. For the first few days, he was alone in the cell. Then the other two cellmates arrived days apart. They exchanged first names and hometowns, but little else. None wanted to say anything about their backgrounds or what they might have done to get there. Bjørn learned in his Scotland training of a Gestapo tactic of planting prisoners in cells to ferret out information. In exchange, the snitches received extra food or favors. His commando instructors had hammered home that he should trust no one if he were arrested.

Bjørn didn't feel like talking anyway.

———

After his cellmates' arrival, Bjørn watched in horror as they were seized by prison guards and hauled off. They were returned early the next morning bloodied, battered, and in pain. He spent agonizing hours and days waiting for his turn.

Then it came. He was awakened by footsteps, and two figures appeared in front of the cell door. Bjørn's eyes grew large. He could only see shadowed silhouettes at the door. It was dark in the cell except for subdued light shining through the bars from the corridor. He dug his upper teeth into his lower lip. They could be no one else but guards.

Heavy keys were shoved into the lock and the door clanged open. His fellow inmates rustled their thin bedcovers. Who were they after? The guards knew. Both went right for Bjørn. They pulled him out of his bunk and bound him in handcuffs. He winced. His body still wore the effects of its abuse in Bergen.

The guards hustled him out of the prison's front door to a waiting car and two plain-clothed thugs. *Just like in Bergen,* he thought. Bjørn had little doubt where he was going and who would be waiting for him.

It was a quiet ride. No one spoke. It was not long, either. The vehicle pulled in front of a stately four-story building. Even in the darkness of night, Bjørn saw enough to recognize it. Victoria Terrasse, Gestapo headquarters. He knew it from the photos he saw during commando training. He knew all about what had been occurring within its walls.

Victoria Terrasse, another place that had seen better times. Built in the late 1800s, it was a fashionable apartment for the well-to-do of Kristiania, as Oslo was called until 1925. Even famed Norwegian playwright Henrik Ibsen once lived there.

When the Nazis took over, they had moved in the Gestapo. The building had taken on a sinister reputation as another chamber of horror. A few prisoners were known to have jumped from the fourth-story windows to their death instead of facing interrogation and torture.

Once they entered the building in an open lobby, the Gestapo men who drove Bjørn there followed him up two flights of stairs. As he climbed, Bjørn felt a firm shove in the back by his handlers to pick up the pace. They deposited him in a third-floor room.

The room was stark and windowless with only a table and chairs. There were two men. One sat behind the table and with an outstretched arm directed Bjørn to stand across from him. The other man stood at one end of the table.

Both were dressed in suits, plain and dark. The one who sat introduced himself as Fehmer. Bjørn assumed it was his last name. Fehmer spoke Norwegian, but Bjørn heard an accent he suspected was German.

Fehmer opened a file and studied it. He then lifted his head and with shadowy, ice-cold eyes held a stare on his prisoner.

"Take off your clothes," came his sudden command.

Bjørn did as he was told and stood naked before the two men. His body still showed the welts and bruising from his earlier beatings. The once-muscular frame had begun to thin from a starvation diet and inactivity.

Fehmer showed no surprise as he sized up Bjørn's condition. "I see you have been through this before." Bjørn saw squinty eyes looking up at him with a sinister smile. "So you understand

what we do when you don't tell us what we want to know." The
Nazi then made a sudden move up, scraping his chair back. "Or
if you lie."

Fehmer's demeanor flashed into anger. "Your life means nothing to us. You are no more important to us than piss on the floor.
If we cut off your ear, we're taking off a dog's ear. If we take out
your eye, it's a dog's eye. Your only chance to stay whole and avoid
pain is to tell us what we want to know.

"We know your organization. That we have proven. We don't
need your confession. We want you to tell us who else belongs
to it.

"Tell us, please, to save yourself." The last statement was
polite, but it carried the weight of the blackjack Fehmer's partner
held in his right hand.

Bjørn read the words as a bluff. He convinced himself that
they knew nothing about him. The sabotage, weapons cache,
assassination. Nothing. He now was firmly convinced that Jens
Grutermann was behind his arrest, fingering him without knowing any of his activities. It was nothing more than that. The
Gestapo could prove nothing. Because of Grutermann, he had
suffered greatly and might well die.

Bjørn stuck to his story. "All I am is a farmer," he told them. "I
am nothing more than that. I've done nothing that you say."

The man who held the blackjack went to work. He moved rapidly toward Bjørn and smacked him across the back. The inmate
felt a painful shock through his entire body and the sensation
that he had no air to breathe. He collapsed to the floor.

He was pulled up, and Fehmer again demanded names of
other resistance workers. This time, Bjørn answered with a weak
headshake. It produced another hit that dropped him again. Next
came boot kicks hard enough to inflict bruises and breaks to his
already-cracked ribs. When Bjørn suffered the rubber baton's
whack to the back of his head, he lost consciousness.

When he came to, the accomplice pulled him up. Bjørn felt groggy and weightless. He had to be held up. Fehmer slapped him hard across the face.

"The next time, you must tell us things. It's the only way to save yourself." His tone told Bjørn that, for now, the Nazi was resigned to getting no answers.

Bjørn's escorts appeared and hauled him away, dumped him in the rear seat of the car, and took him back to Møllergata 19. The pain was unrelenting and the throbbing in his head was excruciating. Fehmer and his fellow Gestapo thug proved just as deranged as his Bergen tormenters, he thought.

He downsized his judgment of the Gestapo. They offered no evidence they knew of his commando activities. Their brutality may have proved effective at forcing other captives to confess and give up names. But they seemed inept at compiling evidence. If they suspected someone, they assumed that individual was guilty. Guilt or innocence was immaterial.

For days afterward, Bjørn found it difficult to even make the slightest movement. He just lay in his bunk. Pain was constant, particularly around his rib cage. His headache was nonstop.

In subsequent days and weeks, he was delivered again and again to Victoria Terrasse. Questioning continued, accompanied by more beatings, compounding his misery. Like in Bergen, the later sessions didn't seem to him as brutal as the first one. Perhaps, he thought, they wanted to keep him alive in hopes of breaking him. They seemed to see him as someone with information they wanted. Bjørn wondered how much longer he could hold out.

—

January 1945

The morning's first light seeped into the cell. Bjørn shivered in cold, dank air. One thin blanket made of paper was woefully insufficient to keep him warm. The damp chill signaled winter, but he had no idea of the month.

He and his two cellmates stirred at the sound of a guard's approaching footsteps. The guard unlocked the door and swung it open. He was big and burly, a stature ideal for a prison custodian. The three inmates made futile efforts to disappear under their flimsy covers.

"1338, put on your shoes, now," the guard said.

"Where am I going?"

"Say nothing. I only know that I have been ordered to fetch you."

He did what was ordered and accompanied the jailer out the cell door, fighting to stay upright.

When they reached the first floor, he was joined by eight other prisoners. They were handcuffed before shuffling out the lone prison door to the street. There was a guard for each inmate. Nine for nine. The guards, who usually were unarmed, all holstered pistols. This summons was different. The change of routine unnerved Bjørn.

A fresh thought consumed him. Was he going to his grave?

Outside, Bjørn and the others were greeted by a genuine Oslo winter. Biting cold. A light breeze compounded the frigid sting. Several inches of snow covered the ground, and light flakes were falling. The prisoners were marched down the left side of the prison building. Where the building ended stood a large courtyard enclosed by a ten- to twelve-foot-high concrete wall. The captives were ushered in.

The courtyard was roughly half the size of a *fotball* field. It was stark. The ground was covered by snow, though a few taller blades of grass managed to protrude through the white. An exercise yard? Bjørn wasn't sure.

At first glance, Bjørn didn't recognize the other prisoners. Suddenly, he picked out one. The man he knew only as Hammer. His colleague had been arrested. Like him, Hammer looked different. Bjørn knew him as a warrior with a strong determination. Now, he was starved, beaten, and worn. His face had no life. When at last Hammer noticed Bjørn, he looked away.

The guards who escorted them to the courtyard took the prisoners to a far wall. As they neared the wall, Hammer and Bjørn got close to each other. In a low-pitched voice, Hammer told his fellow commando, "I didn't give you up."

"Me, either," Bjørn whispered.

The guards chained the cuffs holding his hands behind him to a ring protruding from the wall. The same was done to the others. They were spaced between five and six feet apart. He looked back at the wall and saw pockmarks and divots. Small chunks of concrete littered the base of the wall, mixed in with the snow. Bjørn realized what was about to occur. Others had died on the ground where he stood. Now it was his turn to die.

The rest of the prisoners appeared to have figured it out, too. But there were no cries, tears, or pleas for mercy. The Norwegians stood stoically as they were hooked to the wall, their faces washed out as if they were already dead.

Final thoughts flashed through Bjørn's head. Would Åsta learn of his fate? He thought of Truni and wanted her to survive. Every other care drifted from his mind. He no longer felt the frigid elements.

The prisoners stood motionless at their assigned spots for several minutes. Bjørn was transfixed. He felt no fear. A sense of calm came over him. *How strange*, he thought. It would be over soon.

A group of uniformed, rifle-toting German soldiers marched into the yard led by an officer. Nine of them. The execution squad. They stopped about twenty paces in front of the prisoners and turned to face them. They unshouldered their rifles and held the weapons stiffly, diagonally across their chests. The guards approached the prisoners and draped black hoods over their heads.

Blinded by the hood, all Bjørn heard was someone barking orders in German. Suddenly, he felt his hood being removed and his handcuffs unchained from the wall. Two guards yanked him away. One other prisoner also was pulled from the lineup.

Bjørn trembled. He was at a loss for an explanation. His eyes blinked wildly. Everything was a blur. He couldn't feel his legs and stumbled forward. The guards literally were carrying him to stand near the officer and the other guards. He still believed he would die.

The German officer spoke to one of the guards in German, and the guard called out in Norwegian to the prisoners against the wall. "Any final requests?"

A single voice sounded. "Take off my hood."

"*Ja,*" another followed.

The German officer nodded to the guards. Hoods were removed from all seven left at the wall.

The soldiers now faced their victims, eye to eye.

Rifles were aimed. Bjørn kept his head directed toward the prisoners. He didn't look away, but he closed his eyes. He couldn't bear the coldhearted bloodshed. The order was given and rifle shots echoed off the wall. The loud snap of rifle fire forced his eyes wide open.

It was over quickly. But Bjørn saw cement splinters fly and seven men fall. He saw Hammer's head reel back and tear apart as the bullet struck. A head shot. His body dropped straight down, and he hung by his arms handcuffed to the wall. The others died much the same way.

The soldiers shouldered their weapons. The officer pulled out his Luger pistol and stepped forward to inspect the carnage. He checked each man for life, and put a single bullet into one of the prisoners to ensure death.

Bjørn's legs gave out and he fell to the ground. A guard came over and lifted him, muttering in very audible Norwegian, "Stand up." When he perched upright, the guard's tone changed and, in a kinder voice, said, "You Norwegians. Brave men."

Bjørn was taken inside and back to his cell. His cellmates were curious why he had been suddenly taken away and opened up with questions. But he waved them off without a word. He fell to his mattress. He curled up, unmoving and silent. His spirit to live and to fight on was gone.

CHAPTER 33

February 1945

Bjørn drifted off to a short, light sleep before awakening to the dread of an anticipated trip to Nazi headquarters at Victoria Terrasse. At any minute, he expected to hear the boot steps of guards pounding the concrete corridor toward his cell. He lay in his bunk wrapped in a thin blanket that refused to keep him warm. His eyes opened to darkness. He waited.

His restlessness had been like that every night in the few weeks since his last Gestapo interrogation and beating. The interrogations had stopped, and guards no longer appeared at the cell door in the dead of early morning. The nights now came and went without interruption. Even so, Bjørn's mind still seemed programmed to keep him edgy and restless. He couldn't shed the anticipation of another Gestapo ordeal.

Following that cold morning when he had been led out to the firing squad and forced to watch other prisoners die, he had faced three more Gestapo inquisitions. He had thought them not as severe as his earlier interrogations. But the battering from these sessions had had its effects. His body still ached, and blotches of black, blue, and red still covered parts of his body. But he noticed normal flesh tone gradually returning to his sagging skin.

Not only did he fear the night now, but Bjørn also channeled his anxiety to the morning's first light. He anticipated that guards would arrive and march him to the same courtyard in front of the same squad of killers. He pictured himself chained to the wall staring at the barrel of a Mauser Karabiner bolt-action rifle. Every time he heard pounding boots along the prison corridor, he trembled.

However, prison custodians now came to his cell every few days only to exchange the waste bucket and the stench that went with it or to deliver an occasional meal amounting to next to nothing. They also entered his cell from time to time for inspections, demanding he and the other occupants stand at attention military style. The guards took human inventory, studying inmate numbers sewn on prison outfits and checking them off on a list. There wasn't much left to see of the malnourished prisoners.

Once every couple of weeks or so, the prisoners were allowed a single shower. Bjørn was marched down—it was more a weak amble—with other inmates, ordered to strip and to hurry through the cold water flowing down on him. Barely enough to get wet, let alone clean, but it was something. There were no towels. He and the others had to stand in the cold and shake off a little bit before putting their prison clothes back on.

The prison population had expanded. One of his cellmates had overheard a guard saying Møllergata 19 had more than 500 inmates in a jail built for about 150.

Four prisoners now shared the cell with him. Bjørn's cellmates more readily identified themselves. There were Torlief Karlsen, a fisherman from Stavanger, and Karsten Kjelberg, a teacher from the small village of Stabekk west of Oslo. They were Bjørn's original cellmates. Olav Saarlof, a laborer from Kongsberg, came next. Later, Bjarne Woldsnes of Oslo arrived. They, too, were badly banged up from their own interrogations and beatings.

To accommodate five, two crudely built bunk beds stood on each side of the cell. For Woldsnes, a worn mattress was thrown on the floor in the middle. Bjørn kept his bunk on the lower left side. The waste bucket was placed at the end against the wall. There was no privacy for anything.

With the disappearance of nightly beatings, Bjørn found himself more freely conversing with his cellmates, and they with him. The fear of snitches had seemed to subside. Bjørn let down his guard and described his farm at Erlikvåg. He spoke nothing of his flight to England and service with Kompani Linge. He assumed his cellmates were involved in some form of resistance work. Why would they be imprisoned in such a notorious place as Møllergata 19 if they weren't? But, like him, they only talked about themselves, not their activities. Their conversations helped crack the boredom of inactivity.

Time in prison meant nothing. Bjørn and his cellmates lost track of it. The month, the day of the week, and the specific time all ran together. A two-foot-square window high on the back wall became the clock. But it showed them only whether it was night or day. Kjelberg began keeping track of days by ripping a razor-thin piece of coarse brown toilet tissue. But he eventually gave up from disinterest.

The inmates had little or no sense of what was happening in the outside world. News dribbled in on rare occasions. When Woldsnes was added to Bjørn's cell in February 1945, he brought fresh snippets of developments in the war. He said Allied forces crossed the Rhine River at a place called Remagen. The good guys were on German soil. Russian forces were approaching from the north. It was just a matter of time before Nazi Germany fell.

Prisoners developed methods to communicate with inmates in cells around them. A shoe became a tool to send messages in Morse code. They would stand at the cell door's bar-covered opening to tap and slide the shoe's toe, creating letters and words.

Three quick taps meant the next word. They used it almost every night as soon as the window showed darkness. One night, they heard a message from a nearby cell: "Italy falls, Mussolini dead."

Food arrived once a day if it came at all. Portions were minuscule, usually one raw herring preserved in salt and a small potato for each prisoner. As a farmer, Bjørn recognized the potato had been frozen, which turned it black. Then it was boiled. By the time it reached them, it was cold.

The inmates quickly learned the best way to eat herring. They ate it whole, bones, guts, and all. There was no knife or fork to separate the meat. The rations of food were so meager, prisoners needed every part of the fish. Even the innards provided nutrition. They ate the head first, the toughest part to get down. They moved with small bites to the tail, which was the last piece consumed.

Woldsnes at first couldn't fathom eating the insides of the herring. He went to great lengths to tear the flesh with his fingers so he would pick off the small amount of meat. He couldn't bring himself to eat the head, tail, and guts.

"If you're going to do that, give me the rest," Karlsen told him.

Woldsnes did initially. But as hunger gnawed at him, he devoured the entire fish like the others.

Sometimes when their hunger grew too much to endure, they tore off toilet paper and stirred in a small amount of what little water they received. It created a mush-like texture for them to eat.

Bjørn faced hunger philosophically. People who didn't have to skip many meals had no concept of starvation and unrelenting hunger, he reasoned. Under normal circumstances, hunger is considered a good thing. A good appetite exists, the human body desires food and prepares to receive it and burn it. But when you cannot satisfy hunger, it stays with you like a despised constant companion. It becomes a form of torture. It forces you to accept any food no matter the type, amount, or condition.

When Bjørn fell sick, he tried to prevent vomiting. To survive, he had to hold in whatever nourishment he ate. What he did get was never satisfying and fell far short of what his body demanded.

The air was cold and stuffy with the stench of sweat, human waste, sickness, and death. It smelled of human bodies wasting away. Anyone entering the cellblock fresh from the street would certainly retch. But starvation and inactivity dulled the inmates' senses. Bjørn didn't even notice the foul, putrid air anymore. When he could smell the ripe conditions, he tried to recall another smell, the salty sea air carried by a light breeze from Osterfjord up to the farm. He longed to breathe that kind of air again.

Bjørn kept his brain stimulated through reflection. He questioned what inhabited the minds of Gestapo agents. Why had the interrogations suddenly stopped? Why had they kept him alive when he gave them nothing? Had they believed his story? Had he fooled them? Then again, perhaps his execution would come any day.

With the Nazis facing a final crushing blow, Bjørn pondered whether their thirst for blood was dissipating. He didn't really believe that, though. They stopped the beatings but continued the torture by letting him waste away in prison. A skeletal frame surfaced through what once was thick muscle mass. There didn't seem to be any bulk beneath the skin. They were carrying out a gradual execution through starvation. They were positioning his body so he was unable to hold off sickness under such putrid conditions. The Nazis now didn't need a firing squad. They could save their bullets and still achieve the same result.

Bjørn's mind rekindled flashbacks of watching Hammer die from a firing squad's bullets. He was curious about his fellow commando. He knew virtually nothing about him. Hammer's real name. His home and family. What he did. Bjørn didn't consider him a friend. But they had shared experiences as commandos and with Nazi interrogation and imprisonment.

Bjørn agonized over the welfare of his own family and friends. Åsta, Arne, and Jon. The fate of Jonas and Anton Seversen. He even wondered how trawler captain Anders Kongsgaard fared in shuttling refugees, commandos, and supplies back and forth across the North Sea. He owed the skipper a debt of gratitude.

Bjørn harbored most of his concern for Truni's predicament. He so wanted her to live and be spared from the brutality and abuse he suffered. Bjørn frowned and his eyes closed tight when he thought of her. He loved her but realized she likely would never forgive him for his sabotage. Would it matter anyway? He probably would never leave Møllergata 19 alive.

Many times, he had believed dying while imprisoned was not only inevitable, but it would come soon. He had recognized his body was creeping toward death. Sometimes he had willed for it to happen. Get it over with. But whenever his thoughts had turned to Truni and his family and friends, he yearned to live and see them again.

The information reaching him and his cellmates gave them hope an end to the war was near.

But which would end first—the war or his life?

CHAPTER 34

May 7, 1945

Bjørn was awakened by an escalating commotion outside his cell, a fast-paced stomping of boots bounding down the corridor. He awkwardly rolled his aching body over and stared at the cell door. In a blur of activity, a guard unlocked it and swung it wide open before his pounding footsteps moved on. Bjørn then heard the clang of another door unlocking and, after that, others in quick succession.

He scratched the whiskers on his sunken, craggy face. Strange activity for guards. Something was afoot. He glanced at Woldsnes, who lifted his head from the mattress on the floor and looked at Bjørn, ruffling his eyebrows inward.

Bjørn heard Saarlof rustle his bedcover in the bunk above. His voice sounded wary. "What is it? What's happening?"

"Don't know," Bjørn said.

He slid to the edge of his bunk and swung his feet onto the floor. His legs flinched when he put weight on them. He thought they might give out. But he maintained enough strength to shuffle past Woldsnes and reach the open door. In a gradual motion, Bjørn leaned forward and popped his head out for a look down the cellblock corridor. Other inmates started emerging from their cells to do the same. Up and down the corridor, there was not a guard in sight.

Bjørn turned back to his fellow captives. They remained in their bunks staring at him, frozen within the familiar confines of their cells.

"What do you see?" It was Saarlof again. Bjørn just shook his head. He was too consumed by his thoughts to answer.

In the corridor, more inmates began to congregate. It seemed no one was there to order them back in their cells. Quizzical voices rose as more prisoners filtered out. Bjørn spotted several either crawling out or, unable to stand, being held up.

Bjørn reset his feet and shuffled out the door onto the wide third-floor balcony. He managed to reach the balcony railing, gripping it as tightly as he could to steady himself. His cell-mates eventually followed his lead and crept out single file. Their mouths hung open. It appeared to Bjørn they were free to mingle in the corridor.

Bjørn turned back to the railing and glanced at a large, open, indoor courtyard below that was ringed by four floors of cells. The courtyard was nothing more than a concrete floor. No vegetation, no benches or chairs. Only dull-gray cement.

He watched a steady stream of inmates assemble on his floor and those above and below his third-story cellblock. The growing numbers looked around with the same eager curiosity he was showing.

Then directly across, one floor above him, a man in a well-appointed double-breasted suit appeared in the center of the balcony. He didn't look Gestapo. The man had Scandinavian features. He was of medium build with a square face, flat forehead, and puffy pink cheeks. His dark hair was combed straight back, and a pair of black glasses sat on his nose. Bjørn placed him in his forties.

The man picked up a megaphone that was wired to an ampli-
fied loudspeaker. "Could I get your attention," he called out in a
dialect of Swedish. His voice reverberated throughout the prison
blocks. "I wish to speak to you. Please give me your attention."

On all floors, the noise from the now-crowded balconies
faded to a low hum.

"My name is Harry Söderman. I'm a Swedish policeman who
has temporarily assumed the duties of police chief here. I have
the privilege to announce to you that the war is over. German
forces have agreed to cease hostilities. You are all now free."

The inmates hung on his words in complete silence for several seconds. Then a low mumble surfaced in a whispered pitch.
There was no cheering or shouting.

"This must be a trick?" Bjørn heard someone say.

Söderman continued. "At ten fifteen last night, Lieutenant
General Franz Böhme, commander of German forces in Norway,
announced the termination of military operations. He ordered
his soldiers to put down their arms."

Bjørn released a large breath. His head felt light. A rising
murmur of voices surfaced from the cellblocks. Söderman raised
his free hand, appealing for silence.

"Attention, please, it is important for you to understand what
I say," he said. "We are presently making arrangements to release
you from this prison. I ask you to be patient. There are many of
you and it will take time. We have documents that need to be
filled out and signed by you. And you will need to pick up articles
of clothing and personal possessions that have been kept for you.

"Outside this jail, we will have buses waiting for you. They
will take you to Grini." His reference to the Grini prison camp
raised a dull buzz from the once-hushed prisoners. Grini, too,
was notorious thanks to the Nazis. Söderman once again admonished the prisoners that he needed their full attention.

A COAT DYED BLACK

"The prisoners from Grini are being released from there. We need this jail for those who have committed crimes against Norway and against you. We must take you to Grini because we have doctors there to look at you. Some of you may need to go to the hospital from there.

"We will provide what food and water we can for you. You have been starved here. So we can give you only as much food as your bodies can handle. Finally, we will need to arrange transportation to return you to your homes.

"I know these have been difficult"—Söderman's voice caught in his throat as he paused to take in the faces of prisoners near him—"most difficult days for you. I wish you all good days ahead. Thank you."

With that, Söderman stepped back from the rail and disappeared into the crowd. For Bjørn, his fellow prisoners, and the whole of Norway, the five-year tyrannical nightmare was ending.

——

The prisoners were free men now. There was no loud jubilation at Söderman's announcement. With most everyone out in the corridor, Bjørn saw firsthand evidence of the size of the prison population. Hundreds of inmates. Most everyone appeared in the same condition. Their skeletal frames moved at a sluggish pace.

Along the cell blocks, they lined up in single file in front of their cells just as they were ordered to do when headed to the shower during incarceration. This time, as Söderman directed, they trundled down the stairs to the ground floor to process out of Møllergata 19. Many needed help staying upright, and the going was slow.

On the ground floor, they reassembled in long lines in the indoor courtyard, queued up in front of a scant handful of tables.

Haggard human figures in identical garb melded together in one massive cluster of prison whites with blue stripes.

Sitting behind the tables were the same guards and other prison officers who'd confined them. They wore familiar custodial uniforms. Bjørn no longer found the guards menacing. They appeared humbled, timid, and even polite as they questioned prisoners, filled out documents, and sent their former charges on their way.

The wait was painstaking. Bjørn shuffled forward at a slug's pace. His patience was waning. But he and the others stayed with it. It was all they could do. Every step toward the tables got them closer to freedom.

Several weak prisoners collapsed. Women with white armbands tended to them. Some of the weaker prisoners were helped to the front of the line, and chairs were commandeered for them to sit on while they waited for paperwork to be completed. Prisoners ahead of them in line yielded without complaint.

Ahead of Bjørn, several men armed with Sten guns stood ten to fifteen paces behind the tables manned by the former Nazi captors. They were Norwegians. Recalling the citizen army he had recruited and armed before his arrest, he assumed the armed men belonged to similar groups and were there to keep watch over the Nazis and maintain order if needed.

Bjørn, too, felt like his legs might give out. He worried that if he fell forward or back, he might create a domino effect and tumble bodies in front and behind him. Some men sat on the cold concrete and scooted forward. The thought of his release from prison seemed to buy Bjørn a little strength. And his cellmates lined up behind him took turns supporting him and each other.

At last, he reached the front. As he neared the desk, Bjørn pulled out a few sheets of the thin, rough-grained toilet paper he had stuffed in his pocket before leaving his cell. He then grabbed a pen from the table just ahead. He and his cellmates exchanged names and addresses by writing on the sheets.

"I will never forget you," he told them.

Just before his turn came, Bjørn overheard one of the guards telling another that he was growing tired and was taking a break. Another inmate heard it, too. As that guard began to rise from his chair, an inmate stepped up from another line, grabbed the guard by his collar, and shoved him back down in his chair.

"Keep on writing," the prisoner said. "We've been waiting a long time. You'll have plenty of time for rest later in the cell I had."

That brought several cheers from other inmates nearby. The men with weapons advanced a few steps from their positions but didn't intercede. The guard shrugged, lowered his head over the table, and resumed work.

———

Bjørn was stunned. He looked at it in disbelief. His watch. He got it back along with his wallet, a pair of pants, his shirt, and the black-dyed coat. The kroner in his billfold was gone. But the Nazis had stored the rest of his personal things and kept a record of them. He hadn't expected to see any of it again.

Moments earlier, he had given a Nazi custodian his personal information and signed a discharge paper. He had exchanged handshakes with his cellmates lined up behind him. He doubted he would ever see them again. Then he had shuffled to a nearby storage room packed with shelves. After saying his name and inmate number, another Nazi guard had retrieved his items from a shelf.

Before leaving the prison, he stripped out of his prison stripes and labored to put on his civilian clothes, cinching the belt as far as it could go around his bony waist. He ripped the inmate number from his prison garb and shoved it in his pocket. It and the names of his cellmates written on toilet paper were the only prison souvenirs that he thought might be worth keeping. He left his prison clothes on the floor where they dropped.

Bjørn put on his coat and trudged out the front door into the street. Mother Nature blessed liberation day with warmth and sunshine. He squinted in the sunlight. He didn't need his coat, but he kept it on anyway so he wouldn't have to carry it. Six months had passed since his arrest. Bjørn now was free.

His saunter was awkward. His body ached from all the unaccustomed standing and moving he had done waiting to get released. He was determined to make it on his own now.

Just outside the prison stood a small army of men in plain clothes and white armbands. Bjørn presumed they were resistance fighters. They were positioned in front of the building armed with Sten guns, Tommy guns, and pistols. Some of them stood behind several massive logs forming a barrier near the prison doors. Two grenade launchers were set up behind the logs.

The jubilant voices of a large celebrating crowd rang out. The revelers waved from down the street and held Norwegian flags high above their heads. For the first time since he had learned of liberation, Bjørn smiled.

Nearby, unarmed German soldiers milled around just outside the prison. They kept to themselves as if they had no place to go. He could only wonder what they were feeling. He didn't care. Some of the released inmates taunted the soldiers as they headed toward a line of buses. "Swine," they shouted. The soldiers showed no reaction.

Bjørn headed toward waiting buses that would take him to Grini. Step by step, he limped closer to them. Before he could make it, Bjørn's body succumbed to fatigue and weakness. He collapsed to his knees on the pavement. He rocked forward and caught himself with his hands.

He heard a voice next to him. "You all right?" He looked up and saw a resistance fighter shouldering a Tommy gun.

Bjørn acknowledged him with a nod.

The fighter's eyes were soft. "I can see you've suffered. Let me help you to the bus."

He gently lifted Bjørn to his feet with a firm and careful grip. "Are you Milorg?" the man said.

Bjørn was shaky and unsteady. "Kompani Linge."

The fighter showed a toothy smile. "Me, too. You were lucky to survive in there. So many of our comrades were executed."

Keeping his steadying grip on Bjørn with one hand, he used his free right hand to gently shake Bjørn's hand. "I'm Gunnar Sønsteby, number twenty-four, lead agent in Oslo. I go by Cheeks."

It took some effort for Bjørn to get his words out and introduce himself. He gave his number, eighty-three, and code name, Ram.

Sønsteby nodded in recognition. "Bergen?"

"*Ja*, near there." Bjørn meekly swung his arm and motioned to the other resistance fighters. "Why are you guarding the prison?"

"There were reports that some Nazis were going to storm it and try to kill as many of you as they could," Sønsteby said. "So, my gang hurried here, set up these barriers, and got ready to defend against that. Must have been just a rumor. No Nazis showed up.

"Now, we are under orders to arrest Nazis, both Germans and Norwegian traitors. We have an intelligence list prepared by our allies. We took the Nazi police chief of Oslo into custody this morning."

The Oslo-based agent studied Bjørn's condition. "I'll contact the commanding officers at Kompani Linge, let them know you're alive and that you'll be at Grini. I wish you a good recovery."

Sønsteby helped Bjørn board a bus for the Grini prison camp.

———

Bjørn spent just one day at Grini after his prison liberation. A doctor checked him and immediately moved him to a hospital. The physician told him he was only a week or two away from death.

"I don't see how you survived," the attending physician said. "It will take a considerable period to recover from your injuries. Your insides are damaged, and I believe your kidney function will be affected. You need a specialist."

Bjørn spent a week and a half at the hospital. Nurses injected fluids to nourish his body. He still felt weak, and his thin frame was shocking to him. But when he moved his limbs and turned over in bed, it became less of a chore. Doctors weren't ready to release him. They wanted further improvement before letting him travel home.

During his second week of hospitalization, the nurse announced he had a visitor. Bjørn looked up to see Konrad Brittvik standing in the doorway. The officer entered the room with his straight-up posture and stoicism and slid a chair beside Bjørn's bed. Two silver stars gleamed bright atop the striped green epaulets of his uniform. He had been promoted to lieutenant colonel.

With his usual military formality, Brittvik said that King Haakon VII had appointed him to an Allied delegation that had flown to Oslo the afternoon of May 8 to deliver the German occupiers conditions for their capitulation. Brittvik had helped to arrange the formal surrender, which had taken place later that day in Lillehammer, between German General Böhme and British Lieutenant General Andrew Thorne, temporary commander of Allied forces arriving in Norway.

"Gunnar Sønsteby told me he met you outside Møllergata 19," Brittvik said. "When I found out where you were, I wanted to see you."

Bjørn told Brittvik about witnessing the execution of fellow commando Hammer. In front of the officer, he kept his reserve. But he trembled at the memory.

"The Gestapo beat me up pretty good and tried to pull information out of me. I gave them nothing."

"Indeed, you paid a price for keeping your silence." Brittvik took a long pause. "But doctors say you'll eventually heal."

"I stood with Hammer facing a firing squad. For some reason, they pulled me out, but made me watch." Bjørn's throat tightened. "I keep asking myself why I was spared."

"You'll never know," Brittvik replied. "They've done that to others. Who knows why you and not someone else. Gestapo had their ways. They may not have known what you did, but they thought you had information they wanted. Holding your tongue probably saved your life."

Brittvik stared at Bjørn with serious focus. "There are some things that should remain unspoken. What happened to Herre Hoggemann will be classified. Do you understand?"

Bjørn returned the stare. *"Ja, jeg forstå."*

The colonel grabbed Bjørn's hand. "You should feel no regret," the officer said. "It had to be done. It saved lives."

Brittvik sprang to his feet. "Well, you need to rest." He turned and strode toward the door.

Halfway across the room, he stopped, pivoted, and faced Bjørn. "I forget to tell you that all Gestapo and SS members are being interned in Norway. They won't be allowed to return to Germany until their wartime activities have been evaluated. Those charged with crimes will be tried and sentenced here. So there will some justice for those who did this to you."

Brittvik straightened up and saluted Bjørn, who returned it with a weak raise of his arm. It wasn't the snappy salute an army lieutenant colonel might demand of someone with less rank. But when Bjørn saw his former commander initiate the salute, tears welled up in his eyes.

Bjørn was released from the hospital a week later. Before boarding a train at Oslo Central Station bound for Bergen, he put on the crisp new army uniform that Brittvik had supplied. Draped over his thin body, it looked rumpled. He didn't care about the fit. He proudly touched the lieutenant stripe on his shoulder. He added a crowning touch, a smart-looking beret.

When he examined himself in a mirror, he studied his face. He hardly recognized it. The shape looking back at him was sullen and gaunt. His cheekbones protruded from faded, translucent-appearing skin. The eyes were dark and recessed.

It was not the way he wanted people to see him, or how he wanted to see himself. But he was going home.

CHAPTER 35

May 28, 1945

Bjørn stood on the *rutebåt*'s foredeck as Erlikvåg came into view. The wind created by the moving boat swept back his dark hair. He raised his head and closed his eyes, inhaling a deep whiff of sea air. He was coming home a free man. The village, his farm, his family and friends, and his country were finally unshackled from Nazi tyranny.

He had been gone slightly more than six months after his arrest. It had felt excruciatingly long to him. A little more than three weeks had passed since his release from Møllergata 19. He still suffered the ill effects of an emaciated, mistreated body. Doctors told him his physical wounds would mend over time, but he likely would have lingering psychological effects. Haunting memories of imprisonment and torture were fresh. Bjørn feared he might never recover from those mental scars.

With every wave the boat sliced, his excitement grew. In prison, he had feared he would never see his family, friends, and the farm again. Now, he was certain his sister, Åsta, would be waiting at the dock. So would Inga, his sister-in-law, and niece, Kristi. They had faced no recriminations after his arrest. He had also learned that his brother, Arne, survived a concentration camp in Poland and would be headed home soon. The farm was intact. All welcome news since his release from prison.

He still had questions. What of the others? Jonas Seversen and his brother, Anton, who were arrested with him? Friend Jon, who escaped arrest? He was anxious to know how Truni fared.

As the *rutebåt* pulled into the Erlikvåg community dock, Bjørn readjusted the beret of his uniform. He caught sight of his welcoming delegation. Åsta and Inga were front and center. Kristi held a miniature Norwegian flag. Jon, too, was there, flanked by Jonas and a handful of villagers. There was no sign of Truni.

Bjørn's steps were short and wide as he fought to maintain balance down the gangway that bounced moderately with the waves. On the dock, a unified chant hailed him: *"Velkommen hjemme, velkommen hjemme."* Bjørn beamed. For the first time, he felt like a war hero.

Åsta greeted him first, gently wrapping her arms around him. He felt the pulse of her cry as she buried her head in his shoulder. Bjørn, too, failed to hold back tears in that moment of joy.

"God has given us a gift," she whispered. "You are that gift."

Bjørn pulled back from the embrace. Gripping her arms, his eyes met hers. "I love you, sister. You've been like a large stone holding everything in place."

His tongue moistened his cracked lips. "When will Arne be home?"

"It should be a week or so. He's now in Sweden. He's in good shape, good spirits."

Bjørn had been worried about his brother's health. He breathed a loud sigh, went to Inga, and hugged her. "I'm so relieved."

"Ja, these months have been terrible for us," she said.

Everyone formed a procession to greet him individually. He noticed tears in Jon's eyes. Jonas wore a broad smile showing his upper teeth. A front one was missing. The storekeeper's thin body and eyes sullen and set back revealed his own abuse at Gestapo hands. He told Bjørn that Anton had survived as well and was recovering at home.

Bjørn's handsome uniform could not conceal his own suffering. He had noticed Åsta's flinch when she'd first seen him. It was obvious his once-solid 215-pound frame built by vigorous military training now sagged. He knew his slow, unsteady gate couldn't go unnoticed.

"I'm going to take care of you," Åsta said. "But I warn you, I'll be strict. I expect you to do what I say."

Bjørn nodded and kissed her forehead.

He could wait no longer. "What of Truni?"

"She's home safe," his sister said. "She called last week and asked about you." His eyebrows lifted.

Åsta added, "I told her where you were and said you would call her when you came home."

Bjørn shoved out another deep breath. He felt dizzy and faint but held himself upright. "What happened to her?"

"She was at the Espeland concentration camp. They apparently were brutal to her. But like you, she survived. Her voice sounded traumatized. But, you know, she's strong. I think she'll be all right."

"I'd like to see her," he said. "But I don't want her to see me like this."

———

Even before Bjørn's return home, significant events in the war's aftermath had unfolded. After a warrant was issued for his arrest, Norwegian Nazi leader Vidkun Quisling had turned himself in the early morning of May 10, arriving at Møllergata 19 in a silver-plated Mercedes-Benz. His name already had become synonymous with the word "traitor."

From his hospital bed after his release from prison, Bjørn had listened to the live radio broadcast on May 12 when three British cruisers arrived in Oslo harbor. One carried Crown Prince Olav. He stepped ashore to a cheering crowd estimated at two hundred thousand.

The prince's home just southwest of Oslo at a place called Skaugum had been sullied during the royal family's exiled absence. Reichskommissar Terboven had occupied it since the beginning of Nazi rule. It was there that the ruthless Nazi administrator went to bed at about eleven p.m. on May 5, two days before the German surrender. Setting his spectacles on the nightstand, Terboven lay in bed with explosives beside him. The man who had led Nazi street gangs in the 1930s while his friend Adolf Hitler rose to power lit a three-minute fuse and blew himself up.

After Bjørn returned home, the Huldra had once again become a morning and evening companion for him and Åsta. It delivered a steady diet of postwar news. The radio was no longer hidden under a pile of potatoes in the basement and had taken its traditional place on the living room side table. The news came not only from the BBC but also NRK and Bergen radio, no longer outlets of Nazi propaganda.

On June 5, Bjørn and Åsta tuned in to a live broadcast of the homecoming of King Haakon VII aboard the British cruiser *Norfolk*, five years to the very day he had been forced to flee Norway on the same ship. In ceremonies at Akershus Castle, British General Thorne formally transferred power from Allied forces to Norway's constitutional monarch.

The king's return gave way to more exciting news that day. Inga received a telephone call from Arne. He had just arrived in Oslo from Sweden. He was to arrive in Bergen by train on the afternoon of June 6.

Inga, Kristi, and Åsta were there at Bergen station to greet Arne when he arrived. Bjørn stayed home to convalesce. Arne returned thin and malnourished, but without Bjørn's skeletal appearance. He hadn't suffered repeated beatings and torture. As Arne described it, his hardship was more psychological than physical.

In the ensuing days, the brothers spent a lot of time catching up. Arne reported he first was imprisoned in the Espeland camp south of Bergen for about two months following his arrest and then spent another month at Grini. He and the Bergen officers arrested with him became part of a larger contingent of more than 250 policemen rounded up throughout Norway and shipped to Stettin, Germany, aboard the ship *Donau*. That ship had gained notoriety earlier by transporting 540 Norwegian Jewish people to their deaths at concentration camps in Germany and Poland. Arne said he ultimately ended up at Stutthof concentration camp near Danzig.

At Stutthof, Arne said, the police officers were treated much better than Jewish and Romani prisoners. He and the others were housed in a special section of the camp overseen by a Danish SS officer. Arne felt fortunate that the Dane was not the strict disciplinarian that other SS officers were. But still, there was little to eat, and they were forced to work on farms.

"One morning, they marched us to the fields," he said. "We passed by bodies stacked and layered between pieces of wood. We were told later there wasn't enough capacity in crematoriums to dispose of all the dead prisoners. Germans piled up bodies, poured gasoline on them, and burned them. From the camp later, I could see smoke rising from the fields."

Bjørn saw torment and a faraway look in Arne's eyes.

Arne contacted diphtheria near the end of the war and was sick when the Germans moved him and the rest of his fellow prisoners as Russian forces closed in. He was marched toward

Germany, then was put on a barge and ended up in Nazi-occupied Denmark. Eventually they were liberated by British troops.

After the war's end, Arne and the others had spent time in Sweden, where they were kept in quarantine while being treated for their illnesses and diseases.

———

In the weeks since arriving home, Bjørn's physical condition crept back to strength despite many ups and downs of good days and bad. Åsta fulfilled her commitment to restore her brother's health. She had started him on a broth-only diet. She then had graduated to a soupy mix of mashed-up potatoes and soft vegetables. On occasion, she had served him small portions of fish. He refused herring. Memories of prison were too raw.

He got strong enough to stroll around the farm. Occasionally he would help with light chores. But he still needed frequent rest.

The farm was springing back to life. The large garden produced ample amounts of vegetables, enough to sell a share of produce through Jonas's store. Åsta had traded some produce for a rooster and a hen, and had built a small brood of chickens for eggs and supper-table poultry. The Erliksen farm had also been promised two piglets from a forthcoming litter on a neighboring farm.

Jon became a frequent visitor, and they renewed their companionship. He led Bjørn on short walks in the forest.

"I didn't know that you, Jonas, and Anton had been arrested until sometime later," Jon said during one of their strolls. "I had to flee quickly and had no idea what had happened. When I heard, I feared I would never see you again."

When the Nazis came to Erlikvåg, Jon said, they initially went to a house near the dock and commandeered one of the three cars in the village. Villager Johannes Rasvik was walking by when he overheard the Nazis' demand to use the vehicle. He had suspected that Jon and some others in the community were involved in resistance activities, and feared Jon was targeted. Rasvik had mounted his bicycle and pedaled for all he was worth on a short-cut path to the farm. He had arrived ahead of the Nazis to warn Jon of the danger.

Jon had fled into the woods with two weapons and some food. He scrambled up the tree-laden hillside and perched behind a large fir, watching the house from there.

He had benefitted from the Nazis' mistake of going to the wrong farm. They stopped at a place farther down the road and seized another guy named Jon. By the time the mix-up was cleared up and the Nazi team finally reached the intended farm, Jon was nowhere to be found.

He said the Nazis searched every room in his house with submachine guns drawn and found no incriminating evidence that might have put Liv and his son in jeopardy.

After the Nazis left, Jon had packed for a long stay away from the farm at a *hytte* deep in the mountains. He occasionally snuck home, but only to get food and necessities and briefly see Liv and Mikal.

One brutally cold winter day in January at his hideout, Jon said, a man had seen smoke rising from the forest and had stopped at his *hytte*. The man said he was going to a place called Stordalen in the Matrefjelle mountains, about fifty miles north of Bergen. The Norwegian commandos had established a base there.

Jon grinned. "Strangely enough, they called it Bjørn Vest, but I don't think they had you in mind, Bjørn."

Jon had accompanied the traveler to Stordalen and ultimately joined the resistance force, which had numbered 250 men.

"Just days before the end of the war, the Germans attacked us," he said. "We succeeded in holding them off. They had to retreat."

The Germans had attacked other places nearby, and he and other fighters were ordered to withdraw before the war ended, Jon said.

When Bjørn told of prison and interrogations, Jon's squinted eyes were solidly fixed on him. He remarked, "I can tell you suffered. You aren't yourself."

Bjørn dropped his head. "You're right. I'm not right in the head. At night, I'm filled with bad dreams. This may last the rest of my life."

"Time can be a good healer," Jon advised. "Give it a chance to work. And remember, you have a family who loves you. I love you as a brother. Don't forget that. We're all here to help."

———

Jonas also visited Bjørn. The storekeeper presented a bag of flour as a homecoming gift. Jonas limped from a broken hip suffered during Gestapo beatings. And one of his top teeth, indeed, was knocked out.

"I was shocked to see you on the boat during our arrest," Jonas said. "You kept a good secret from me."

Bjørn asked him why he and Anton were arrested.

"The best I can figure, it was from our efforts to feed people. I think you know about supplying the military-aged men in the mountains."

The storekeeper said he had a friend who operated a barge that took flour from a mill in Mellvaaga, a town in the northern reaches of Osterfjord. The mill owner was a quisling who ground wheat and barley he got from farmers, bagged the flour, and hired the friend's barge to transport it to Bergen.

"The miller paid the farmers next to nothing for their crops," Jonas said. "All the flour went to the Germans. The Nazis gave him a good price. I worked out an arrangement with my friend to stop his barge on the fjord near Ostereider. We sent a boat out to haul off bags of flour from each shipment, and we used the flour to feed people. I gave a little to Åsta.

"The Germans got wind of it when the miller realized that not all of his flour was reaching German hands. I got a visit from our quisling sheriff, who asked me about it. I denied everything, of course. Then the Gestapo came."

Bjørn clenched his teeth. "I believe Jens Grutermann was behind my arrest. He probably snitched on you and Anton. He's a traitorous bastard. He proved to be a dangerous man."

"That sounds about right," Jonas replied. He told Bjørn that he and Anton, too, underwent torturous interrogation in Bergen before being imprisoned at Espeland.

"Look at us, Bjørn," he said. "We suffered cruel treatment. But we're here, and we can hold our heads high. Jens Grutermann can only hang his."

———

Within a week of Jonas's first visit, the storekeeper returned, this time with two other elderly men. One of them looked familiar. Bjørn squinted and focused his gaze beneath the old man's puffy red cheeks and Saint Nicholas beard to place him. The man broke into a wide beam at being sized up. Bjørn's memory then clicked into gear.

"You're the ferry captain," he said.

Jonas chimed in. "*Ja*, and he has brought you something."

Bjørn's voice slid to a high pitch. "*Lensmann*?"

The old man nodded. His ever-widening smile further reddened his cheeks.

He reminded Bjørn who he was, Hjelmaar Ostlund. With him was his friend Erling, who owned an old fjord boat that had towed *Lensmann* down Osterfjord to Erlikvåg.

"I kept your name, so it was easy to find you," Ostlund told Bjørn. "Your boat is in pretty good shape even after these difficult years. A German officer had it. Used it for his own pleasure. Kept her in the same boathouse in Bolstad where the harbormaster stored her. The German officer took pretty good care of it."

They immediately left the farm and walked through the village to the boathouse that had been empty during the five-year German occupation. Bjørn opened the door and found the boat tied up. He let out a huge sigh. Its varnished surface looked faded and worn. But he saw no structural damage.

A small piece of Bjørn's torn life had been stitched.

———

Lindås District Sheriff Johan Asheim called on Bjørn for an official purpose. Asheim, who had been demoted and replaced by the quisling sheriff under Nazi rule, had been restored to his old position following liberation.

It also was Asheim who, as a deputy, had given Bjørn a key to the community center so that he and Jon could retrieve Nazi-confiscated radios from the loft.

Now in full police uniform, Asheim said he was there on instructions from the Bergen police chief to interview Bjørn about his captivity and interrogations. Asheim explained that the information from Bjørn and other prisoners would be used to prosecute Gestapo agents, SS, Stapo officers, and other conspirators who committed crimes against Norwegians and the state.

Entering Bjørn's living room, the sheriff pointed at the Huldra radio and chuckled. "Have you had it for long?"

Bjørn returned the smile. "*Ja*, and I must remember to thank the person who enabled me to have it."

The interview lasted an hour. Asheim fired many questions, requiring Bjørn to relive the pain of his interrogations. He was able to identify Wolter and Gartner, his primary interrogators in Bergen. The sheriff said both were in jail awaiting trial.

"Evidence against them of war crimes was piling up," Asheim said.

Bjørn also named Fehmer, the only tormentor he could identify at Victoria Terrasse. Asheim promised to forward the name to Oslo authorities.

He also told the sheriff his belief that Grutermann reported him to authorities. "I would like to have a talk with him."

Asheim leaned forward in his seat. "I strongly advise you not to see him. We're looking at him and what he's done. He will have to account for his actions. Stay away from him."

Bjørn gritted his teeth. He moved forward in his chair and started to speak. But he settled back and stayed silent. He replayed his thoughts from prison. He remembered how he had entertained himself thinking about what he would do to Grutermann if he survived. He had rehearsed in his mind how he would pulverize the Nazi's face with repeated punches. Disable both of Grutermann's knees by stomping on them with heavy boots. Bjørn had even envisioned slashing Grutermann's throat. He had killed one Norwegian Nazi. He could do it again. He wouldn't take pleasure in it. It would purely be out of vengeance.

Now, with Asheim waving him off any confrontation, he wondered whether it would be worth it. His thoughts in prison perhaps achieved what was needed, bolstering his will to survive. His days of challenging bullies in the schoolyard were behind him. He was no longer a commando. And he was in no condition to challenge a Nazi snitch.

Bjørn broke his silence. "All I want to do is tell Grutermann that I know he was the one who turned in me and the others. I wouldn't hurt him."

Asheim's eyes stayed focused on Bjørn. "If you were to see Grutermann, even to talk, nothing good could come of it. Stay away from him. Let us handle it. Let justice work."

Bjørn stared back at the sheriff, whose eyes stayed fixed on him.

"Promise me, Bjørn."

Bjørn frowned, but his eyes softened. "All right."

CHAPTER 36

August 1945

Bjørn stared into the mirror and realized a good transformation had been taking place. Restored muscle tissue stretched out his sagging skin. He had felt his strength return as his work activity around the farm increased. Hikes through the forest had lengthened. There was renewed spring in his step.

Mental wounds were still sticking with him in dreams during many restless nights. He replayed unpleasant events of prison and Nazi torture. Often, the storyline of the dreams rewrote itself. In one, he had crashed through the window of Victoria Terrasse to plunge to his death. But he had snapped awake before reaching the pavement.

Dreams aside, his thoughts often returned to Truni. Had she forgiven him? Could she understand why he had destroyed her family's factory? Could he restore their relationship?

Soon after returning home in late May, he had called her. Truni had seemed distant as they talked. The sabotage hadn't come up, but he had sensed she still held resentment.

During the call, both had expressed a desire to see the other. To him, that was a positive sign. But he hadn't been ready for her to see him in his beat-up condition. They had agreed to let more time pass so they could recover from their wounds.

On this warm summer afternoon, a knock on the door woke him with a startle from a nap. He scrambled to the door.

It was Truni.

Their reunion got off to a slow beginning. No warm embrace. No hug.

This was a different Bjørn from the one she'd last seen at Gestapo headquarters in Bergen. She stared at him without speaking, taking in the changes. Gone were the bloody bruises and welts on his battered body and face. So were the swollen eyes and split lip that she had witnessed. He was thinner. His clothes fit like they belonged to someone a size or two larger.

Bjørn, meanwhile, noticed lingering signs of her suffering. Malnutrition during her concentration camp imprisonment had cost her some of her strong, shapely physique. Her once-rosy cheeks had faded pale.

"Would you like to sit here on the steps?" he said. "The sun is out and the warmth is good."

"*Ja*, I'd like that."

They sat on the top front step of the farmhouse, side by side, close together but not touching. Their gazes were fixed ahead, not at each other.

She spoke first. "When I saw you in that jail cell, I thought I'd never see you again. Knowing you're alive makes me happy."

"I remember how frightened I was for you," Bjørn responded with a soft smile. "They had you. I didn't dare show my concern. The Gestapo was watching our reactions."

Truni nodded.

He looked at her and decided to put his heart on his sleeve. "I'm sorry about everything. I should have never included you in anything I was involved in. The feeling that I played a part in your arrest and what happened to you"—his mouth felt like it was stuffed with cotton—"well, it has made it difficult for me to look in the mirror."

Truni touched his arm. "You're not responsible. I made my own choices, and I have no regrets. Like you, I believed I had a duty to do something. It's why I formed my group. Some were arrested with me. They all survived the war.

"And remember," she said, "I insisted on being a part of the Hoggemann operation."

Her eyes were on him as she continued. "I've had time to think about things. I understand why you destroyed my father's factory. I'm still angry about it. It's been difficult for me and my parents. You knew that my father didn't feel right about making things for the Germans. But it was our only means of income, for us and his employees."

Bjørn dipped his head. "I didn't feel good at all about doing it. I was ordered to do it. I thought I had no choice. I had to put my feelings aside. I felt worse by not admitting it to you when we were last together. I believed I had a duty to keep quiet. Now I must live with the guilt."

Truni had listened patiently. She said nothing when he finished.

He wasn't quite ready to ask her what he really wanted to know. And he wasn't sure he was prepared for her answer. Bjørn bought a little time by asking, "How are your parents?"

Truni shifted her gaze from him and looked out toward the village and Osterfjord. "They're fine. They were very angry, as you can expect. They knew it was you. I didn't have to tell them. It will take them some time to forgive."

"Can your father rebuild?"

"He thinks so. He's looking into borrowing money. It's been difficult for all of us financially, but we're getting by."

She turned toward him and smiled. "My father's also considering what he can do to manufacture things that will be more profitable than what he did before. It may turn out better."

Silence hung in the air briefly. Then Bjørn summoned courage and got to his question.

"So, where do we stand? You and I?"

Truni leaned back, resting her elbows on the concrete porch. She cast her eyes skyward. Bjørn drew in a deep breath, waiting. His question dangled.

"I don't know," she said at last.

Truni looked into his eyes. Her smile was ever so slight. "When I was in the Espeland camp, I thought of you so much. I realized one thing I knew to be true. I love you, Bjørn. I do."

Then she looked away. "But things seem so different now," she said. "We've both been through a lot."

Bjørn leaned forward, his head down. He sighed and waited for the rest.

Truni sat up straight. "I need time to recover. My thoughts and dreams are filled with the horrors of what happened, especially at night. I can't shake them. It will take me time to get over this."

She turned her head and looked at Bjørn. "I know you have so much of your own horror to deal with. I don't believe either of us is ready for a future together."

Bjørn blinked rapidly to fight the moisture building in his eyes. "This war has ruined everything," he said. "Things I've done. Things that have been done to me, as well as you. I worry I might never be the same."

He scooted a notch closer and moved his arm around her waist. "I love you, too. But I worry I'm no longer the man you fell in love with."

Truni started to say something but stopped. She leaned into him, resting her head on his shoulder. "I might not be the same, either."

Bjørn couldn't hold back. A few tears trickled down his face. He knew it was ending. Not only was Truni ending it. He was ending it. He didn't know why, really, and he knew his heart would break again. But he thought it was for the best.

They sat silent for minutes, embracing and brushing away their tears.

"It's so strange," she said finally. "The war brought us back together. Now that it's over, the war is breaking us apart."

———

Bjørn glanced up the road at the house. It was within a hundred yards, standing in a serene farm setting with open pasture and trees beyond. To reach this point on the outskirts of Nestad, he had trudged six miles from Erlikvåg.

He had never seen this side of the house before. Only the back of Jens Grutermann's farm. The back with the pigpen.

As Bjørn neared Grutermann's farmhouse, he began to question his decision. His footsteps halted. He had to think this through again.

Sheriff Asheim had admonished him to stay away, and he had agreed not to confront the one-time Norwegian Nazi. But his anger, bitterness, and stubborn streak wouldn't allow him to keep that promise. As he mulled whether to face Grutermann, Bjørn placed everything on the former Nazi's head. His arrest, beatings, imprisonment, and being nearly starved to death all rested with Grutermann. All that on top of Grutermann's work in confiscating animals and crops from Bjørn and his neighbors.

He had envisioned it being so satisfying to see Grutermann's reaction to him standing at the door. It would have to be fear. He'd cringe. He would have no Nazi skirt to hide behind. In his mind, Bjørn had seen Grutermann dance around his questions. He'd never apologize. He'd never admit anything. He'd deny it all. *Oh, just one punch, just one,* Bjørn had thought. It would be so satisfying to break that puffy nose, and justified, too.

Now Bjørn stood in the middle of the road glaring up at the house, wondering whether it was a good idea. He hated his conscience questioning his resolve. It was like the devil sitting on one shoulder and an angel on the other. His hands were fisted and he pounded them repeatedly on his legs. What would he gain? Satisfaction. Would he really be satisfied keeping things only to words, not fists? What if it came to fists? He didn't want to risk spending time in jail.

What if he was wrong? What if Grutermann didn't snitch on him? Bjørn had no proof that the traitor was behind his arrest. Bjørn had simply convinced himself that he was.

It also occurred to him that he might be putting himself, not Grutermann, in grave danger. What if Grutermann came to his door armed? Who would have the upper hand then?

Bjørn put his hands on his hips and stared at the house. It was quiet, peaceful. A plain white farmhouse. No trees, shrubbery, or anything of color except a green-painted door. Nothing to show that the Nazis enriched Grutermann.

Bjørn had a decision to make. He could keep going or turn around. He dropped his arms to his sides. He drew a deep breath, held it, then puffed it out with disgust. Grutermann wasn't worth it. The sheriff was right. Let Grutermann pay for his actions the proper way in a court of justice.

Bjørn turned and began a slow stride back to Erlikvåg.

——

The year 1945—a year that marked the war's conclusion—was now approaching its own end. After the bright, warm days of summer and a mild fall, Norway turned cold and wet as December arrived. Erlikvåg had three early-season snowfalls.

During the year's waning months, NRK radio had brought to Bjørn and Åsta news of a nation emerging from its shell and healing from its wounds. In September, Vidkun Quisling had been convicted of treason and murder after a month-long trial. His arrogance as much as his deeds sealed his fate. He was sentenced to death and didn't have to wait long. On October 24, he was unceremoniously removed from his Møllergata 19 cell, escorted to Akershus Castle, and executed by a ten-man firing squad.

Before the first snowfall, most of the 284,000 German soldiers stationed in Norway at the end of the war—the equivalent of one soldier for every ten Norwegian citizens—had boarded ships sailing back to Germany. Many of the Gestapo agents and other troops of the SS remained imprisoned in Norway. Ultimately, sixty had received prison terms, and another twelve were executed.

Among those put to death was Alfred Josef Gartner, who had been found guilty of capital crimes. Karl Wolter, Bjørn's other Gestapo tormentor in Bergen, had been sentenced to a long prison term. Sheriff Asheim told Bjørn that his signed transcript from the sheriff's interview was introduced at both their trials.

Upon learning of their fates, Bjørn had felt tears trickling down his face. No satisfaction or joy. Instead, sadness filled him as he reflected on the lingering pain and death they had inflicted on him and on so many fellow Norwegian patriots.

He had also received word that Siegfried Wolfgang Fehmer, the Gestapo agent who beat him in Oslo, was imprisoned at Møllergata 19, awaiting trial for murderous acts. Also in custody with a trial pending was Ernest Weimann, the SS officer on the military boat who oversaw his arrest and the seizure of Jonas and Anton Seversen.

News accounts reported that roughly ninety thousand Norwegian Nazi conspirators were charged with treasonous crimes. Jens Grutermann was among them. He admitted to charges related to being an accomplice to Nazi transgressions, but he denied giving anyone up to the Germans or Norwegian Nazi authorities. He received no prison sentence, but was fined a moderate sum of five hundred kroner, which was deposited in a government fund to repay Norwegians for possessions the Nazis stole from them. The shuns and taunts that the people of Nestad gave him and his family may have been a steeper price. At the end of 1945, the Grutermanns put their farm up for sale with plans to move somewhere they wouldn't reveal.

—

When 1946 arrived, the country was well on its way toward putting itself back together. Rationing was phasing out as food supplies became adequate to feed a deprived and hungry nation. Clothing, paper products, and other necessities also were being restored. Like their fellow citizens, Bjørn and Åsta believed better times were ahead.

Physically, Bjørn felt mostly up to snuff. His body filled out and his weight was within twenty pounds of what it was prior to the war. In a checkup in February 1946, doctors gave him a clean bill of health, even though they found that one of his kidneys was permanently damaged.

By then, he had returned to full-scale work around the farm. Production continued to increase with the addition of more chickens and livestock to supplement a flourishing garden. Åsta remained on the farm and continued to savor rural life. Just after the new year, she had been offered her old bookkeeping job in Bergen as the factory cranked up. She respectfully declined.

Åsta also found love. A past suitor from Bergen had come to see her in late 1945, and romance had blossomed. Bjørn liked him instantly, and he had become more than an occasional visitor.

Arne, meanwhile, had returned to the Bergen Police Department, which had been purged of turncoats and Nazism. He, Inga, and Kristi had moved back into their old home in the city. By early 1946, a second child was on the way.

While Bjørn had recovered physically by the start of the year, nightmares were frequent. His mood swung from sad and depressed to agitated and angry.

Throughout the winter, he took frequent hikes in the mountains on snowshoes to condition his body and build his strength. In the cold mountain air, he contemplated his life. Bjørn believed change would help him, but he fell short of knowing what that change should be.

He channeled his anger into hatred toward the Germans. He wasn't the only one who did so. On occasions when he gathered around the stove with other farmers in Jonas's store, bitterness surfaced in every discussion.

The war seemed to come up in every conversation. Bjørn found it ironic. Norwegians wanted to move past the war and treat those five years like a bad dream. At the same time, they seemed obsessed with talking about it. Villagers talked about relatives and people they knew who either had died at the hands of the Nazis or were left scarred by malnutrition, stress, and suffering.

Perhaps the obsession was understandable, Bjørn realized after giving the irony more thought. It was a shared experience that he and his fellow Norwegians couldn't suddenly turn off like a spigot. There were too many memories to discard, almost all of them tragic and many of them horrifying.

CHAPTER 37

January 1947

A late-evening telephone call jerked Bjørn out of his chair and sent him rushing down the hall to answer it.

It startled Åsta, too. "Who could it be at this hour?"

Bjørn turned his head and glanced at her from the hallway wall phone with wide eyes. It was an operator-assisted, long-distance call from America. He instantly recognized the distant voice of Anders Kongsgaard.

"I have an offer if you want to accept it," he said. "I'm here in Sitka, Alaska. It's a United States territory. I'm back to fishing. For salmon. How would you like to join me here? To catch fish together."

Bjørn fumbled with the phone. His tongue seemed tied in a bowline knot. "You . . . me? Why?" He remembered what his father had impressed upon him long ago that opportunities are the product of hard work, not good luck. Good things seldom drop in your lap. You earn them, Sigfried Erliksen had said.

Kongsgaard was emphatic. "Crew up here, it's hard to keep 'em. They move around a lot. I'm looking for someone who's steady. Reliable. Will do things the way I want them done. No one I've talked to in Norway wants to come. Then I thought of you.

You showed courage, and I think we could work well together. I'll teach you all you need to know."

Bjørn pulled in a deep breath. He couldn't find the right words to respond. He thought there might be some mistake.

"A job?"

"Yes."

"How . . . how did you get to Alaska?"

"I met an American soldier at a pub in Lerwick," Kongsgaard said. "He was from Anchorage, Alaska. Told me about a fishery teeming with Pacific salmon off the Alaskan coast. Told me there was a lot of money to be made."

The line crackled and popped with static, but not enough to drown out Kongsgaard's voice. "I was risking my life with every North Sea crossing. I was ready for change. Talked to my wife. At first, she thought I'd breathed too much engine exhaust. But she got excited about it. So here we are."

"But how did the *Hildur* . . . You sailed all that way?"

"*Nei*, sold the *Hildur VI* and our house to a friend. Damned Nazis made my home their home, and I didn't want it anymore. But I hated to give up the boat. Had to leave her behind. Well, we moved to Seattle, it's a place south of Alaska, and I bought a new boat. Newer, modern. Best fishing trawler you'll ever see. I come up here to Sitka and fish during the season."

Kongsgaard was wound up. "You should see the salmon, Bjørn. Their meat is deep pink, almost red. Delicious. In high demand. I'll be fishing in Alaska six to seven months of the year. The rest of the time we can relax in Seattle. Nothing to do but keep the boat and equipment ready for the next season."

Bjørn stood motionless. "Oh my. Sounds good, but . . . I don't know."

"I know this is sudden," Kongsgaard's voice squawked through the phone, "but I'd love to have you. All you need is a passport. My immigration lawyer can get you a work permit."

"How will I get there?"

"Passenger liner to New York, then a train across America. Takes longer than you can believe but takes you straight to Seattle. And you'll like Seattle. There are a great many Norwegians there." The skipper chuckled. "Swedes, too. But that's all right. You'll get used to them. What do you say, Bjørn?"

"I say . . . I need time to think it over. I have a farm, I have family. But . . . can I have a day or two to think it over?"

"OK, but not too long. I need a good strong Norwegian mate as soon as I can get one. I want it to be you. How's four days? I'll call then. About this same time. *Ja*?"

"Four days. Good, thank you—" But the line had already gone dead.

Åsta now was by his side with her hand on her chin. "Four days to think something over? It must be something big!"

When Bjørn told her about Kongsgaard's offer, her initial reaction was to laugh it off. "How could that possibly work?" But Åsta closed her mouth as soon as she noted Bjørn's distant look.

———

In the ensuing days, Åsta kept her distance and her silence. Bjørn knew she was well aware of his restlessness. He needed time to mull over the offer.

He did not seek her advice, but he solicited it from others. Bjørn sat and talked with Jon about the prospect.

Jon thought it was a far-fetched idea, but confessed he was envious. Five years of German occupation had brought so much disruption and change. Many Norwegians, repressed by years of war, now felt free to dream big. Jon was so invested in his family and farm, he couldn't consider a broader horizon. While he didn't want his best friend to leave for such a distant place, Kongsgaard's offer was an exciting opportunity.

"If you want to do it, you should do it," he told Bjørn.

Jonas offered his thoughts, too. "You owe it to yourself to at least consider it. Weigh every positive and every negative you can think of. Take some time. This is your future and your family's future."

The storekeeper said he would help him get a passport if he decided to leave.

While he thought about it, Bjørn took long walks around the farm. He hiked in the mountains by himself and sat for hours at the lake below the farm.

On the afternoon of the third day after Kongsgaard's offer, Bjørn and Åsta sat in their chairs alongside a warm fire.

He was blunt. "I've decided to go. It's best for me to leave. This is a chance for me to put things behind me."

Åsta dropped her head. "I knew."

Bjørn grabbed his chin. "You knew what?"

"That you're going. I knew it before you hung up the telephone."

"My sister, I—" Åsta stopped him with a wave of her hand.

"No need to explain. I understand. This is the last thing I wanted to hear. But you've been miserable ever since you came back from prison. I knew it would be a matter of time before you found someplace else to be and something else to do."

He stared at his sister in silence. He'd expected resistance from her and had prepared to defend his decision. But Åsta was good at reading his thoughts. She left him speechless.

He reached across the table and put his hand over hers. "The farm's been doing pretty well. It earns enough so you could hire someone to help out, if you wanted to stay here. If you don't, then I'll figure something else out. What's important to me is that you are happy."

She took his extended hand in both of hers. "I like it here. I'd like to stay and take care of things. If you don't like life in America, you can always come back here."

Bjørn studied his older sister. The struggles to keep the farm alive during the Nazi oppression had aged her. While he was off fighting, she had managed it and given him something to come home to. Now he wanted something else. He would miss her. His love for her ran deep.

His voice softened but remained emphatic. "Then I want you to have the farm."

Åsta's head tilted and her eyebrows furrowed. Bjørn realized she didn't grasp his words.

He continued. "I'm turning it over to you, free and clear."

Now she understood. Åsta gasped. *"Nei . . ."*

He held up his hand with the palm out. "I've thought about this even before Anders Kongsgaard's offer. You should have the farm. You deserve it. You kept it going during the war. Our home survived because of you. This farm is as much yours as it is mine."

Åsta's sigh was deep. "This doesn't feel right."

He smiled. "It is the right thing to do. Åsta, if Father were sitting here now, he would agree with me. *Ja*, this is right. I'm signing the deed over to you."

Bjørn aimed his eyes at the floor. "I don't see myself coming back here. I love this place and being here with you. But bad memories are overtaking the good ones. I go to bed dreading the night. When I'm able to fall asleep, nightmares of the Gestapo kicking the bed keep waking me. Each time, it's a different person. It's the people who arrested me. It's the people who tortured me. Every night, I don't know who's coming for me. So, I have to try to put the past behind me."

He released a burst of air. "Maybe these nightmares will find me wherever I go. But I need to try to bury them."

Åsta looked into his determined eyes. "You think you can escape your memories by leaving. But it doesn't seem to work for anyone else. I don't think it will work for you. I hope you prove me wrong. I hope change will be good for you."

Åsta kept her eyes locked on him and paused before speaking. "If this is what you want, I will be happy for you. Never forget, Bjørn, never forget where you came from. This farm will always be your home, our home."

Signing the farm over to Åsta felt like the finest thing he had done in an awfully long time.

As he had struggled with his decision, his father's words again came back to him. If a gift does indeed drop from heaven, you must be prepared to catch it, or it will slip through your fingers. His father was proven to be right.

When Anders Kongsgaard called back, Bjørn accepted his offer and prepared for his departure.

———

July 1947

Bjørn stood on the ocean liner's side deck, palms resting comfortably on the richly varnished wood rail. He pointed his raised face at the bright afternoon sun. Sea air filled his nostrils. Smooth, rolling waters glistened below him. He recalled how different this was from when he had crossed the North Sea on *Hildur VI* through the eye of a storm.

On this journey, he was crossing the North Atlantic aboard the RMS *Queen Mary*. The liner had been pressed into service during the war, her sleek rich-black hull and gleaming white topside painted a drab navy gray. Antiaircraft guns had been mounted on the deck. The vessel had served valiantly, shuttling American troops between America and England. Now the gray and the guns were gone, and her elegance and majesty were back. Just the day before, the ocean liner had pulled out of her berth in

Southampton, seventy miles southeast of London. This marked her maiden voyage after her restoration back to the white-gloved flagship of the Cunard-White Star Line. Bjørn felt proud to be aboard.

He traveled in tourist class—the cheapest of three levels—and his cabin on a lower level of the ship was cramped. His view out a small porthole was limited. But in Bjørn's mind, this was going in style, and he couldn't care less that his accommodations would be considered steerage to high-paying passengers.

Just one suitcase held his belongings. He had packed only the basic toiletries, money for the various train tickets that would take him to Seattle, a change of clothes, a pair of boots, and a small framed photo of Åsta. His wallet contained the folded toilet tissue with the names of his prison cellmates and the scrap of cloth with his prison number. At the time, he hadn't quite grasped why he ripped off his number stitched to his prison clothes and kept it. So much had been taken from him in Møllergata 19. It had been his sole identity those six months there. A number, not a name. Now it had become a badge of proof that he'd withstood Nazi evil and suffering.

Bjørn also carried his black-dyed military coat. There was something about that coat. It had kept him warm in the winter, and its assortment of pockets was useful on the farm. He couldn't part with it. The coat had been through so much with him. It would prove useful in Alaska.

Five days from now, Bjørn would sail into New York Harbor. Like London, New York City was a place he could only dream of. He'd seen photos of the skyline, the Empire State Building looming tall among the skyscrapers. Bjørn found himself giddy, striking up conversations with complete strangers about the weather and the most trivial things. He couldn't stop rubbing his hands together in anticipation at the beginning of each sumptuous meal.

From the Big Apple, Bjørn's itinerary called for him to cross America by train and arrive at Union Station on the West Coast in Seattle. He had heard the name, but he wasn't familiar with the city. Some people near Erlikvåg had a family member who moved there, he recalled. They had spoken favorably about a Scandinavian enclave called Ballard. Seattle would serve as his home base and the opportunity for a new life.

———

August 1, 1947

The sun was still hidden on the horizon, but it was rising. The silhouette of the New York City skyline was just beginning to appear. Bjørn stood on the *Queen Mary*'s top deck, peering over the rail. His wide eyes stared into the distance. The day had come when the passenger liner would carry him into New York Harbor.

He had slept only a little the night before. His bedcovers were askew from frequent tossing and turning. His heartbeat had kept thumping, and he couldn't get it to ease by lying still.

His watch had told him it was three in the morning when he got out of bed and cleaned up. He had to climb multiple levels of stairs from his cabin in the lower reaches of the ship to the top deck. Few people had stirred when he walked along the deck below the vessel's three gleaming black and rust-colored smokestacks to reach the front of the ship. He had taken his place at the portside rail and waited and watched.

When he saw the cityscape come into view, he became motionless, his eyes transfixed. He worried that if he blinked, he might miss something. The skyscrapers were still mere distant shadows.

It was warm and clear. A soft breeze tossed his hair. He made no move to smooth it. If the breeze brought any early-morning chill through his brown, plaid short-sleeved shirt, he didn't seem to notice. He continued to hold his sight steady on the skyline.

As the *Queen Mary* entered the harbor, the skyscrapers loomed tall and large in browns, reds, grays, and even a pale blue. Bjørn wondered if it all was real. Was he in some fantasy land? Of course, it was real.

His heart pounded. He gulped in breaths of sea air. It seemed to cleanse his soul. Thoughts rushed through his head. He held no regrets about leaving Norway. He'd miss his family and friends. But if he had stayed on the farm, his surroundings would have kept alive memories he needed to shed. He still thought about Truni, but he had to emotionally let her go.

He wanted renewal. A fresh start. A new life.

A voice snapped him out of his daze. It was an American voice. "Hello, mister."

He glanced down. A little boy had come alongside and tugged at his pant leg. Bjørn guessed he was seven or eight. "Oh, hello."

The boy held a small American flag on a stick. "We're coming to New York today."

Bjørn smiled. "Are you going home?"

The boy looked up at him with a wide grin. "Yes."

Just then, a couple and a girl, maybe ten, came up beside him. "Christopher, you must be more careful and stay close to us," said the woman. She looked at Bjørn. "I hope he hasn't been a bother."

"Not at all."

The man held out his hand toward the skyline. "Beautiful, isn't it?"

Bjørn kept his smile. "*Ja*, it is. It is."

"Are you new to America?" the man asked. Bjørn figured his accent had given him away.

"Yes, I'm from Norway," Bjørn answered in English, reminding himself that he needed to buy a book to help him learn the language better.

"We haven't been there, but we've heard it's full of beauty."

The little boy held out the flag. "Would you like this?"

"Oh no, thank you."

"But I want you to have it."

Bjørn felt a surge of emotion. He crouched down to reach eye level with the boy.

He took the flag, pulled it to his chest, and embraced it. "Thank you."

Bjørn rose and looked out just as the Statue of Liberty came into full view. He raised the American flag and waved it at her. He convinced himself that Lady Liberty was staring back at him. Surely, he thought, her extended arm with the torch of freedom was meant for him.

EPILOGUE

Bjørn Erliksen found renewal in America. He obtained a green card and signed on with Kongsgaard as a third crew member aboard his fishing trawler, *Marlene*. After buying the boat from a retiring fisherman in Sitka, Alaska, the skipper told Bjørn that he considered renaming the boat *Hildur VII*. But he grew superstitious and kept the original name.

Thanks to Kongsgaard's orientation, Bjørn settled into a small apartment in Seattle's Ballard neighborhood. He liked the community. Indeed, there were many Scandinavian immigrants from Sweden, Denmark, and Finland as well as Norway. There were other nationalities, too. He didn't quite understand Ballard's nickname, Snoose Junction, but someone told him that people equated it to the Scandinavians' use of chewing tobacco.

He worked on the fishing boat for four years, spending months at a stretch in Alaska netting salmon through two seasons a year. The territory of Alaska's rich fishery proved lucrative. Kongsgaard liked Bjørn's work ethic and how quickly he picked up the skills of the trade. The skipper was generous at sharing the earnings from the catch, and Bjørn's frugality helped him build a healthy nest egg. When in Seattle, he spent part of the time maintaining and repairing the boat and its nets, which were stored in a sizable warehouse space near Fishermen's Terminal.

Bjørn had much free time, and he put it to good use. He bought two English lesson books and studied on his own, enlisting American neighbors in his apartment building for tutoring.

He befriended the apartment building's handyman. The worker pointed Bjørn toward a local electrical contractor who needed a full-time helper. So, in the fishing off-season, he went to work as the contractor's assistant. It turned into a demanding full-time job, and in the late spring of 1951, Bjørn made a change. Kongsgaard was disappointed, but he understood, and the two remained lifelong friends.

The new employment changed everything. Bjørn eventually completed an electrician correspondence course, earned an apprenticeship, and ultimately joined the Brotherhood of Electrical Workers Union Local 46. In 1954, he found work as an electrician for Bensen Boatworks, a mainstay business along Ballard's Leary Way waterfront. Bensen repaired, renovated, and upgraded boats and ships, the lion's share of which belonged to Seattle's budding fishing fleet. Bjørn spent the rest of his working life there.

Bensen Boatworks was where he met his bride. Her name was Elizabeth Jane McKibbon, thirty at the time and of English and Scottish origin. She was a brunette with a nice smile, blue eyes, and a smart head on her shoulders. With bookkeeping experience, Elizabeth had worked for Bensen only four months when she first met him. She was filling in at the receptionist desk when Bjørn walked in for his job interview.

He would never forget what she said to him that day.

"Do you have Norwegian heritage?" She had a wide smile.

"Yes, I'm Norwegian." Bjørn's faced reddened. "My accent must have given it away."

"It was a good guess, wasn't it?" She chuckled. "You know, this is Ballard."

Bjørn learned through subtle inquiry that she was single. She had no steady, as far as anyone knew. One day, he entered the office and saw her in the cafeteria on break with no one around her to overhear. He asked her out, and to his surprise, she accepted.

Bjørn and Elizabeth, who he called Liz, were married on September 30, 1955, and honeymooned at Cannon Beach on the Oregon Coast. She continued working at Bensen until their son, James Sigfried Erliksen, was born nearly three years later. They named him after Liz's dad, James McKibbon. Bjørn's father's name was used for the middle name.

Through the years, Bjørn occasionally spoke of his life in Norway and the experiences of war. He said little about his arrest, torture, and imprisonment. "There are some things I try to forget," he told her early in their relationship. She didn't delve deeper, and told him she knew little about Nazi Germany's occupation of Norway.

They carved out a happy life at their modest but cozy home in the Crown Hill neighborhood just north of the heart of Ballard. They weren't rich, but with his secure job, they were comfortable. No grand vacations to foreign lands, but their car trips to the mountains, ocean, and nearby places were fun and relaxing.

Bjørn remained in contact with his family and he, Liz, and James made one visit to his homeland in 1969. It had taken him twenty-two years to decide he was ready to confront the ghosts of war he'd left behind. His arrival at the farm turned into a community celebration. Virtually the whole of Erlikvåg showed up at the farm for a picnic. Jonas Seversen has passed on by then. But Jon and his family of five were there. He still worked his farm. Bjørn didn't see Truni but learned that she had found happiness. She was married and a mother of two daughters. Åsta and her husband had one son, whom they had named Bjørn. She and her family visited Seattle three years later.

At about age ten, Bjørn and Liz's James hit a growth spurt and, by sixteen, reached six foot five. He went on to become an all-city basketball star at Ballard High and received a scholarship to play for the University of California Golden Bears. It was the 1970s, when free spirits still thrived in San Francisco's Haight-Ashbury district. To his parents' disappointment, James gave up his athletic scholarship, dropped out of Cal Berkeley, and married a young woman he'd met hanging out. He found work and his passion in a small guitar shop in East Bay. He later acquired the store, and the business thrived, building high-quality and sought-after instruments. In 1983, he and his wife gave Bjørn and Liz a grandson, Michael Bjorn Erliksen. Michael's middle name honored his grandfather, with the English *o* substituted for the Norwegian *ø*.

At seventy-seven, Liz died of cancer in April 2001. Bjørn lived on until October 2009 and died peacefully in his sleep from kidney failure at ninety.

Bjørn never forgot his roots, but became a proud American citizen in the early 1960s. At his Ballard home, he encased a sturdy flagpole in cement and flew the Norwegian flag every day just under the American flag.

AUTHOR'S NOTE

Thank you for reading *A Coat Dyed Black*. I hope you enjoyed the story. My approach to the book was to blend the authenticity of history with a journey of a fictional character. Now that you've finished, I thought it might be useful to cover where history intersects with storytelling.

Bjørn Erliksen was modeled and shaped after real Norwegian resistance fighters who told me their stories before they passed on. Most of Bjørn's adventures and predicaments are based on real experiences and actual events.

Captain Anders Kongsgaard and his trawler *Hildur VI* are fictional. But the German transport *Rio de Janeiro* was sunk by the Polish submarine *Orzel* en route to Norway. Fishing boats did rescue surviving soldiers and take them to Lillesand where the survivors told Norwegian authorities they were on their way to Bergen to protect it from a British and French invasion. It provided some of the early evidence that Nazi Germany's attack on Norway was imminent.

The knock on the door by Bjørn's friend and his decision to volunteer and fight is also fictional. In reality, the Norwegian Army's Fourth Division mobilized in and around the mountain town of Voss, and hard fighting occurred there as well as in the mountainous valleys of south-central Norway. The ambush in the fictional valley of Ørhandal, the subsequent retreat over the mountains, and the journey home were fictitious.

Bjørn's thwarted attempt to flee Norway by carrying a sack of potatoes to a house in Bergen was a true account, with some fictional details and enhanced dialogue. His harrowing journey from Hernar Island across the North Sea to the Shetland Islands aboard a fishing trawler through a gale-force storm was real as well, but creativity was required to fill in details.

In London, refugees from Nazi-occupied countries were processed at the reception center in what was originally named the Royal Victoria Patriotic Asylum. The institution, which was built as a girls' orphanage in the years following the Crimean War, still stands and is occupied by a variety of businesses. Interrogations were an inherent part of that process, and Colonel Oreste Pinto was a real British security service MI5 officer who proved effective in unmasking Axis spies during interrogations at the reception center. After the war, his 1950s book, *Spycatcher*, became the basis for a popular radio serial and early BBC television series. His specific interview with Bjørn was fictitious.

Martin Linge was a real Norwegian captain who commanded the Norwegian Independent Kompani No. 1. He died of wounds in a second commando raid on the Lofoten Islands. The unit was subsequently named Kompani Linge in his honor.

Description of the commando training in Scotland was truthful, based on interviews of two Norwegians who underwent the rigorous regimen. German military leaders were aware of commando training and referred to it as the International Gangster School. The Gestapo was active in hunting down these agents and decreed that any commandos captured would be executed within twenty-four hours following interrogation.

Bjørn's return to Norway on the same boat that took him to Shetland is purely fictional. But SOE operatives and Kompani Linge commandos were shuttled across the North Sea on a fleet of fishing boats, which also sent caches of weapons and equipment with them. SOE organized the fleet that became commonly known as the Shetland Bus.

The story of the airdrop of weapons and supplies in the mountains was made up but was based on true personal accounts by some of those who participated in retrieving and securing materials parachuted into Norway by Allied planes. The sabotage of the fuel tanks also was fictional, but loosely based on accounts of a similar act. Bjørn's romantic relationship with Truni and his sabotage of her father's factory were complete figments of the author's imagination.

There was an assassination. In 1944, Norwegian Nazi State Police Officer Olav Njøten was gunned down outside Stapo headquarters in downtown Bergen in the light of day. My story is based on that assassination. While the book generally follows history, the specific portrayal was fictional. I created the fictional character of Amund Hoggemann to enable storytelling. In fact, Njøten did play a role in investigating the arrival of Kompani Linge commandos in the fishing village of Telavåg. Details of the shoot-out between Nazis and the Norwegian agents and the subsequent atrocity adhered to history.

Scenes of Bjørn's arrest and his interrogations and imprisonment at the notorious Møllergata 19 prison closely follow actual accounts taken from my interviews of Norwegians who were arrested and tortured. Fiction was added only to fill in details and to expand the dialogue and storytelling. The interrogation at Gestapo headquarters in Bergen was taken from a transcript provided to authorities by one resistance fighter. His transcript was used in the actual trials of Gestapo agents Karl Wolter and Alfred Gartner, who were convicted of their crimes. Gartner was executed, and Wolter was sentenced to eight years in prison. Siegfried Fehmer was a real Gestapo agent who interrogated prisoners at Victoria Terrasse in Oslo. After the war, he was executed for committing capital crimes. However, Bjørn's interrogation session with Fehmer in Oslo was fictional.

The firing squad scene was largely authentic and based on a first-person account. But Hammer was a fictional character, and Bjørn's exchange with him as well as the description of the courtyard were created. The prison scenes at the war's end are largely accurate. In fact, Swedish police officer Harry Söderman did enter the prison and announce to inmates that the war was over and they would be freed. I must point out that my descriptions of Møllergata 19 are fictional. While I used a general description inside the prison based on an interview with someone who was imprisoned there, I could find no records of what the prison looked like. It was demolished in the 1950s.

The scene of Bjørn getting help from Gunnar Sønsteby is fictional. Sønsteby was a real Kompani Linge commando who is arguably the most famous resistance fighter and certainly the most decorated. He was at the prison on liberation day.

ACKNOWLEDGMENTS

What's a guy with an Italian surname doing writing a book about Norway? The explanation is simple. My wife, Wendy, lost her father to cancer when she was young, and her mother remarried a Norwegian immigrant who became Wendy's second dad. It brought a large Norwegian family into her life. In the 1970s, when my father-in-law first told me stories of his resistance involvement during Nazi Germany's World War II occupation of Norway, I was in the early stage of my newspaper career. From that perspective, I quickly realized it was a story that should be told.

My interest spawned considerable research about the Nazi occupation and led to many interviews not only with him but with family members and others outside the family. I owe them a huge debt. At first, I set out to write a nonfiction book. But I faced difficulties, most notably the steadfast stipulation of the Norwegians interviewed that they not be named. This desire was in line with their belief that their contributions were no more important than those of others. So, my book was literally shelved for decades.

After my retirement from a wonderful career in journalism and public affairs, I rekindled my interest in writing the book. This time, I was able to honor my pledge not to name my sources and tell their resistance-related stories through the genre of historical fiction. This book has brought me great personal satisfaction and joy. If I hadn't captured the stories before these brave Norwegians passed on, their eyewitness accounts and experiences might never have been told.

I wish to thank so many who helped me on the journey to write this book. First and foremost is Wendy, whose love, encouragement, and support enabled me to complete this work. With writing as a mainstay throughout her long career in corporate public and government relations, her continuous advice, suggestions, and keen editing skills made this a far better book.

I also thank my late parents for their early support and for generally guiding the direction of my life and career. Donald A. Pugnetti was a highly respected newspaper editor in the state of Washington. He was the founding editor of the *Tri-City Herald* before becoming executive editor of the *Tacoma News Tribune*. My mother, Frances Taylor Pugnetti, also had a journalism background and was an author herself of *Tiger by the Tail*, documenting the first twenty-five years of the *Herald*.

Huge thanks, too, to our combined families in the United States and Norway, all our sisters and brothers, nieces and nephews, great-nieces and -nephews, and cousins. Their encouragement was and is always appreciated. Given the duration of this project, a special salute to friends old and new who encouraged me at every step. Special recognition goes to the late Arne Forsberg, former newspaper colleague and friend who lived in Norway during the occupation, for his help in translations and background.

Credit Nicolas Nelson of Wordsmith Writing Coaches in Los Angeles for giving the manuscript a thorough structural edit. His comments and recommendations led to a much better story. Author DL Fowler, who has published two splendid biographical novels of Abraham Lincoln, is a friend and mentor whose sage advice enhanced my book. Thanks to friends Stephen Donovan,

Scotsman Ian Robertson, and O'Shea McLaughlin for lending their names for characters in this book.

Finally, I am grateful to everyone at Girl Friday Productions, led by Senior Book Development Editor Sara Spees Addicott, for their skill, professionalism, and dedication in getting *A Coat Dyed Black* published.

ABOUT THE AUTHOR

Don Pugnetti Jr. has had a decades-long career in journalism, public relations, and public affairs. After eighteen years as a reporter and editor at the *News Tribune* in Tacoma, Washington, back when newspaper journalism was in its heyday, he served as chief policy advisor, speechwriter, and strategist for the elected Washington State auditor and had stints managing public and private agency communication operations. He has taught newswriting and other communications courses as a visiting professor at the University of North Florida and as an adjunct instructor at Pacific Lutheran University. Pugnetti received his BA in journalism from Washington State University and MA in communications from the University of Washington. Now retired, Pugnetti lives in Gig Harbor, Washington, with his wife, Wendy, where he continues his passion for writing.